Picker's Bleed

Mark. R. Faulkner

This is a work of fiction. Names, characters, places, and incidents either are the product of the author's imagination or are used fictitiously. Any resemblance to actual persons, living or dead is entirely coincidental.

Copyright © 2021 by Mark R Faulkner

All rights reserved

First edition April 2021

Published by Infested Books

ISBN (paperback) 978-1-8384650-0-1
ISBN (ebook) 978-1-8384650-1-8

www.markrfaulkner.com
Twitter:@MRFaulkner1
Facebook: Mark R Faulkner

Prologue

It was a classic mob, forty strong and dressed in sackcloth. Most of them were brandishing crude horticultural weapons and flaming brands, which were thrust out in front of the procession as it threaded its way between the trees. Angry banter passed back and forth. The crisp pre-dawn air crackled with tension.

The rabble came upon the crooked silhouette of a cottage nestled within the forest. A lamp burned in one of the downstairs rooms, the window a square of light in the cold gloom. The mob funnelled into the front garden, trampling the beds underfoot. Despite there being a frost, the faint scent of sage was detectable beneath the oily black smoke from the torches.

'You don't understand,' screamed the witch when they dragged her from her home, hands bound. Her eyes kept darting back to the cottage, as if more afraid of something left behind.

'Burn her,' went the chant from the mob. 'Burn her.'

'Put her to the stake.'

'Don't do this,' she pleaded. 'You're making a mistake.'

'It's too late, witch.'

And so it was that Ella Jameson was manhandled unceremoniously through the forest. Little heed was paid to the branches and thorns that snagged her skin and hair. Likewise, few paid attention when Ella began a soft chant, under her breath. For a moment or two she convulsed, then went slack in her captors' arms.

As they reached the village, the witch came to, thrashing and biting like an injured tiger, her strength far greater than her size. A string of obscenities issued into the morning dark as they tied her to the pole and set the fire.

Long after the witch should have been dead, a commotion was stirring on the village green. Even the most naïve of villagers had begun to realise something was amiss. Fat was dripping onto the fire, hissing and spitting while clouds of black, greasy smoke rose into the morning sky. The morning smelled more like a hog-roast than an execution. Her body whistled like a sausage as her skin blistered and split, before blackening to a crisp.

And yet she was still pleading for her life. Her tongue protruded and was burnt half away, wagging up and down as she begged to be saved; 'Please let me go. Please. I promise I'm not a witch. Please.' Her words sounded more mocking than sincere.

Gregory Stour wanted to cover his ears, blot out the wretched whimpering; he wanted to be away from it all, but honour wouldn't allow him to run. He needed to appear strong in front of the villagers else he'd risk losing all control, and the favour of Lord Mandeville.

Someone came stumbling into the congregation; half crazed and muttering about being too late. It was one of the villagers who'd stayed behind to search the cottage. It registered in the back of Gregory's mind that the grotesque parody of Ella Jameson had fallen quiet. He glanced back towards her, forcing himself to look. Although her hair was burned clear off her scorched scalp and her ears were like two withered mushrooms, more charcoal than flesh, her eyes were bright. They were fixed firmly on the newcomer.

'I'm too late,' he muttered again.

The witch laughed; a hideous cackle which only faded when her bones fell into the embers, sending clouds of choking, sulphurous ash into the air.

1

Jake Evans stood at the kitchen sink, washing dishes on autopilot while staring out of the misted window above The Discount Freezer Food Store. He used the palm of his hand to clear a circle in the condensation and was watching a chip wrapper gambol up the middle of the grey high-street below when Hannah shouted from the living room.

He half turned, cocking his head in the direction of the door.

'Jake!' she shouted again, sounding half-excited about something.

'Hold on a minute.'

'You okay?'

'Just drying my hands,' he said coming into the living room, wiping off suds with a tea towel. He looked down at the laptop on the tatty coffee table in front of her. A glossy photography magazine was wedged under one of the legs to stop the table from wobbling. 'What've you found?'

She tilted the screen to show Jake an estate agent's photograph of a ramshackle country cottage, complete with thatched roof and oak beams.

'In your dreams,' he said.

'I'm serious,' she replied. 'Sit down,' and she gave him a knowing smile.

He looked back at the screen. 'How much?' he asked, humouring her.

'It's at the top end of our budget.' She raised her eyebrows a touch.

'Really?' Jake's attention was drawn back to the slightly out of focus photograph. The roof looked like it might be damp, or even rotten in places, which they'd need to get checked out, although even if the whole roof needed replacing, the house still stood head and shoulders above anything else they'd seen in the months they'd been searching for a new home. 'Where is it?'

Hannah's smile broadened. 'A place called Picker's Bleed.'

'Picker's what? I mean, that's a bit of a creepy name, if you ask me!'

Her smile cracked into a fit of giggles. 'Picker's Bleed. It's not too far from Marsham.'

'Right,' he said. 'And where the fuck is Marsham? And what's a Picker and why are they bleeding?'

'How the Hell should I know? A farm hand I suppose.'

'But seriously, where is it?'

Hannah switched the map to satellite view and the screen was filled with the greens and yellows of open countryside. She zoomed out, and out again, until the grey sprawl of urbanisation appeared at the bottom corner of the laptop's monitor. At this scale the village of Marsham was too small to be labelled.

'Fuck me it's in the middle of nowhere,' he said, his eyes widening in slight disbelief. They had always dreamed of living somewhere secluded, but never imagined they'd find somewhere which would potentially fit the bill so perfectly, didn't mean moving to the other end of the country, and still be just about affordable. 'Call them,' he said.

They allowed themselves a moment's excitement before reining in their enthusiasm to lessen any impending disappointment.

Hannah said, 'There's bound to be a catch.'

'Only one way to find out,' Jake replied. 'I just hope it's not already been sold.'

'If it has then it wasn't meant to be,' she said.

'Somebody must have died in there or something for it to be so cheap.'

'I don't care. It's perfect.'

'I've got to go early tomorrow, so could you call the estate agent first thing?'

'Love to,' she said.

The next morning Hannah was editing photos and glanced at the clock for the tenth time in as many minutes. It was nine o'clock and the estate agent's office would be open, so she saved her work, picked up her phone and went down to the bottom of the pissy communal stairwell and out into the small yard. She lit a cigarette and took a long drag while scrolling for the number on her phone. Worried the cottage might already be sold she was unconsciously tapping her foot while she waited for the agent to answer.

'Good morning, Albright and Green.' The girl who answered sounded breathless, like she'd run to pick up the phone. Hannah imagined she'd probably got to the office a few minutes late and was making the first tea round of the day.

'Hi,' said Hannah. 'Sorry to ring so early, I'm calling about the house at Picker's Bleed and was wondering whether it would be possible to arrange a viewing?'

'Yes, of course it would,' said the voice on the other end of the line, almost without delay. Hannah could hardly believe it. 'We've got the keys to that one, on account of it being empty. When were you thinking?'

'Erm...' Hannah, taken by surprise, could hardly bring herself to believe she was actually booking a viewing. 'Would you be able to do Saturday?' She would have preferred to have seen the house sooner, but she'd promised the McKenzies they'd have their wedding pictures ready by the end of the week.

'Saturday, hmmm...' came the voice on the other end of the line. 'Let me check.' Hannah could hear the faint sound of a keyboard tapping. 'Yes. Saturday's fine.'

When the call was finished, Hannah took a deep breath to try and calm herself and slow her racing heart. 'Don't get too excited girl,' she muttered. 'It's probably a complete wreck.' But the truth of it was that it would have to be almost beyond repair for them not to put an offer on the table. Rather than being a daunting task, the renovations were something to look forward to.

She flicked her lipstick-rimmed cigarette butt onto the ground and crushed it into the concrete, gave the air a small fist pump and jogged back up the flight of concrete stairs to the flat. Too excited to get straight back to work she went to the kitchen and texted Jake the good news while she waited for the kettle to boil. Her hand was shaking a little when she poured the tea. Her cheeks ached pleasantly from smiling.

The laptop sat open on the coffee-table, next to a greasy pizza box and half-empty bottle of wine. There was only one photograph on the website, which led them to believe the inside must be a complete dump. 'It doesn't matter,' Jake was saying. 'The inside's the easy bit to fix, as long as it's structurally sound.' He studied the pixilated picture on the screen, looking for any clues as to what they might find, squinting to try and better see the thatched roof and keeping his fingers crossed in the hope it wouldn't need replacing because that might tip the cottage out of their budget. Although he hadn't the foggiest idea how much it actually *did* cost to replace a thatched roof.

'We'll have to wait and see,' said Hannah, reading his mind. She gave his arm a small squeeze, trying to be pragmatic when in reality she was more excited than he was. 'It is stunning though,' she said wistfully.

The higgledy-piggledy cottage was surrounded by an overgrown hedge and the front garden was choked with brambles and weeds. Hannah drifted into a daydream, imagining what might be revealed when the garden was cleared.

Dogrose and ivy were growing up the front of the cottage, framing the windows and the slightly askew front door. Beyond the back corner of the house, at the very edge of the photograph, was what appeared to be an overgrown orchard; its stunted fruit trees melding with dense natural woodland beyond.

'It's a fairy-tale house,' mused Hannah.

2

Saturday morning found Hannah and Jake driving along a raised road, traversing an expanse of fields and marshland, which was punctuated infrequently by small stands of trees and isolated hillocks. In a vast sky, vapid wisps of cloud drifted slowly in isolation and did nothing to lessen the sun's oppressive heat. The air-con' was long broken and so all of the car's windows were open.

'There's a crossroads up ahead,' said Jake. 'The turning's got to be around here somewhere.' As they neared, he slowed the car to a crawl.

'This is the same one we were at half an hour ago.'

'Are you sure?' Jake turned the engine off and they both got out, leaving the car's doors open.

'Think so, I recognise that tree there, with the bit of barbed wire wrapped around the bottom of it.'

'Balls,' he said. 'We've been driving around in circles for hours now.'

'We've got plenty of time to make the viewing,' said Hannah, 'as long as we find out where we are soon.' She sighed. 'What are we going to do?'

Jake shrugged his shoulders.

Hannah looked up and down both roads. They hadn't seen another car in hours.

'I've got no signal,' Jake said. 'I just checked,' but he glanced at his phone again, out of habit.

'Me neither,' she said.

'Fuck me it's hot,' said Jake, shading his eyes and squinting up at the sky.

'Shit, fucking, cunting bollocks!' Hannah took a deep breath, trying to find her zen. Just as she was coming to terms with never making the viewing, she spotted a car driving towards them, little more than a distant speck but getting larger.

The maroon Range Rover - of the old, boxier style - pulled slowly into the left turn where they were partially blocking the road and came to a halt, rocking back and forth on creaky suspension before coming to rest. The man who got out was a rangy gentleman with thread-veined cheeks. He wore a short-sleeved shirt and knee-high wellingtons. A curved pipe hung from the corner of his mouth and he briefly shielded his face while he put a match to the tobacco. 'Do you need a hand?' he asked in a puff of smoke, using the mouthpiece of his pipe to gesticulate towards their car.

'You could say that' said Jake with genuine humility. 'I think we're a bit lost.'

'Lucky I passed by then.' The man took another drag on his pipe and exhaled the smoke in a ring - which was lazily borne away on the scant breeze. 'Where you off to then?' he asked.

Hannah had been looking at the shortening shadow cast by a nearby telegraph pole and fretting about making the viewing on time. 'A place called Picker's Bleed. You don't happen to know where it is, do you?'

Enough of a look passed across his face for Hannah and Jake to exchange a quick glance. 'What would you want to go there for?' he asked, sucking on his pipe and quickly regaining his composure.

'We're off to look at a house,' answered Jake.

'Well, there's only one house there,' said the man, 'and you can't miss it.' He pointed off down the road with his pipe, while climbing back into his car. He carried on through the open window. 'About four and a half miles that way and you'll come across a lane going off to the right; Follow it for another mile or two and take a left; there's no other roads before it. Follow that and it'll take you straight there. Good luck.' He gave a small, backhanded wave as he gunned the engine and drove away, leaving Hannah and Jake standing in the road. His departure seemed a little abrupt, but they thought little of it.

'I'm fucking glad he came along,' said Jake. 'Good job we set out early, I reckon we'll only be twenty minutes late.'

'Well, we'd better get a move on then,' said Hannah, already back in the car and buckling her seatbelt.

'Righty-O.' Jake gave the roof of the Fiat a light slap and hopped into the driver's seat before setting off in the direction the man had pointed.

The first turn only appeared from out of the endless fields of gently swaying wheat when they were upon it. Jake stomped the brake as hard as he dared and flung the car into reverse, quickly backing up before, with a short squeal from the tyres, they headed along the road they needed to be on. 'I'm sure we've already been down here,' he said. 'I really don't know how we missed it?'

'Slow down a bit!' said Hannah, clinging to the door handle. 'You don't want to end up in a ditch, do you?'

Jake grumbled under his breath and eased his foot slightly off the gas. The breeze coming through the windows did little to quell the mid-morning heat. Up ahead they could see a stark treeline running parallel with the road; a sudden boundary where in one direction a forest stretched out to fuzzy the horizon, while in the other lay the endless green and brown fields they'd become accustomed to. They'd been driving for another ten minutes or more when they came upon the next turning. It was more of a track than a road, which plunged beneath the trees and was marked with a blue sign as unsuitable for long vehicles.

The broadleaf canopy reached right across the lane to form a tunnel. Jake tapped the brakes while his eyes adjusted to the change in light, from the glare of the afternoon sun to dense shade. 'I hope we don't meet anything coming the other way,' he said, noting how the trees and scrub encroached upon the road, forming high hedges full of thorns and stout branches, with no passing places. Then he considered the length of the grass down the middle of the track and thought it unlikely they'd meet other traffic.

Jake had the beginnings of a headache coming on. He breathed deeply, savouring the cool, earthy air blowing in through the windows, bringing blessed relief after the oppressive sun of the open country.

'Are you sure this is the right road?' asked Hannah. 'It looks more like a farm track to me.'

'I think so. Didn't the chap say there were no other roads to take?'

'I can't remember.'

Just then they crossed over a small, hump-back bridge which spanned a gurgling stream, its small but steep banks verdant with mossy boulders and ferns. They slowed the car to a crawl, just squeezing the Fiat onto the bridge. The stone walls on either side were too low for him to see from the driver's seat. Hannah was looking through the window into the miniature gorge the stream had carved below and wondered how many millennia the process had taken. 'That's stunning,' she said.

Jake stopped the car so he could see for himself without fear of scraping paint along the side of the bridge. Looking from his side of the car he saw the river tumbling down a series of small waterfalls before it passed beneath the trunk of an uprooted birch that spanned the stream like a bridge. His response came in the form of a satisfied sigh. After they'd savoured the view for long enough Jake said, 'It's a bit nice 'round here innit.' The stress of the journey had all but melted away, although his headache was worsening, putting a taint on his mood.

Fifty yards further on they came to the cottage. 'Is it this one?' asked Hannah.

'Certainly looks like the picture,' answered Jake. The cottage, its gardens and the orchard formed a clearing in the woods. Just like the estate agent's photograph, wild roses and ivy grew up the front of the house, framing the front door and one of the downstairs windows, fanning out to tickle the windows above. A line of rooks adorned the sagging roof, cawing loudly.

Hannah and Jake had set out to find somewhere secluded, but this house was isolated to a degree neither of them thought possible. 'It's miles from anywhere,' said Hannah in a faraway tone whilst stepping out onto the potholed tarmac to open the rickety double gates.

The paint had peeled off the gateposts a long time ago to leave the wood soft, porous and home to numerous plants, animals and fungi - an entire ecosystem was flourishing in and around the rotten wood. The gates' hinges had sagged so Hannah needed to lift them to drag them open, flattening a swathe through the long grass. Saplings sprouted from the overgrown lawn, acting as forerunners for the encroaching forest.

Jake slowly pulled the car onto the unkempt drive, following in old tyre tracks which must have been made weeks before. 'Estate agent's not here yet,' he said through the open passenger-side window when he'd brought the car creeping to a halt outside the peeling, green front door.

Hannah leaned in with her arms crossed on the car's roof. 'They probably can't find the bleeding place. Come on,' she cocked her head towards the house. 'Let's take a look around.' The rooks cawed louder, disturbed by the incursion into their territory. Agitated, they kept alighting the roof and landing again, as if the thatch was hot.

By the time Jake was out of the car, Hannah was already standing in front of one of the downstairs windows, trying to peer inside through cupped hands. 'I don't suppose you've got any ibuprofen, have you?' he asked. 'I've got a banging headache.'

'Afraid not,' said Hannah and she stepped back from the window to wipe the glass with her hand in an attempt to clear away some of the grime, which seemed to mostly be on the inside. The view wasn't much improved. Little could be seen of the house's interior past the dirt and yellowing net curtains, which were hanging just inside. 'I need to pee,' she said. 'Keep an eye out for the agent, will you?'

It was Jake's turn to try and see through the opaque window while Hannah pushed through tall weeds and disappeared around the corner of the cottage. 'Shout if they get here,' came her voice from just out of view.

While she was gone, Jake stepped back to take a better look at the house, squinting through the bright sunshine and his worsening headache. At some point in its history the cottage had been rendered with lime mortar, which was now cracked and peeling away from the wall where the damp had taken hold. Moss grew under the windowsills, which in places, like the gate, had gone porous with rot. A large crack ran up the chimney, following the line of the brickwork where a tenacious sapling was growing from the masonry. Bundles of twigs could be seen poking from the crooked chimneypot, most likely shoved there by the rooks which were flapping about on the roof. Jake wondered how much extra they'd have to pay for a comprehensive survey before committing to buy.

Just then Hannah poked her head back around the corner of the house. 'Come and have a look around here,' she said. 'We'll hear when the estate agent turns up.'

'If they turn up.' Jake looked at his watch, 'Give it another ten minutes, then we'll try to call.' He already knew there was still no phone signal.

They were in the orchard, where wizened apple trees were just beginning to sag under the weight of their fruit, wading through thigh-high grass and picking their way between bramble patches as best they could. Thorns snagged them with every step, leaving scratched skin and pulled clothes. Jake's eyes alighted upon a damson tree and his thoughts turned to emulating his granddad's infamous wine. He plucked an apple from an overhanging branch and gave it a quick shine on his tee-shirt.

'They're nowhere near being ripe,' said Hannah.

'I know. I'm just trying one.'

'You'll give yourself gut ache, you daft get.'

Jake had been expecting to bite into something hard and sour, but instead his teeth met little resistance and snapped together, forcing fetid mush, the consistency of semolina into his mouth. He retched and spat the rotten apple out, throwing the remainder to the ground where it split, disgorging maggots into the long grass. Jake wanted to be sick, but vomit wouldn't come.

Hannah's 'Fucking hell,' was long and drawn out. 'That's grim. You okay?' she asked, genuinely feeling sorry for him where usually she would have laughed.

'No,' he said. 'And where's this fucking estate agent.'

'I don't know,' she sighed.

Before Jake could answer they heard a car approaching. It was still someway distant and faint, but the sound of the engine highlighted how quiet the day had become, as it only can on the hottest of summer days. Any hint of a breeze had long gone and there was not even a rustle from the forest.

Jake was repeatedly spitting as they pushed back through the undergrowth to the front of the house, trying to clear his mouth of rot. Before he spoke again, he went to the car and rummaged in the foot-well until he found a bottle of water. The first two mouthfuls he swilled around and spat into the grass and only drank some when he was satisfied his mouth was as clean as it could be. There was a putrid aftertaste when he swallowed. *I don't like this house,* he thought.

3

Almost a full three minutes passed before an orange Citroën Saxo swung, too quickly, through the open gateway. The wide-bore exhaust split the peace of the day asunder and the rooks finally took flight towards the woods. 'Sorry I'm late,' the agent said as he was getting out of his car. He was a young man; in his early twenties, possibly younger, with sideburns which were trimmed close and angular. The collar on his neatly pressed shirt - white with pale pink stripes - seemed far too large and elaborate and he wore big, square, gold cufflinks. 'I didn't realise how far from...' he glanced around at the woods, '...anywhere it was.'

'Yes, I know,' said Jake.

The estate agent pulled a small bunch of three keys from his pocket, two Yale type keys and a long one with an oval hoop at the end. 'Shall we?' He stepped towards the front door, trying to keep out of the undergrowth as best he could. When he brushed past Hannah, she noticed he was wearing too much aftershave.

The first Yale key didn't work and so he tried the next,

but that didn't work either and so he tried the first again, giving it a wriggle as he attempted to turn it. 'Probably needs some oil.' There was a hint of nervousness in his voice. 'Shall we try around the back?'

'After you,' said Jake, pointing the way.

The group of three navigated the long grass and brambles, fighting their way to the back door. 'Been empty a while has it?' asked Jake, trying to ignore the taste of rot which still pervaded his mouth.

'I have no idea,' said the agent, speaking over his shoulder as he encouraged the longer key into the backdoor lock. 'It's being sold through the bank.'

Like the rest of the cottage the door was in a bad state of repair. Paint which had once been green, had peeled years before and the wood beneath was warped, damp and wore a mossy coat. An oblong of moulded glass – with a concentric circle design and made opaque through time and neglect - was set into the door at head height and carried a crack which ran diagonally between opposite corners.

The long key didn't turn either. The agent sucked his lower lip and gave a short nervous giggle, trying not to reveal his frustration while surreptitiously trying to force the lock.

'Don't do that,' said Hannah, addressing the agent like he was a child. 'You'll break it.'

The young man, suitably chided, released the pressure he'd been exerting on the key and looked at her, his eyes slightly downcast; embarrassed and annoyed with himself.

'Here, let me try?' Before he had chance to reply, Hannah had nudged him out of the way and had her hand on the key which was still protruding from the door. Without undue effort on her part, there was a light clunk and the door was unlocked. She pushed down on the corroded, black wrought iron handle and, with the aid of a small kick to the bottom of the door, it swung inwards. 'There you go,' she said, stepping aside to let the estate agent enter first and making no effort whatsoever to conceal her smugness.

The kitchen was thick with gloom. Motes of dust glinted and danced in the shaft of golden light from the door, but the sun's influence didn't penetrate far into the room and beyond it the dust lost its glint, hanging like an ancient veil on a desiccated corpse. The agent sneezed. 'This is the kitchen,' he said, holding a finger under his nose.

Jake gave him a curious glance. It was obvious that the agent knew precisely as much about the cottage as he and Hannah did. The dust that filled the air was a fraction of that which coated all the surfaces.

Beneath the window was an old Belfast sink, with wooden tables at either side rather than modern worktops. The linoleum covered floor was stained dark with age and dirt, as were the walls. Cobwebs hung not only from the corners of the ceiling but from all over the rough plaster, reaching towards the floor like grey, gossamer Christmas decorations, swaying in the air turbulence caused by the three people entering the cottage. Jake noted the Aga, positioned against the thick set chimneybreast and for a moment he saw past the dirt and the grease and some of the house's worth was redeemed.

'Any questions?' asked the agent.

Hannah, who was picking errant cobwebs from her hair, shook her head and they moved as a group into the hall. Jake tried the light-switch, but wasn't surprised when it didn't work and so the hall remained illuminated only by the dim red and yellow glow of sunlight shining through the faded stained glass above the front door. There were three other doors leading off the hall. Two, they assumed, opened into reception rooms and the other was a smaller door with a crooked lintel. The little door was nailed shut in a crude fashion. Nail-heads were sticking out of the wood at all angles. Dark stains coated the wall around the door.

'What's in there?' asked Hannah

'I'm ... erm ... not sure.' The agent stared at the floor plan he was clutching. The door wasn't marked. He said nothing about it. 'It's probably just a cupboard under the stairs.'

Meanwhile, Hannah's attention had been drawn to a faded painting which was hung on the wall opposite. It was of a small girl, with rosy cheeks and an old-fashioned bonnet, there was nothing special about the painting, but she gazed at it with a sense of déjà vu, sure that at some time in the past, she'd stood on the same spot and stared at the same picture.

Having given up on the nailed-up door, Jake and the agent shuffled further along the hallway, but Hannah stood for a moment longer, transfixed by cobwebs fluttering around the edges of the picture frame, before she snapped back to her senses. With a shrug, she followed the other two towards the next room.

They were in a sitting room of sorts, devoid of furniture apart from an old grubby two-seater sofa. The bare floorboards seemed sound enough and Jake took a moment to admire the large open fireplace, with its cast iron grate. Twigs were poking down from the chimney.

As the trio surveyed the room Hannah's sense of déjà vu was still present, but it was by no means an unpleasant sensation. Despite the cottage's decline and isolation it already felt strangely like home, as if she were merely returning after a protracted trip away. She reached for Jake's hand and gave it a light squeeze while looking up to meet his eyes with a smile on her face that said, *I love it*.

The other downstairs room was almost a mirror image of the first, although the fireplace was slightly smaller. An upright piano was pushed against the wall. 'You've always wanted a piano,' said Hannah, giving Jake's hand another squeeze.

Jake still wasn't a hundred percent sold on the cottage. There were some features, like the open fireplaces and the Aga which added charm to the place, but in his mind the amount of work needed to make it habitable might prove to be a deal breaker. And although they desired seclusion, the remoteness of Picker's Bleed made him uneasy. Unlike Hannah, he didn't find the cottage welcoming at all. He gave her hand a light squeeze in return and tried to conceal his growing doubt until they'd at least seen the rest of the house.

The bare wooden staircase creaked as the trio ascended, the young estate agent tentatively leading the way. Their footsteps echoed through the empty house. No one spoke and all of them were almost creeping, as if they were intruders rather than prospective buyers. Fresh dust bloomed with their passing. The estate agent sneezed again, making both Hannah and Jake jump and all three burst into giggles, the tension temporarily broken.

While the air downstairs had carried a slight chill, the heat on the upper floor was oppressive, which was noticeable the instant they stepped onto the landing, which doubled back from the top of the stairs. There were three doors leading off it, all with matching brass knobs and all of them closed.

The first door they tried, which stood adjacent to the top step, led into the bathroom which was decorated with grimy, not-so-white tiles and lino', stained the colour of long dried blood. Beneath a horizontal slit of a window stood a cast iron bath, on short but decorative curved legs. The toilet was on the shorter wall and opposite was a free-standing ceramic basin beneath a long, dusty mirror. Spider webs clung to every surface in a grey mat, filled with the detritus of flies and shed spider skins. No one bothered to lift the toilet seat for closer inspection.

As the intrepid explorers moved along the landing towards the other doors, the air became heavier.

'It's warm up here,' said Jake, stating the obvious, before turning the knob on the next door.

It was the second bedroom, according to the floorplan. Plaster was peeling off the damp walls, revealing the lathes beneath, which showed through like the ribs of a decaying whale. Their footsteps echoed on the bare floorboards. Behind the door, so they only saw it when they were in the room, was a baby's cot, its slats yellow with age.

Jake thought it was creepy, but Hannah was viewing the house as if it were already theirs. Despite the dirt, she was filled with a sense of pleasant well-being.

When they opened the next door all of them stopped dead in their tracks. The agent looked decidedly sheepish, and a little afraid.

At first it appeared they were peering into nothing, but as their eyes adjusted they saw that the entire room was painted black. Not just the walls, but the floor, ceiling and even the windows were coated with a thick tarry substance. The agent fumbled for the light-switch (it too was painted black) but when he flicked it no light spilled from the bare overhead bulb. Being as none of the other bulbs had worked the absence of light came as no surprise.

'Do they even have mains electricity around here?' asked Hannah, not complaining but simply curious to know if there was a generator somewhere.

The agent looked flustered, as if unsure of the answer. 'I'm sure they do,' he said. Then he paused and squinted at the pieces of paper in his hand, struggling to see if electricity was mentioned in the house's details.

Hannah's mind was racing with possibilities. 'We could put solar panels on the roof, or a small wind turbine in the garden,' she was saying, the excitement evident in her voice; relishing an opportunity to live off grid.

'Maybe,' said Jake, who was only half listening. His attention was fixed on the black bedframe that jutted into the even blacker room from the longest wall. The aged slats conjured images in his mind that were darker than the room itself. He gave a small shudder and turned to the agent, whose voice had tailed off, he too seemingly mesmerised by the curious black room. 'Is that all of it?' asked Jake. 'I think I've seen enough.'

4

'Careful you don't get that one wet.' Hannah shouted the instruction from the living room and Jake wondered how she could possibly know which box he'd picked up. He shrugged it off as one of life's little mysteries and carried the box out of the front door and down into the rain that had fluctuated all day between heavy and torrential. The sale had gone through remarkably quickly and the day had arrived for them to move.

And what a foul day it was. Jake was feeling melancholic; 'I'm going to miss this place,' he said.

'But look at what we're moving in to. It's amazing.'

'I know,' he said. On paper it was true, the cottage was everything they'd dreamed of, but no matter how hard he tried, Jake couldn't get excited about Picker's Bleed.

'But?'

'I'm fine,' said Jake, but he didn't feel fine. He often thought back to the day of the viewing and wished he'd been more insistent about not buying the cottage, but at the time Hannah's enthusiasm had been infectious. The instant they'd climbed back into the car she was telling him how much she loved it.

"Really?" he'd asked, surprised at first because it was unusual for them to hold such polarised feelings about something so important.

"Oh," she had said, a little crestfallen at his reaction. "Yes, don't you?"

"There's a lot of work needs doing," Jake had said, fumbling for reasons not to like the house.

"I know," said Hannah. "It'll be more than worth it. Imagine you and me, surrounded by all that countryside. We could get a dog and go on long walks through the woods. It's a place I could see us raising children."

Jake raised an eyebrow. They had always said one day they'd move to the country and have a large family. It had always been Hannah who was against the idea. He'd given her knee a gentle squeeze and for a while they drove without speaking, and with distance from Picker's Bleed Jake's feelings of unease tapered off until eventually they were just a memory, and just like the memory of pain, the sensation lost potency. "It would have to be a cheeky offer," he'd found himself saying. "To make it worthwhile with all the work that needs doing."

"But what if they don't accept it?" she'd asked, with a hint of apprehension.

"Then the house isn't supposed to be ours."

Hannah hadn't been completely satisfied, but it transpired she needn't have worried because their offer had been accepted without hesitation and the survey they'd paid for showed the house, structurally at least, to be in reasonable condition for a property of its age, which considering the cottage was over five-hundred years old, really didn't say a lot.

Now it was too late for protests.

Jake's hands gripped the faux leather steering wheel as they traversed the countryside. Wind raced across the fields, trying to bully the car off the road and driving rain into sheets of water which obscured the way. Even with the wipers on full, he was forced to slow the Fiat to a crawl, hunched over the wheel, concentrating on keeping the car in the middle of the road. Hannah's fingernails were starting to dig into the foam of the seat by her sides. Behind them the back seat had been folded flat to make space for the boxes of valuables and fragile stuff they didn't trust to the removals company.

Jake's mood was darkened by more than the weather. He had the beginnings of a headache and still couldn't shake the feeling they'd done the wrong thing. 'Do you reckon it's safe?' he asked. They'd reached the turn-off into the woods and stopped for a moment to assess the situation before entering the trees.

Both of them eyed the canopy above. The branches were still fully laden with leaves and thrashed wildly in the storm. The journey had already been arduously long and the thought of turning back was enough for them to take a chance.

With a shrug, Jake edged the car onto the track. The noise of the forest was tumultuous and Jake feared for their safety. Looking across to Hannah, he could see her quietly gnawing her top lip. His hands were clammy, and his shoulders ached from tensing.

The nagging anxiety he'd been suffering since they'd completed on the sale was worsening. 'I'm sure something's trying to stop us getting to this house,' he muttered.

'What's that?' asked Hannah.

Jake repeated himself, but louder.

'Why?' she asked.

'Well, it just is. It shouldn't be this hard.'

Somewhere outside the car a crack pierced the cacophony of the storm. 'Fuck!' shouted Jake and slammed his foot on the brake. Even though they were only travelling at a snail's pace the car almost slid sideways on the wet road.

Hannah let out a small scream. 'Fuck. Fuck. Calm down. For fuck's sake,' she mumbled to herself.

Both of them craned their necks to see out of the back window. Behind them the lane was cut off by a mass of leaves and twigs where a sizeable tree had succumbed to the storm. 'That was close,' said Jake quietly, his voice almost lost to the racket outside the car.

'Well,' said Hannah in an equally reserved tone of voice, just slightly louder to make herself heard over the screaming cacophony outside, 'there's no going back now.'

They pulled away at a crawl, wanting to go fast to escape the woods, but afraid of hitting another fallen tree or skidding off the road.

'Do you reckon the removal van's come though this?' Hannah said.

'Fuck knows. They might have come in from the village end, but I doubt it. Try and give them a ring if you can, but I bet there's still no signal all the way out here though.' Jake was thinking moving to Pickers Bleed was definitely a bad idea, and he could feel his wits beginning to fray.

Hannah reached down into the foot-well and cursed herself for not cleaning her bag out more often. When she did finally extract the phone, she took one look and threw it into the glovebox. 'Damn.'

'Here, try mine.' Jake tentatively took one hand off the wheel to fish his own mobile from out of his coat pocket. The inside of the pocket was damp and cold and when he handed the phone to Hannah it was filmed with moisture and coated with bits of soggy tissue. She gave it a wipe on her sleeve and confirmed the lack of signal.

When they reached the babbling brook they'd paused to admire a couple of months previously, they found a torrent straining to escape its miniature gorge. Water was backing up where it met the bridge and flowing across the parapet. Jake stopped the car for a moment. The water across the road's surface didn't look too deep and just before Hannah voiced her concerns Jake said, 'Fuck it,' and stomped the accelerator, driving through as fast as he dared, hoping the bridge wouldn't choose the moment of their crossing to be washed away. Water sprayed up either side of the Fiat and he felt resistance through the steering wheel. For a moment he panicked that he might have misjudged the depth, but moments later they were off the bridge and the car's tyres were sloshing through regular puddles again.

It was with more than a little relief that they reached the cottage. Standing in a small clearing it seemed hunched against the storm, hugging the scant protection offered by the straining trees around it. The gates stood open, almost buried amongst rich, flowering grasses, which were now sodden and bent. It was safe to assume no-one had been there since the surveyor. Why would they?

Grass was up to the car's windows as they pulled through the gate. Jake guessed where the drive should be and aimed the car in the general direction of the house. When he dared go no further they both took a moment to breathe a sigh of relief at arriving, and to listen to rain hammering on the car's roof.

'You got the keys?' he asked.

Hannah held them up and gave them a jingle. 'Ready?' she said and gave him a little smile.

Both of them paused for a moment, poised and ready.

'Go.' Jake flung open his door. A fraction of a second

later Hannah did the same and they dashed across the short distance to the house - *their house* - and into the relative shelter of the small, open porch canopy. Luckily, the first key Hannah tried slid effortlessly into the keyhole and turned with the minimum of fuss. They bowled into the hallway, giggling, and slammed the door closed behind them.

All of a sudden it was quiet, as they shut out the storm and were pitched into gloom a shade or two darker than dusk. They could taste the dust they'd disturbed and felt it adhering to their damp skin.

'Wonder if there's power yet?' asked Jake, reaching over and flicking the light-switch. As expected, nothing happened.

'Lucky I brought these.' Hannah fetched three plain, white candles from her handbag.

'You're a genius,' Jake told her and moved forward to give her a kiss.

'Get off,' she said. 'You're all wet.'

'You'll be wet,' he said.

'Dirty bastard,' she giggled.

5

The candles did little to banish the deep shadows which lay thick around the room, fluid in the flickering light. 'We could do with opening a couple of windows,' said Hannah. 'It doesn't smell too fresh in here.'

'Damn right. It doesn't matter too much if the rain comes in.' On the way past, Jake tugged on the little door under the stairs. 'We're going to have to get this open,' he said. 'I'm dying to know what's in there.'

When they reached the kitchen, Jake reached over the deep, heavy sink to lift the latch on the wooden window frame. The frame must have warped or swelled and at first it wouldn't open. He gave the half-rotten wood a little help with the heel of his hand, afraid the glass would fall out if he gave it too much of a jolt. After four attempts - each harder than the last - the window jerked open and was caught by the wind. Jake needed to be quick to catch the edge of the frame before the window swung all the way and shattered against the outside wall. Somewhere else in the house a door slammed.

It was a struggle to pull the window closed enough to fix the metal catch, a feat made worse by the shards of cold rain lashing at his face and running down his neck. The window rattled and the catch threatened to wrench its screws free of the wood. In the short time it had been open a puddle had formed on the windowsill, which was over topping and trickling down behind the sink. 'Hope that holds,' said Jake.

'We'll be needing new windows anyway.'

'Still, I'd rather not break any on our first night, I think there are a few more important jobs to be getting on with.'

'Well of course, but I'd rather chance it and have an aired house, that's all,' said Hannah.

Jake couldn't disagree with her. 'It's a bit daunting, isn't it?'

'What is?'

'The amount of work needed to make this place into a home.'

She looked up at his face, beaming. 'But it's our house. There's no rush, we'll just do one thing at a time. It's going to be brilliant turning it into a home. But I think we'd better get the camping stove from the car before getting stuck in.'

Jake peered at the dilapidation surrounding them and felt small and a little bit afraid.

'Don't worry,' she said as if reading his mind. 'As I said, we don't have to do it all at once. It'll be fun.'

They raced back out to the car for a couple of boxes of essentials and a small camping stove they'd had the foresight to pack. Hannah went about opening more windows while Jake's first port of call was back into the kitchen for water. With some effort he turned on the ancient cast-iron tap above the sink. There came a juddering through the pipework, which seemed to emanate from all over the house, making its way to the kitchen from all directions and culminating in an ejaculation of thick brown sludge, which splashed back when it hit the bottom of the sink. Some hit him in the eye, and another drop wetted his bottom lip. Jake felt a little defeated. His headache was worsening by the minute.

After a while the pipes ceased trembling and the flow of water became more constant. He waited as the stream steadily ran clear and, when he deemed it clean enough, Jake swilled out his mug, letting the water run a few moments longer before filling it again and drinking. The water still tasted of dirt, but he filled the kettle anyway and carried it back through to the sitting room.

They enjoyed tea and biscuits while sitting cross legged on the living room floor. A break in the clouds filled the room with enough watery sunlight for them to be able to snuff the candles. Neither of them had been able to get a phone signal to call the removal firm.

'Hope they can get through,' lamented Jake, wishing he'd packed a dry change of clothes in the car. The ones he was wearing were wet, cold and uncomfortable.

'I'm sure we'll manage,' said a cheery Hannah. 'There's loads of food in the car, well, some sandwiches and crisps and I think there's a bottle of Fanta still. And maybe some more biscuits.' As usual she'd over-packed for the journey, but they were both glad of it, else they'd have been hungry as well as damp.

'Right.' Jake downed the last of his tea, swallowing a soggy lump of Hob Nob which had sunk to the bottom of the mug, 'let's get this place sorted shall we.'

Slightly refreshed, they took advantage of a lull in the storm to unload more boxes and bags from the car and pile them in the living room next to the camping stove. After several trips in and out of the front door both of them were soaked from the waist down from pushing though the long grass. One of the boxes was full of cleaning products and while Hannah selected a few things from it and got busy scrubbing the kitchen, Jake wandered upstairs, stooping halfway up to avoid bumping his head on the low ceiling.

Like the kitchen, the window in the first bedroom - the one they dubbed the nursery because of the aging cot - didn't open easily, but after a minor tussle he was trying to secure the catch. Fortunately, the front of the house seemed to be a little more sheltered than the back and so he thought there was a chance the frame would hold and he could leave the window open. Wind whistled through the house, making filamentous cobwebs flutter and dance.

For a few moments - minutes perhaps - he ignored the rest of the room and leaned out of the window, letting the wind ruffle his hair and even though it was strong, it carried the clean scent of rain and earth. When he'd had his fill of fresh air, Jake turned his attention back to the room.

He contemplated the cot for a moment. Once upon a time it had been painted gloss white, but the slats had long since yellowed and behind them faded wallpaper had peeled away to reveal the damp, crumbling plaster beneath. As he crossed the room towards it a floorboard creaked loudly under his weight.

The noise made him acutely aware of his surroundings, the wind, the musty smell and ultimately his own physical presence. Now everything seemed too real and he felt on edge as he got down on one knee to peer underneath, expecting to find something, but unsure of what.

Jake recoiled from what he saw. Two glass eyes stared back from behind a thick layer of dust; and yet they managed to retain a glint. The teddy-bear was not some antique, like a Steiff, but was obviously old and quite threadbare in places. A large, but harmless house-spider crawled across one of the teddy's ears and Jake got back to his feet, leaving the creepy old bear where it was and shaking his head.

The next room Jake went into was the 'black' room. Within two steps of the threshold he was smothered with gloom as if he'd walked into a cave. The air was musty and humid and he wouldn't have been surprised to find diverse ecosystems of fungi growing in the shadows where he couldn't quite see what was hidden. He peered around anxiously, half expecting to detect movement in the dark corners. After fumbling for the window, he quickly realised there'd be no way of opening it without the aid of tools. The seal of black paint was too strong an adhesive.

Behind him the door slammed shut. The dark was absolute and Jake had the overwhelming feeling he was no longer alone in the room.

'Who's there?' croaked a woman's voice, from right beside him. It sounded crow-like in its hoarseness.

Panic was upon him in an instant and in his rush to reach the door, he became disorientated and smashed his shins into the black bed frame which was jutting into the room. A stream of obscenities left his mouth as he fell forwards and became tangled in the bed's springs, thrashing, not caring if he ripped his arm open on any stray points of metal or wood, such was his need to escape.

There was cackling laughter at his plight.

Within a fraction of a second he was up and feeling along the wall and soon located the doorknob. The knob didn't turn in his grip and his hand slipped off.

'Remember, this is my house,' said the voice.

Jake tried the knob again, but his hand kept slipping and it refused to turn. Tears sprang to his eyes as he hammered the inside of the door with one fist while tugging the knob with the other. His panic was too out of control to allow for rational thought.

Hannah was already coming along the hallway, having heard the commotion from downstairs and within moments she'd flung the door open from the outside. Dim light flowed into the room and Jake's fear subsided.

'What the bloody hell's wrong with you?' she asked.

'There's somebody in there,' he stammered.

'No there's not, silly.' Hannah peered into the room.

'I swear I heard someone.'

Hannah gave him a concerned look and Jake was left struggling for an explanation. 'The door slammed and I tripped over the bed in the dark,' he said while bending to rub his sore shins.

'Prat.' She gave him a half-confused smile. 'You scared the crap out of me. Now, how about you make a start on cleaning the bathroom while I carry on with the kitchen?'

'No worries,' he said, giving the door knob a twist on his way out of the room. It turned without resistance. 'Bloody thing.' He swung the door closed on the black room.

'Doesn't look like the removal van's going to get through today, does it?'

'Nope,' replied Hannah.

'I'll have to take a drive I suppose, to see if I can get a signal anywhere.'

'We'll be okay until morning,' she said, looking out of the window and thinking the break in the weather was possibly the eye of the storm. The sky had darkened to twilight although it was only four in the afternoon. The wind was once again increasing in power, trying to uproot trees or at the very least, strip them of their leaves and lesser branches.

'You sure?' Jake had no desire to go out in the storm, but he was conscious of the fact they only had a couple of cheese sandwiches and half a packet of biscuits to eat, and the sandwiches were going stale. They also had no bed; the one already upstairs wasn't an option, and all their blankets, pillows and duvets were somewhere en-route.

'Of course I'm sure,' she told him. 'If the removals van can't get through then you're not going to be able to.'

'I was going to go the other way. On the map the lane wriggles into Marsham after a couple of miles.'

'And what happens if a tree falls on the car? I'll be here all by myself, not knowing if you've been squished. I'll be too worried if you go, and I don't want to risk going out in this.' As if to answer her fears there came a flash of lightning. She counted to seven before the low rumble of thunder came rolling over the treetops. 'There's every chance the other way's blocked too.'

'You're right,' he said. 'I'd better go and close the windows then, before they all get blown off the hinges and rain floods the house.'

The room with the cot felt much fresher for being aired but a faint smell lingered, which he couldn't quite place. Before returning back downstairs he looked along the hall to where the door to the black room stood slightly ajar. He thought nothing of it and was simply glad he didn't have to venture back in to close the window. 'I hope we've done the right thing,' he mumbled to himself, not for the first time. *Bit late now. Better learn to love it.*

Jake refused to sleep upstairs and so they spent the night on the sitting room floor. They chatted away most of the night but eventually they tried to sleep. Dusty floorboards made for an uncomfortable night, wrapped in each other's arms and wary of splinters. Wind whistled through the draughty house, causing bangs and rattles. Jake was awake with Hannah's head on his bare chest. She was gently snoring.

A flash of lightning lit the room and the instantaneous thunderclap was felt as well as heard. In the diminishing rumble there came the sound of children in the house; a miserable whimpering which floated through the empty rooms like a will-o'-the-wisp. Jake almost cried. *This living in the country is going to take a bit of getting used to*, he told himself. It must have been the wind, or a tree blowing about outside. There came another peal of thunder and rain hammered the windows with increased ferocity. Glass rattled in the frames.

The empty house was giving him a bad case of the heebie-jeebies.

6

At some time before dawn he must have fallen asleep because Jake woke with a numb shoulder. Beside him Hannah was still snoring, playing lead to a chorus of birdsong from the surrounding forest. Although the window was grimy, there was enough sunshine coming through to tell it was a glorious blue-sky morning outside. Something rattled down the chimney, no doubt dislodged by the rooks congregated on the roof above.

The need to urinate forced Jake to try and slowly untangle his limbs from Hannah's without waking her, a task in which he was unsuccessful. She opened her eyes and began to stretch out her numerous aches. 'What time is it?' she muttered, groggy beside him.

'No idea.' Jake dug his phone from the pocket of his jeans, which were heaped on the floor next to where they'd slept. The battery was still dead.

'We got a plan?' she asked, climbing to her feet and brushing dust and cobwebs from the clothes she'd slept in. 'I need to get my clothes from the removals people. I must stink.'

'No change there then,' he quipped.

'Cheeky bastard.' She looked for something to throw in his direction, but there was nothing to hand.

'We'll drive until we get a signal I suppose,' said Jake, getting back on topic. 'I'm sure we'll be able to sort something out to get our things. We'll pick up some paint and stuff too, so we can get something done with that bedroom. I reckon it'll need a new window as well, but we can make a start on the other bits and pieces.'

While Jake crouched on his haunches over the camping stove, waiting for the kettle to boil, Hannah pulled on her shoes and went out into the garden. It was still early and mist was rising from every surface at the merest touch of the sun to hang in thick wisps above the forest canopy. The air was fresh and clean and carried with it the faint scent of honeysuckle. Hannah went into the orchard, paying no heed to the dew and rainwater soaking through her shoes from the overgrown vegetation.

Something rustled off to her left, making her start. It sounded large, perhaps a fox, badger or maybe even a muntjac. An instant later the grass was still again and Hannah was alone with the birdsong coming from the woods and the cawing of rooks from the roof.

For a while she stood and listened. A green woodpecker laughed amongst the twittering of tits and finches. A broad smile lit her face at owning her own small corner of Eden. Her smile broadened further when Jake came wading through the grass carrying two steaming mugs of coffee. After handing one to her he placed an arm around Hannah's waist and pulled her close so they could enjoy the splendour of the morning together. 'We'll have to pick up a bird table while we're out.'

'There must be all sorts living out here,' she said, thinking about the creature she'd heard scurrying away, 'I think we ought to buy a trail cam as well. I'd love to see what comes out of the woods at night.'

The density of the forest made it difficult to see far past the first disorderly ranks of gnarled trees. 'I can't wait to go exploring in there either,' said Jake. He peered around the overgrown garden and orchard, 'but we'd better get this lot sorted out first.' He let out a small sigh.

'One thing at a time dear. The garden will be easier to fix in winter anyway.' Hannah was just finishing the dregs of her coffee and despite the rapidly warming morning she breathed out a plume of vapour. 'Right. Shall we make a move then?'

'Best had.' Jake swallowed back what was left of his drink and set to closing up the house.

'Bloody hell, it's only ten-past-seven!' It was only when Jake turned on the car's ignition and the dashboard clock lit up that they had a way of telling the time.

'Never mind,' said Hannah. 'It's a beautiful morning and we can have a bit of an explore around the village and stuff.'

It was indeed a morning of the finest quality, especially after the previous night's storm and by the time they were reversing out of the gate the mist was burned off to merely a few thin wisps that hung gossamer around the treetops.

'Which way do you reckon?'

'Well, we know that way's blocked,' said Hannah, nodding in the direction from which they'd arrived at Picker's Bleed. 'So, there's only one way we can go.'

They'd already started moving when Jake began rummaging in his pocket for his phone before plugging it into the charger dangling from the cigarette lighter socket. Hannah rolled her eyes but stayed quiet, wondering why he hadn't done it before they'd set off. Dappled sunlight shone down in patches onto the lane that wound through the forest. Grass was growing up the centre of the road, which was littered with twigs and debris from the storm.

'Balls. There's another one down!' Jake stopped the car inches from a tree blocking the lane. The uneven light had meant his eyes were having a difficult time adjusting and they'd almost run straight into it. He sighed and while he was waiting for his phone to power up, Hannah got out of the car.

There was no chance of them moving the fallen tree by hand, it was simply too large and Hannah suspected that even if they had a Land Rover with a winch, the old beech would prove too cumbersome. On one side of the road an enormous disc of roots and earth reached skyward where they'd been torn from the ground and the other side was a mass of leaves and splintered logs; many of them from neighbouring trees which had been unfortunate enough to be in the way when the large one fell.

Not one to be disheartened, Hannah clambered up onto the fallen trunk. With her eyes closed she tilted her head back to catch the morning sun as it penetrated the newly made clearing. The bark was smooth beneath her fingers.

'Still no signal.' A dismayed looking Jake emerged from their car, peering longingly at his phone as if mind-power alone could make it work.

'How far do you reckon we've come?' she asked, lazily glancing down at him.

'I didn't clock it. A mile, tops.'

'Well, by my reckoning that leaves about another mile or so to walk. That's not so bad.'

Jake grumbled, feeling a twinge of anxiety. Born and raised in the city, he found something quite disconcerting about being out of touch with the world. Hannah on the other hand, found it all quite liberating and hopped off the log, eager to get going.

'Do we need anything else from the car?' Jake returned to remove the keys and to make it secure, although he couldn't think who'd come along to steal anything from it.

'Is there a drink?'

'Think so.' Jake rummaged about in the rear foot-well and found some cup drinks – the type with a thin plastic straw Sellotaped to the side of the carton. He couldn't remember how long they'd been there but they were better than no drink at all. He hoped. 'Do you reckon the car will be alright here?' he asked with a backwards glance.

'I'd have thought so,'

'What if someone comes to clear the road?'

'Then they'll have to come and find us. I'm sure it'll be easy enough.'

'Wait!' He quickly strode back to the car and unlocked it again. Hannah tutted, becoming impatient but forgave him when she realised he was fetching a pen to write down the number for the removals firm before his phone ran out of battery again.

The walk into Marsham was more than pleasant and in the sunshine it didn't take long for Jake to stop fretting about their abandoned car, missing belongings or creepy house.

As they wandered towards the village the track appeared even less used than it did in the other direction from the cottage. Trees and bushes crowded in on either side and nettles grew in patches from clods of dirt in the middle of the road. More than once they heard unidentified creatures scuttle away from them off to the side of the lane, just inside the thick-growing forest. Rabbits hopped away at their approach. One time they rounded a slight bend to see, not many yards off, a deer standing in the lane. The animal stood as tall as they were, resplendent with velvety antlers. They froze in awe, but also partly afraid of the deer's size. The animal also paused for a moment to study them before it bounded off into the undergrowth and despite its bulk, within seconds there was no indication, sound nor sight that it had ever existed.

After they'd strolled for about half an hour the trees came to an abrupt and definite end, leaving them with an open vista of fields, criss-crossed with ancient hedgerows and sprinkled with the occasional veteran oak. Ahead lay what they presumed was Marsham, which from a distance appeared as little more than a collection of squat stone buildings congregated around a church spire, silhouetted against the sky. A weathervane glinted on top, flashing golden in the sunshine.

The sight of the village spurred them on and their pace increased. The sun beat down and after the cool shade and pleasant sunbeams of the forest they were surprised by its intensity.

Marsham was larger than it had appeared at first glance, but only just. First they came across sporadic houses which became more frequent with proximity to the village, until both sides of the street were lined with squat, terraced cottages. The lane came out at the village square. On one side of the junction was a public house, The *Bull's Head* -A freshly painted sign of its namesake was hanging above the studded oak door – and on the other was the village store. 'It's like something straight out of Miss Marple!' Hannah exclaimed. An elderly lady was struggling out of the shop with her wheeled basket and despite the heat of the morning she wore a long, brown-checked, woollen overcoat.

Directly opposite was the imposing *Church of Saint Augustine*. The church was built of the same grey, stone blocks as the rest of the village, although it appeared to be infinitely older; pitted with age and the corners rounded with wear. Gargoyles peered down from the roof, these too were eroded so they lacked any hard features.

In the middle of the square was a raised island of stone with a memorial in the centre and benches around the outside, facing outwards, all surrounded by a moat of double yellow lines. When they wandered over to have a closer look they saw there were no names on the memorial.

'What time is it?' asked Hannah, wondering at the general lack of people.

'No idea. I'd have thought there'd have been a few folk about by now.' The old lady, having successfully negotiated the shop door, was long gone.

'Go and get us a drink and ask in the shop, will you? I'll wait out here.'

A single 'ching' from the bell above the door announced Jake's entrance and a stout woman, with her grey hair in a tight bun and wearing a floral apron, came shuffling out of a back room, seeming ever so slightly out of breath. She took a seat on a tall stool behind the counter.

'Morning,' said Jake.

'Morning,' the woman curtly replied. Not exactly unfriendly but not welcoming either and while Jake perused the cold drinks he could feel her eyes boring into his back. He didn't take it personally because he got the distinct impression she was the same with all her customers, particularly any who were strangers.

He grabbed two bottles of Sprite and took them to the counter where the woman punched the amount into the cash register - which was one of the old, pre-digital age ones with clunky buttons and digits which shot upwards into a glass enclosure on the top – all the time making him squirm under her scrutinous gaze. 'That will be two pounds forty please?'

'Thank you,' he said as politely as he could muster and placed the correct change in her upturned palm. She didn't reply and again, he could feel her gaze at his back as he left, the bell once again going 'ching' on his way out.

'Here you go.' He handed Hannah her drink.

'Thanks. What time is it then?'

'Bollocks. Forgot to ask.'

'You'd better go back in then.'

'I'm not going back in there! I reckon I'd end up in a pie or something.'

'That bad?'

'Worse.'

'Surely not?'

'Well, you go in then.'

Hannah peered in through the plate glass door to see the empty shop. The old woman must have gone back into the back room. 'Nah,' she said, thinking that if the shopkeeper was as unfriendly as Jake was making out she didn't want to risk disturbing her. 'The time's not important anyway. Let's go for an explore shall we?'

Exploring turned out to be a quick activity. Apart from the *Village Store* there was the *Bull's Head,* the imposing church and a butcher's shop. Once, there had been a post office as well, but it was long since converted into a house, the only indicators to its history were the words *Post Office* neatly inscribed into the lintel above the front door and a red pillar box on the pavement outside. Beyond these few frontages, terraced cottages reached for sixty or seventy yards in either direction. Opposite, just outside the church gates, there was an old, red phone box.

For such a small village, the *Church of Saint Augustine* was unfeasibly grand, as if its architect really wanted to put their stamp on the surrounding landscape. Hannah turned the hoop on the wrought iron gate and the hinges let go a squeal as the gate swung inwards to admit them. The sound rang too loud in the still morning air, highlighting just how profoundly quiet the village was. Within the churchyard the silence seemed thicker still. Nothing stirred, as if a giant invisible duvet smothered everything.

They sauntered between yew trees, trying to read names and dates on the headstones, speaking in hushed tones. Eighteen sixty-two was the oldest date they found, but some of the graves looked much older, their inscriptions faded to indiscernible indentations in worn sandstone, encrusted with colonies of green and yellow lichen. As they neared the church's ornate wooden porch, the headstones became grander and included an eight-foot carved angel and a smattering of sarcophagi of untold age.

Jake and Hannah paused for a moment to see if there was anything of interest in the glass fronted noticeboard which was housed in the church's porch. Harvest festival was coming up and someone in the village was running a yoga class.

Jake took the iron hoop which served as a handle in the studded oak door and turned it. He gave the door a bit of a rattle before realising it was locked. The sound echoed loudly inside the church, which spoke of a large unoccupied space within. With a shrug he backed out of the porch, caught his heel on an uneven paving slab and fell flat on his arse with a heavy thump, much to Hannah's amusement.

From his position on the floor Jake looked up at the church. Despite its size and once elaborate decoration, the church's windows were remarkably narrow, slit-like even; each filled with the tall figure of a saint in stained glass. The steeple rose high above, faint wisps of cloud passing behind it, which gave it the vertiginous illusion of movement.

At the rear of the church the grounds were less well tended, grass grew up around the headstones and some were completely obliterated beneath low hanging branches from errant trees and shrubs. A dozen or more headstones stood up against the crooked and warped brick wall which surrounded the graveyard, as if they'd been moved in order create room for more bodies.

'Do you reckon it's late enough to call the removals people now?' asked Jake.

'I'd have thought so.' Hannah took a quick glance around at nothing in particular. 'Come on then, let's go.'

The payphone was not as antiquated as the box it was housed in and needed a credit card rather than coins. 'Is that a seven or a two?' Jake was holding the crumpled piece of paper he'd had the good sense to write the removal company's number on.

'Seven... I think.'

The phone rang out three times before a lady answered with a husky, forty a day, kind of voice. 'Good morning, Timmings Removals!'

'Hi,' Jake began. 'We were supposed to be moving yesterday but there was a storm...'

'Oh yes. Is that Mr Jenkins?'

'That's my partner's name, but yes. A tree came down and I think it might have stopped the van from getting through.'

'Yes, bit of a blow that...'

Aware of the cost of phone charges Jake interrupted her before they got into a conversation about the weather. 'Do you know when our stuff might be delivered?'

'Has the tree been moved?'

'Shit!' It was the most fundamental question and yet it hadn't crossed his mind.

Sensing his embarrassment, she answered for him. 'Do

you know when it might be moved?'

'Erm... Soon, I hope.' The realisation dawned on him that he and Hannah were probably the only ones to know the lane was blocked. Life in the country really was going to take a bit of getting used to.

'Do you want to call back when it's cleared?' She sounded friendly enough, as if she had all the time in the world.'

'Yes, I better had.'

'Not good news?' asked Hannah after he'd hung up, sensing the way the conversation had gone.

'We've got to ring back when the tree's been moved.'

'Well, how do we know when that will be?'

'When *we* move it, I suppose.'

'Bollocks.'

'Bollocks indeed,' he said. 'What shall we do now? I don't fancy walking back just yet.'

'If we don't get our clothes, we'll stink.'

'Are you sure there're none in the car?'

'Yes, I'm sure.'

'Balls.'

'Do you reckon the pub opens at eleven?' asked Hannah.

Jake's eyes lit up. 'It might do, you know.'

'They'll probably have a number for the council or something.'

'Bound to have. They might even let us use their phone. I think this one just cost us a small fortune.'

'We could just ask in the shop?'

'I suppose you're right,' said Jake with a sigh. 'I don't fancy our chances though, but we could do with some more supplies if we've got a long wait.'

'Oh, hello again,' said the shopkeeper. This time she

actually appeared irritated when she came shuffling out of the back room.

'Hi,' said Hannah. 'I don't suppose you have a number for the council do you?'

The shopkeeper answered slowly, as if deliberating whether to answer at all. 'No,' she said.

Hannah suspected she might be lying. 'Only we moved into a new house yesterday, but the road got blocked by a fallen tree in the storm and the removals company still have all our stuff so...'

'Sorry, can't help you.' It was obvious by the way the woman was looking at Hannah that she was going to offer no effort in finding a number. She seemed to be scrutinising her.

Jake appeared from the back of the shop, carrying a couple of pre-made cheese sandwiches, bottles of water, crisps and a multipack of Snickers. 'I should have got a basket,' he said, trying not to drop the teetering pile of snacks.

It was a distraction which prevented Hannah from saying something she might live to regret, especially as it was the only shop for miles around. The shopkeeper very deliberately keyed prices into the cash register without a word, while Hannah relayed to Jake that she didn't have any numbers to offer.

'Pub then?'

'Bloody hope they know someone.'

7

It was seven minutes past eleven when the pub was unbolted from the inside. Jake had been on the verge of banging the stout door, but any hint of impatience disappeared the instant it swung inwards and they were greeted by the jolly looking landlord.

'What'll it be?' asked the landlord after he'd secured the door and followed them into the taproom, where Jake was appreciating the qualities of a 'proper' pub. It was like something from antiquity, with a low beamed ceiling and floorboards that were worn smooth by the passage of countless feet. Although smoking was no longer allowed in pubs the room carried the mellow aroma of old tobacco smoke, ingrained into the wood across the centuries.

The landlord had the look of a man who drank his fair share of the profits. His face was rounded, on the verge of developing jowls beneath his glossy cheeks and his nose had started to take on a bulbous quality. A red, checked lumberjack shirt was tucked into the waist of his faded blue jeans so his ample belly hung over, straining at buttons and seams.

After a few moments studying the small placards on the pump handles, Hannah and Jake chose their respective tipples – pints of ale for both of them – and Hannah began the conversation. 'I don't suppose you have the number for the council, do you?'

'Oh, why's that then?'

'We've just moved into a cottage up the road and...' Hannah began to recount the story and an odd look flashed across the landlord's piggy blue eyes and he leaned forward to rest his elbows on the bar, attentive. '...the lane's blocked so we can't go anywhere.'

'Was a bit rough last night.' A wry grin curled his lips. 'Which place you moved into?'

'Picker's Bleed. Do you know it?'

'Yes. Yes, I know it alright. Been empty a long time that place has. How you finding it?'

'Good,' said Hannah.

'It's a bit damp and it needs a lot of work, but it'll come good in the end,' chipped in Jake.

'Sure it will,' said the landlord. 'I'm sure it will.' Something in his voice suggested there was something Hannah and Jake were as yet ignorant of. 'Wasting your time calling the council though, they'll have their work cut out and your cottage isn't going to be top of their list.'

'But...' Hannah started, about to complain about her lack of clothes.

'Old Les'll be along shortly,' the landlord cut in. 'And he's often as not got a chainsaw in the back of his pickup.'

'Do you think he'll help us?'

'For the price of a pint, I'm sure he will.'

'What time do you think he'll be in?' asked Hannah, given fresh hope but acutely aware the day was passing while she was keen to get to work on their new home.

'Anytime really,' said the landlord, vaguely. 'You just

enjoy your drinks and I'm sure he'll be along shortly.'

'Fancy another?' They had nursed their pints for as long as possible, until all that remained were warm, flat dregs.

'May as well,' said Hannah, impatient but resigned to the wait.

As Jake approached the bar the landlord, as if he'd been watching from somewhere unseen, appeared from the back room. 'Same again?'

'Please.'

They were still the only customers in the pub and while they spoke they were mindful to keep their voices low. Not that they were speaking of anything worthy of being eavesdropped upon, but rather just to preserve the peace and quiet. Nearby, a grandfather clock ticked away the seconds.

The next pint went down much faster than the first and it was soon Hannah's turn to go to the bar. 'I don't suppose you have a number for the chainsaw guy, do you?' she asked the landlord when he was topping up the ales.

'I don't believe I do, I'm afraid,' he said with a slight shrug and trying to look as apologetic as he could. 'But I'm sure he'll be along shortly.'

Hannah sensed he wasn't being entirely honest but didn't know why. She bit back her frustration and headed back to the table, not caring too much that a small amount of beer sloshed over the top of the pint pot where it would leave a sticky puddle on the polished floorboards.

Just as she placed the drinks on the table and was sliding onto the bench the door opened and an aging yet obviously physically fit for his age gentleman entered. He was wearing a khaki green pullover and a flat cap, from under which protruded an ample set of ears. He didn't seem to notice Hannah and Jake sitting near the back wall.

'Morning John,' hailed the landlord, already fetching a

dimpled pint-pot from a hook behind the bar and beginning to fill it with best bitter. The two exchanged pleasantries then leaned into one another, speaking in hushed tones before they both turned to look at Jake and Hannah.

Jake leaned forwards on his short stool, expectant that the man was the chap they were waiting for, but even as he opened his mouth to speak the new arrival at the bar turned away and returned to muted conversation with the landlord. Despite Jake's and Hannah's best efforts to catch the landlord's eye he steadfastly failed to glance in their direction.

The older man eventually scraped his stool back on the floor and came over. 'So, you've moved in over at Picker's Bleed, have you?' he spoke with a thick, native drawl; born and bred. He stood near Jake's shoulder, wringing his cap in both hands until Hannah indicated to the empty stool at their table. Just as the man sat down the landlord came over and set down the dimpled tankard, freshly filled, before assuming a position behind the bar, where he pretended to clean glasses with a tea-towel. 'How're you finding it?' asked John, without waiting for a response to his first question.

'Don't know yet,' Hannah answered.

'We've not even moved in,' added Jake. 'The lane's blocked by trees, brought down by last night's storm.'

'Worst luck,' said the old man, his tone genuine.

'Apparently there'll be someone along *shortly* who'll be able to help us though,' said Hannah.

'Oi Tom.' John left what he'd come over to say for another time, instead hailing the landlord, who looked up at hearing his name. 'You've got a number for Les, haven't you?'

'Erm…' The landlord's face was a mask of innocence. 'I don't believe I have.'

''Course you have.'

'Must have lost it,' he lied.

'Likely story,' the old man grumbled, fishing an old *Nokia* from out of his coat pocket. 'Now let me see...' he held the phone up in front of his face, almost at arm's length and squinted at the screen while he scrolled through the many contacts and started the call. When the person on the other end answered, John shouted loudly into the handset and had to bring the phone back around to his ear to listen to the response. 'He'll be here shortly,' he said after he'd hung up.

'Brilliant,' said Hannah with enthusiasm, although they'd already heard both sides of the conversation perfectly clearly. The person on the other end of the line must have been shouting just as loudly as the old man. She made a mental note to ask what phone network he was on.

'Time for another?' Jake asked, tilting his glass.

'Always,' said John.

'Your round,' said Hannah to Jake.

The old man still had over half a pint left but downed it and handed the tankard to Jake as he stood to go to the bar. 'Same again,' he said.

'So, you know Picker's Bleed then do you?' Hannah asked as an icebreaker while Jake was at the bar.

The man shifted uncomfortably in his seat. 'Let's get another drink in us first, shall we?'

'Oh,' said Hannah.

Just as Jake returned to the table the door swung open again and a couple walked in, dressed for the outdoors. 'Morning Tom,' the woman called to the landlord and as she glanced around she saw the trio seated at the table. 'Morning John,' she said turning an enquiring gaze to his companions.

'Morning Mary, Pete,' replied Tom. 'These are... I'm terribly sorry,' he said. 'I didn't quite catch your names..?'

'Jake.'

'Hannah.'

'... They've bought the cottage at Picker's Bleed.'

A look passed between the newcomers, 'Oh,' said the woman. 'How are you finding it?'

John spoke before either of them had chance to reply, 'They've not moved in yet. Tree's blocked the lane. We're just waiting for Les to come and help us shift it.'

'Oh, he's just pulled up outside,' said Pete, who's eyes kept shifting from Hannah to Jake and back again. Both of whom sat forward in their seats at the news help was imminent.

Just moments later the door swung confidently open. 'Ey up Les,' greeted John. 'Get yourself a drink and pull up a pew.' And then, with six people, seven including the landlord, the cosy taproom came alive with chatter.

Les wasn't old at all, Hannah put him as being in his early thirties. He had the look of someone who worked continually outdoors in all weathers. He was lean, wiry even, but obviously strong. His eyes were ever so slightly squinted, but sharp as a weasel's. He wore rigger boots and jeans and gulped down half of his lager before he'd crossed the short distance to the table, taking the stool next to Jake with a satisfied sigh. Neither Jake nor Hannah thought it would be good manners to ask him outright when he was going to help; they would have to wait for him to offer in his own good time.

'Slide up, there's room enough for both of you.' They were eventually climbing into the front of Les' old Toyota pickup. Hannah got in first with Jake clambering in after, pulling the door closed once he'd swung both legs in.

'Are you sure you should be driving?' In no way sober herself, she recalled Les downing at least three pints before they'd left the pub, laughing their goodbyes to the landlord. Behind them John hoisted himself onto the flatbed and scuttled forwards, slapping the roof twice to let them know he was holding on tight and ready to go.

'Do you want this tree moved or what?' Les put the dash mounted shift lever into reverse and they pulled out of the village square. Behind them John stumbled and struggled to keep his balance.

Jake's head slumped against the window and he could have nodded off, but no sooner had his eyes gently closed he became aware of coming to a stop. Hannah nudged him in the ribs, 'Come on, you can't pass out yet, we've a tree to cut up.'

'I'll do the cutting,' said Les.

'Probably for the best,' answered Jake, finding the door handle and giving it a pull. The pickup's door sprung open and Jake spilled out into the lane, much to everyone's amusement. John was already hopping off the back of the truck, holding a sturdy set of loppers.

While John set to work on the thinner branches Les was pulling on a pair of Kevlar over-trousers and visor. Jake nodded appreciatively at the safety measures.

It must have been getting towards mid-afternoon and the shadows were lengthening when the chainsaw revved into life. Hannah almost felt apologetic for disturbing the peace and quiet of the woods. Once they got going it didn't take many minutes of cutting and heaving to have the vast majority of the fallen tree moved to the side of the lane, leaving just a smattering of leaves and small twigs in the road.

'Take care,' shouted Les as Jake rifled through his pockets to find his car keys. With nowhere to turn around, the pickup reversed back along the lane. Hannah and Jake's car was still facing towards Marsham, away from Pickers Bleed.

'Want me to drive?' Hannah asked.

Jake knew he was well over the limit, but convinced himself that there'd be no other road users and they'd be fine. 'You're in a worse state than me,' he said.

'You're probably right.'

When they reached the village the occupants of the two cars waved goodbye out of their respective windows and the pickup parked up for Les and John to return into the Bulls Head.

'Shall we get some take-outs while we're here?' said Hannah.

'Top idea,' Jake replied, and so they parked the car and went back into the pub, which was snug and homely.

'We could just stay in here for the evening?' Jake asked.

'Nah,' said Hannah. Let's get back to our house.' She smiled. '*Our* house does have a ring to it.'

Jake didn't feel so attached to the cottage yet, and he wasn't sure he wanted to be. 'But there's no furniture yet. And it's damp.'

'But it's ours. Besides, if you have another drink we'll never get home alive.'

'Good point,' he said, and they got their carry-outs and left.

8

Jake woke first, having jerked out of a nightmare; one where he was being mauled by an unearthly black dog with glowing red eyes. His mouth was dry as a bone and he felt like his throat was clogged with dust from the bare floor. Hannah lay asleep next to him and he disentangled himself from her limbs and climbed unsteadily to his feet. The creaking of his joints was audible.

He pressed a hand to his temple in a vain attempt to ease the pain which ebbed and flowed there, as he headed down the hall towards the kitchen, running the other hand along the wall to steady himself. It wasn't only his hangover making him unsteady, but the slightly odd angles of the hallway. Where the walls met the floor and the ceiling, there was not a single true line in the passage and the overall effect was disorientating.

Hannah didn't fare much better and was grateful for the coffee, despite grumbling about being woken. The night before, when it had seemed like a good idea, they'd agreed to leave early to get their chores done and so, less than an hour after rising, they were in the *Village Stores,* picking up copious bottles of water, energy drinks and pastry products. It was another hour before they reached the relative civilisation of an out-of-town retail park.

It was a productive morning and when they were done they had paint, scrapers and an assortment of other tools, including an axe for chopping firewood and a crowbar to investigate what lay behind the small door in the hallway.

They'd also phoned the removals company, who'd agreed to deliver their belongings in two days' time due to other obligations, which Jake and Hannah, although inconvenienced, thought was fair enough. They'd trawled the charity shops for clothes and had bought enough ill-fitting jumpers and trousers to last a few days. Underwear was purchased from the supermarket at the same time as they stocked up on groceries. They'd also managed to make inroads to getting the power reconnected while they were able to use the phone. By the time they'd finished and returned to Picker's Bleed it was only just gone two o'clock and they both felt much better for their excursion, especially after driving home in the sun, with the car windows open and music blaring.

When they got home, Hannah and Jake stood in the hallway, eager to get started. Motes of dust swirled around them, glinting red and yellow in the light from the grimy stained glass above the front door.

Jake's eyes alighted upon the crooked, little door beneath the stairs. 'First things first,' he said. 'I absolutely need to know what's behind here,' and without delay he forced the crowbar between the door and its frame near the lock, compressing the wood and making splinters as he wiggled it into the gap until the steel tip was embedded far enough for him to apply some pressure. He was pushing on the end of the crowbar with all his might, using both hands and leaning into it until, with the squealing of nails pulling free of the frame, the door sprung open and Jake cannoned into the wall in front of him, hitting his knuckles and swearing loudly, but his curses were short lived.

Dark seemed to spill out of the doorway rather than any of the weak light from the hall penetrate the space beyond, so they still couldn't see what lay just inside. Hannah stepped forwards into the void, confident.

'I'll grab the torch,' said Jake. 'Wait there a second.'

'Okay,' replied Hannah.

She'd already made her way inside the door by the time Jake came back and was standing in the dark, on the top step of a flight which led down into a cellar. At first Jake couldn't see her and experienced a flutter of fear in his chest, but when he pointed the torch through the door it shone directly onto her face. Her breath billowed across the narrow beam of light. He fumbled around for a light-switch, found one and flicked it before remembering the cottage was still without electricity. Hannah's breath was testament to how much cooler the cellar was than the rest of the house.

At first the cold gave welcome respite from the lazy, autumnal warmth of the cottage, but as they crept carefully down the steps, feeling their way with one hand on the wall, the chill slunk into Jake's bones until he was shivering. His teeth were chattering.

The chill didn't seem to bother Hannah as they headed downwards. The torch cut a straight beam through the dark, in which dust floated in lazy whorls. The light was pointing towards their feet and all it illuminated was the next crumbling step down.

Near the bottom of the brick staircase the hair on Jake's neck began to prickle. Faint gossamer threads tickled his face and he kept trying to brush them away or grasp them between his fingers. Much to his frustration, he continually failed.

Despite the cold, the atmosphere was stifling and oppressive. Jake was keen to escape, but Hannah was already groping her way along the nearest wall, feeling damp mortar crumble beneath her fingertips. The dark space welcomed her like an old friend.

'Come on,' Jake said. 'Let's get out of here.' Anxiety was tugging at the edges of his mind. The torch was trained on Hannah's back, the beam flitting up and down her body, revealing only part of her at a time. He briefly swung the torch around in a wide arc to try and gauge a sense of what the cellar looked like, and from the snatches afforded him, his mind formed a rather unimpressive picture of it. The cellar looked to be about the same size as the footprint of the cottage and was littered with the usual shelves, boxes and old furniture. The ceiling was low and vaulted, made of the same crumbling, red brick as the walls.

He flicked the torch's beam once again in Hannah's direction, to check she was following, and when the light touched her face Jake let out a screech. For an instant it wasn't Hannah standing in the torchlight. It looked like her but much paler, gaunt, her face stretched back taught over prominent cheekbones and jaw to show too many teeth in an evil grimace. Her hair seemed longer and matted and the eyes which reflected the light back to him were predatory.

Involuntarily, he recoiled and blinked away the image. When he reopened his eyes she was just Hannah again; the whole episode had all happened in a fraction of a second.

'What is it?' she asked, alarmed. 'Shine that bloody thing somewhere else would you?' Hannah lifted her arm to cover her eyes.

'Sorry,' he said. What he'd seen must have been a trick of the light, a hallucination caused by shadows on shadows. 'I'm giving myself the creeps, let's get out of here.'

'Lead the way,' said Hannah with a deep sense that the cellar was somewhere she'd like to explore at her own leisure.

Stepping back out into the hallway was like coming into a hot kitchen on a snowy morning, but without the comforting smells. A definite ache had taken up residence in Jake's fingertips. 'Fuck. It's freezing down there.'

'Is it?' Hannah hadn't noticed the cold, or been affected by it.

'Surely it's not just me?' He thought Hannah must have been being sarcastic.

'Must be,' she said.

'Something odd's going on here!'

'Like what?'

'I don't know,' he said, bemused.

'You feeling okay?' she asked him.

'Yes, fine. I think. It's this headache putting me out of sorts.' Jake realised he couldn't remember the last time he *didn't* have a headache.

With the brief exploration of the cellar done it was time to begin the next pressing task, which for Jake was to paint the black room. While they'd been out shopping he'd picked up no less than four tins of white emulsion. Hannah had mocked him for it, but he knew that just this one room would probably use all of it, and he wouldn't be at all surprised if it wasn't enough. It was with a little trepidation he opened the door and peered in.

Despite the bright afternoon sun shining outside, the black room was dim, gloomy and actively unwelcoming. The painted glass in the window glowed a weak dull grey, and a little light was coming from the open door. His first task was to rectify the lack of light, and for this he'd come prepared. As well as paint, rollers and brushes, he'd also brought the crowbar up with him, intending to use as a last resort if he still couldn't get the window open by less coercive means.

Jake used two full paint tins to prop the door open before venturing inside and despite the stuffy heat, in total contrast to the cellar, a chill ran down his sweat-filmed spine. It was with purpose he strode to the window and wrestled with the catch, steadfastly refusing to acknowledge the creeping fear which was bubbling up inside him.

Despite consciously reminding himself there was nothing to be afraid of, Jake wasn't spared a small hint of panic when the window catch wouldn't budge. As a result he might have been a little hasty to use the crowbar. With minimal leverage the rotten joints parted ways and the pane of glass cracked down the middle, before tumbling into the long grass below.

'Bollocks,' he muttered under his breath, but wasn't really sorry the glass had broken; there was fresh air in the room and the light spilling in was golden and glorious. He leaned out of the broken frame, careful to keep his neck clear of the jagged shards of glass which poked from it in places.

The sun was about to descend below the tree line and the afternoon had started to cool. The forest rose from behind the few wizened short trees of the orchard, starting to take on its autumnal coat of brown, red and yellow. Jake couldn't help but think it was more as if the surrounding trees shied away from the cottage, rather than hemming it in, although it didn't feel that way at night. A handful of cawing rooks circled above.

Behind him, the door slammed. Jake jerked his head back through the window. Broken glass snagged his earlobe on the way. By the time he'd spun around his hand was already clutched to the side of his head, to stem any potential blood. 'What the...' He expected Hannah to be standing in the doorway, but there was only the bare, black, back of the door. 'What the...' he whispered again but in a different tone of voice, this time quieter and more subdued, knowing instinctively that Hannah was still downstairs.

When he tried the door and it opened without resistance he could have wept with relief. In the hallway the two pots of paint sat on the bare floorboards, just outside the door. 'Fuck this shit,' he mumbled, eyeing them suspiciously while touching his ear in an attempt to assess the damage. There didn't seem to be too much in the way of blood and so without further ado, after propping the door open again, he set about the walls with white paint. It was the only colour he could envisage working in the black room, a complete transformation.

Meanwhile, downstairs, Hannah was tearing wallpaper off the living room walls, bringing great chunks of plaster down with it and revealing the thin wooden lathes beneath. She hummed a merry tune, content in her work and excited about the prospect of restoring the cottage to its former glory. She'd had much less trouble opening the downstairs windows than Jake had in the bedroom and they were all wide open, clearing dust and cooling the air.

The noisy rooks were distant above the forest, far enough away for it to be a peaceful sound. Somewhere between them and the cottage a woodpecker laughed.

9

Almost two months had passed since they'd moved to Picker's Bleed and autumn was marching into winter.

In that time Hannah and Jake had made good progress with the renovations. Tradesmen had come and gone, and they always seemed to finish ahead of schedule, in a hurry to move onto the next job. The chimney had been repaired and cleaned, much to the annoyance of the rooks and jackdaws. Now the nights were drawing in the open fire was cosy, although a constant cold crept up from the cellar. They'd replaced the broken door with a cheap pine one with a flimsy wire latch, but no matter how many draught excluders they piled in front of it, the chill remained.

The black room had taken all four tins of paint, but now it was dazzling white and new windows completed the look to make it seem, on the surface, light and airy. The black bed was in a broken heap in the garden, providing shelter to a family of hibernating hedgehogs. Their own king-sized divan stood in its place, on a comfortably deep beige shag. A small pile of logs was stacked neatly by the fireplace.

The cottage was becoming a home, but Jake was losing his mind. The headaches, which had plagued him since the day they'd moved in, had become more or less constant. He'd spent more time looking for misplaced tools than he had decorating. He was becoming more irritable by the day and he wasn't sleeping. The nights were an endless cycle of tumultuous nightmares and lying awake, listening to the peculiar, unsettling noises the cottage made at night.

At first he thought there must have been rodents in the walls, for there was always tapping and scraping, but other sounds were more difficult to rationalise. Floorboards creaked. Doors opened and closed. There was often a breathy whistling which he put down to the constant draught blowing up from the cellar. More than once he heard a dog padding around downstairs, or occasionally snuffling about on the landing outside the bedroom door. There were also voices. Usually, they were present as a muttering at the edge of his perception and, although he couldn't say whether he was dreaming or not, there were times when he heard children, right there in the room. Twice he heard the piano in the sitting room strike a dis-chord while Hannah lay snoring next to him.

Most nights Hannah slept like a log, oblivious to the noises and she'd told Jake more than once it must just be the house settling. There had been times he'd shaken her awake, but each time, as soon as he did, the noises subsided to only natural creaks and rustles. In the end he gave up trying to convince her and spent every night terrified.

'I can't believe it's time for you to go, already,' said Hannah, kicking up partially mulched litter, which was too damp to rustle underfoot. They'd got up early and after breakfast had wrapped up warm against the autumnal weather and headed out into the forest, not bothering to lock the front door behind them. Cold mizzle filled the air. The forest was quiet apart from the cawing of rooks, muted in the almost fog. The damp air smelled earthy and fresh. Soon they found themselves following a narrow deer-track that wriggled its way amongst the trees and in time the path opened into a small clearing, fringed by ancient, gnarled blackthorn; all bare branches and exposed spines dripping with lichen. The light rain had settled into fog and the trees on the opposite side of the clearing were little more than indistinct, looming shadows.

Jake peered up into the balding trees, pretending to watch a small brown bird flutter between branches. 'I'll be back for Christmas,' he said, guilty that a large part of him couldn't be more pleased to be leaving. Touring would do him good; a few weeks on the road, away from Picker's Bleed and its ghosts. He'd spent most of last night lying on his back, staring up into the dark. There were none of the usual whistles, rustles or creaks that had kept him awake almost every night since they'd moved in, only the monotonous ticking of the clock from downstairs, marking off every second of his insomnia. It was almost as if the house was waiting impatiently for him to leave.

'Are you sure you're going to be okay?' asked Jake as they were arriving back at the cottage.

'Don't worry about me,' she said. 'I'll miss you, but I'm going to get stuck into some work myself. I've had a few ideas for an exhibition.'

'Great.' He felt exonerated, even if he couldn't quite understand how she could be okay with staying on her own at Picker's Bleed.

She gave him a sideways glance; 'Are you sure *you're* alright? You've been acting off for weeks now.'

'Yeah, I'm okay, it's just these headaches, that's all.'

'You need to see a doctor.'

'If it's not better in a week, I'll go.'

'You'll be on the road then.'

'I'm fine,' he said.

'I'm worried, that's all,' she replied and took his hand in hers. 'You've been on edge since we moved in.'

'I'm fine,' he said, but wondered whether he was.

The cab arrived ten minutes late, which took them both by surprise as they had both expected it to be much later. Jake put his cup of tea on the side and went running out onto the overgrown drive to let the driver know he'd found the right address.

'I was wondering,' said the driver, 'you not been in long? It looks abandoned from the front.'

'Yes, I know. Hang on there and I'll carry out my things.'

'Need a hand?' chirruped the driver.

'It's okay, I can manage,' said Jake. It took four or five short trips to where he'd stacked his gear just inside the front door and then they were loaded up and ready to go.

'I'll call soon,' he whispered in Hannah's ear as they hugged on the doorstep, before he climbed into the cab. After a short conversation with the driver, the taxi bumped off the drive and, as it pulled onto the road, Jake turned to wave through the window.

10

Over the next week or so Hannah decided to make the most of the peace and quiet to throw herself into her work. In the evenings she carried on with decorating, cleaning and generally turning the cottage into a home, but ever since they'd moved to Picker's Bleed, the cellar had been playing on her mind. For some reason she'd been putting it off, but as the days wore on she found it more and more difficult to resist. So, by the following weekend Hannah let curiosity get the better of her and she found herself making her way down the crumbling brick steps and into the depths of the cottage. The pockets of her cardigan were stuffed with candles and she was carrying a camping lantern, which cast a dim, swinging glow as she descended into the dark.

Hannah tried the short cord on the lightbulb. To her surprise the bulb lit, giving off a variable light which ranged from dim to dimmer and cast thick, pulsating shadows. She turned off her feeble lantern and placed it carefully on the bottom step where she'd be able to most easily find it when the overhead light inevitably failed.

Propped against one wall was a set of rustic looking shelves, which were jam-packed with coloured bottles and old clay flasks. Hannah was on her way across the room to take a look when she caught her toe on something and went sprawling to her knees. The light wavered. The palms of her hands stung and she checked for grazes before scouring dirt from the floor to find whatever had tripped her. She found the small iron hoop with the tip of her little finger and let out a yelp.

Hannah got to her feet and pulled at the metal ring, but whatever it was didn't budge, so she dropped back to her knees and started to scrape away some of the dirt, feeling around the edges of the trapdoor – for that's what she was sure she'd found. Her hands were filthy and sore. She paused for a few moments before trying again. Eventually she felt movement and yanked harder on the ring, tugging until, bit by bit, more dirt was dislodged. Eventually, with a final gargantuan heave, the trapdoor lifted.

A dim glow came from below, making a luminous square in the floor. *Phosphorescent rock?* she thought. *Or some kind of glow in the dark fungi?* A cold draught was blowing up from the hole; arid and carrying with it what she equated with centuries' old death as it caressed the pale skin of Hannah's face and tousled her hair.

She poked her head through the trapdoor. A crude ladder, un-sanded, full of splinters and bound with ancient rope, led down a shaft, six or seven feet down through the bedrock.

With a nervous gulp she descended. Dirt, which she'd dislodged, trickled around her and fell into the space below. With each step the ladder creaked horribly. Twice, the rungs gave a resounding crack, but fortunately they held and soon she was standing on compacted earth. Hannah spent a few moments pulling splinters out of her hands with her teeth while she took stock of her surroundings.

She was in some kind of subterranean grotto, which had been roughly hewn out of the bedrock. The cave was empty, apart from a stone pedestal and a full-length mirror, with an ornamental, carved frame. It was the mirror which was oozing the sickly, directionless light.

The pedestal was carved from the same rock as the walls and floor, as if the cave had been chiselled around it to work the altar from the bedrock. On it was a book, and by the look of its cracked brown binding, it was ancient. Hannah reached out and when the tip of her middle finger touched the cover a shudder passed through her. The pages were made of something thicker than paper, but less supple than leather.

The text was of thick, ornate calligraphy, written in a language she didn't recognise. For a few moments she thought it might have been some variation of olde English, where S is written like f, but upon closer inspection she couldn't decipher any of it. She traced the letters with her finger, feeling how they were raised off the page and rough, like scabs. Hannah didn't need to understand the writing to know the words held power.

She let her fingers brush against the ancient pages while she looked more closely at the mirror. The glass was remarkably clear for something that had been underground for untold years. Hannah was peering at the reflection of the grotto for some time before the realisation dawned on her that she couldn't see herself reflected. She gave a little gasp of surprise and left the book where it was while she leaned right up to the mirror, staring at the cave behind her.

Hannah felt a slight shifting of her reality, like she'd stood up too fast, but when the bout of dizziness passed something had changed. There was an unsettling, hypnotic effect about the mirror in front of her and the more she stared the more she became disassociated from reality, being drawn into the scene until she was immersed.

The image in the mirror blurred, then dissolved, drifting like smoke before ever so slowly coming back together, coalescing into new shapes and images. The underground grotto disappeared and in its place was her bedroom, painted black like it had been when they'd bought the cottage.

In the black room sat an old woman in a rocking chair. At her feet was a great, black dog with burning red eyes and scarlet blood dripping from its fangs. There was the faint, but unsettling noise of children, crying and snivelling. Hannah looked harder into the mirror, unable to tear her gaze away, and she saw them, hiding in the corners of the black room. Hannah was overcome by a bottomless sense of sorrow, like an open pit where her heart should have been.

The hag, all of a sudden, seemed to become aware of Hannah and stopped rocking, shifting in her seat to fix her with a stare full of twisted malice. The look jolted Hannah back to her senses and her sorrow turned to icy dread.

She backed up to the ladder, picking up the book on the way, unable to take her eyes off the images in the mirror, eerie in the dim glow. From it the old woman stared after her.

Hannah forced herself to look away and scrambled up through the shaft as quickly as she could while carrying the heavy book.

***

Shortly after seven the following morning, after a sleepless night spent pacing the cottage and trying to figure out what the hell she'd experienced, Hannah was pulling into the soft floodlights of Tesco's car park. She chose a space near the few other cars huddled near the supermarket doors and left the engine running while she started her phone. There were a few missed calls and messages from Jake, asking how she was, and to say he was getting worried. She glanced at the time and decided to wait until later in the morning to call him.

The supermarket lights brought her back down to earth

and for a while she mindlessly wandered the isles, browsing vegetables and stocking up on enough bits for the week; milk, bread, toilet roll and the like. By the time she was done, there was still half an hour to kill before the library opened, so she went back to peering at her phone, but her Google searches were fruitless.

The library was a new, glass fronted building in the middle of town. The librarian was young, fresh faced and extremely apologetic when Hannah marvelled how few books there were. 'Well, they got rid of a lot of them when we moved out of the old building. Apparently they looked tatty,' he said.

'Oh,' said Hannah. 'So, do you have any local history?'

'That shelf there.' The librarian pointed to a shelf about four-by-four feet. Local history took up half of the middle shelf.

'Oh.'

'But if you need anything specific you could try the records office in the town hall.'

'Thanks, I might just do that.' Hannah thanked the librarian for his time, went to the toilet and left. The records office was in the next doorway of the same glass fronted building.

'Of course you can make an appointment,' the lady at reception said. 'What about a week Tuesday?'

Hannah couldn't be bothered to argue. 'That'll be fine,' she said, knowing full well the wheels of bureaucracy wouldn't bend for her and so she left, slightly disheartened.

Just outside the council building Hannah found a concrete bench to sit on while she called Jake. The reception was bad and kept cutting in and out. After the opening chit-chat she wanted to tell him about what she'd found, but just as she started to talk about it the line crackled a few times and went dead. She tried to call back but couldn't get an answer.

Hannah was in a curious predicament. She was desperate to find out what she'd discovered beneath the house and until she knew something, she was reluctant to go home at all. But there was nowhere else she could think of going and so she wandered town a bit; browsed in Sports Direct, Millett's and Primark. She bought a cuckoo clock from a charity shop. It was brightly painted with a farmhouse scene; a sunrise, haybales and a large, brown rooster all featured prominently. She thought it would add charm to the kitchen. There was a small gallery she spent a while in, which was selling overpriced prints and originals from local artists. She made a mental note to speak to them about possibly displaying a couple of pieces. By mid-day she reluctantly headed home.

That afternoon, Hannah busied herself painting, cleaning and generally putting the cottage to rights. By the time she'd finished, the house was looking homely. Not once did she venture down into the cellar, and she tried to think about what was down there even less. All the time she was busying herself, she tried as hard as she could to ignore the strange book which was now on their wonky coffee table. By about teatime she was tired, but in a good way and so she showered, changed and walked along the lane into the village.

11

About the same time Hannah was exploring the cellar at Picker's Bleed, Jake's guitar lay abandoned mid-stage, artistic feedback just making the transition to an ear-splitting squeal. Guitar-tech, Justin, pushed an ice-cold bottle of Kronenbourg into his hand before rushing out onto the darkened stage and pulling the plug. Feedback gave way to rapturous applause. Justin walked back off stage, high-fiving Jake, a grin lighting up his sweaty face.

The crowd chanted for more. Jake closed his eyes and leaned back against the wall, heart thudding; revelling in the moment at the same time as trying to catch a breath. Another bead of perspiration rolled down his temple, but it was one of many and went unnoticed; his tee-shirt was wringing with sweat. The beer was refreshing. The audience could chant all they liked, there would be no more songs. The headliner's amplifiers were already being wheeled past him and onto the stage.

'Nice set.' Somebody he didn't know paid him the compliment with a firm slap to the shoulder.

'Cheers,' said Jake, but his mind had turned to Hannah and a sliver of anxiety took the edge off his euphoria.

All of a sudden the air was oppressive, too thick to draw a proper breath. The large free-standing fan opposite where he was leaning seemed to concentrate the hot air into a jet which continually pushed across Jake's face, threatening to suffocate him. The noise from the auditorium muddled his senses. All of a sudden he needed to be outdoors.

Pushing past the jumble of people gathered backstage, making their way to and fro, he found an emergency exit and shoved the bar, crashing out into the autumn chill, where the sleek tour-bus was parked in a side-street. His sweat-coated body cooled quickly and the cold air he'd been craving tickled his throat and made him cough. Still, it felt good.

'You okay mate?' Childhood friend and vocalist for *Dead Man's Handle*, Alex, was standing against the wall, smoking a joint and chatting to the remaining two band members, Adam and Dave.

'Mate, it's fucking boiling in there.'

'Tell me about it. Fucking awesome show though.'

'I'm fucking buzzing,' said Dave.

Jake allowed the smile to return to his face. 'Hold on a minute, I've just got to make a call.' He'd left his phone on the bus, so he entered through the back door and made his way up the narrow stairs to his bunk. As luxurious as the bus was, with wide screen TVs, games consoles and the like, his bunk was one of ten lining the top deck. Eight of the others were occupied by band members and road crew. And although it was cleaned and aired daily, the bus smelled faintly of stale farts and marijuana smoke. Still, he paused to look around in slight disbelief and to bless his good fortune. It was a far cry from Dave's battered Ford Transit, which they usually toured in.

Jake's phone was stashed in the little mica-veneered

cabinet next to his bunk and he had to climb up the first two steps of a short ladder to reach in and fetch it. A brief glance at the screen showed he'd received no missed calls or messages and although dismayed he wasn't surprised. He clambered onto his bed to make the call.

It had been almost a week since he and Hannah had last spoken, and for the past four nights he'd tried calling but got no answer. It wasn't surprising there was no reply on the mobile, because of the poor signal at Picker's Bleed but she could have at least made the effort to get in touch when she was able. Although they'd had the landline connected, service had been intermittent and so he wasn't surprised he hadn't been able to get through on that either.

Anxiety snagged the edge of his mind, tugging and rubbing until it made a small blister of anger. Anger that Hannah wasn't calling, even to let him know she was okay. He was angry they'd moved somewhere with no neighbours he could call to check in on her. Jake found himself wondering how long he should leave it before calling the police. He tossed the mobile back into the cabinet, rolled himself a joint and went downstairs in search of beer, good times and a little piece of oblivion.

The phone's ringtone woke him. It had been a night of heavy drinking and it took a while for his sleeping and woozy mind to process the sound, and even longer for him to realise it existed in the real world. Once he'd rolled over and found the phone it was a race against time to answer before the call diverted to voicemail. In his haste he fumbled the phone and almost dropped it. 'Hi,' he groaned. The constant whine of the engine and the bus's gentle rocking let him know they were travelling at speed, most likely on the motorway.

'Hi,' she replied. 'How's things?'

'Hungover.' He tried to keep his voice quiet because

people were sleeping.

She laughed a little. 'Back into the swing of things then?'

'You could say that.'

'Staying off the drugs though?' A hint of concern tinged her voice.

'Yes,' he said, as if for the thousandth time. 'The hard stuff anyway.'

'Well, that's good.'

'So, tell me what you've been up to then?' he asked, changing the subject. 'Anything interesting?'

'As a matter of fact, yes. I found some weird shit in the cellar.'

'Like what?'

An annoying crackle developed on the line. 'Sorry you're breaking up a bit,' said Jake. He could hear an indiscernible babble of voices in the background. Distant.

'That's not really surprising.'

'I guess not. Anyway, you were saying...'

'Yes. I went down the cellar yesterday...'

'I can hardly hear you,' he said. The crackle was getting worse, and the incoherent jumble of voices louder, so he was straining to hear what she was saying.

'Interesting... ...Bizarre... ...Kids...' One of the crossed line voices was becoming distinguishable from the dull cacophony. It was humming a tune.

'Can you say that again, Hannah. I can hardly hear a word you're saying now.'

And then, clear as day, a woman's voice came on the line; old and cantankerous. Vile even; the way some folks get after a long life of being mean. 'That's enough of that,' said the voice and the connection was suddenly lost. He'd heard the voice before, in the black room, and his blood ran cold.

'What the fuck?' Jake looked at his phone's screen, wondering what had just happened. He tried calling straight back, but got an automated message *'The number you have dialled has not been recognised.'*

'Damn,' he said.

The bus braked suddenly, the engine whining as it moved down through the gears and there was a hiss of air from the brakes. Jake clung to the thin edge of his bunk for support, letting go of his phone as he did. It went spinning across the cabin and connected heavily with the corner of the small table opposite. There were a few grunts as various members of the band and crew peered out from under their duvets.

There hadn't been a crash or any other kind of mishap, rather the traffic had stopped as it is apt to do on the M6, just North of Birmingham and they were now crawling along at a snail's pace; bumper to bumper; stop-start. With the revelation there was no drama unfolding, most people on the bus rolled back into their sleepy cocoons and Jake was left alone with only muffled grunts, snores and one disgustingly flamboyant fart for company.

The inevitable hangover was making itself known. Jake's head felt like he'd happily chop it off and there was a sickness in his belly. He tentatively clambered down the short ladder to retrieve the phone. On hands and knees he furtled under the table, hoping not to find anything disgusting, until his fingers alighted upon the handset.

Cracks spread out like a spider-web from a nasty dent in the centre of the screen and despite his best efforts he couldn't get it to turn on. The broken screen stayed blank.

Resigned, he slid the broken phone onto the table and pulled himself back to his feet, holding onto his bunk-ladder for a few moments until his head stopped spinning and a bout of nausea passed.

12

There was a man near the front step of the Bull's head, trying to light a cigarette with his parka pulled up tight against the wind. They politely nodded to each other, sharing an oddly loaded moment as she pulled open the pub door.

The bar was livelier than she'd expected. The warmth of a real fire welcomed her in. Laughter was coming from a nook by the window and Hannah glanced around to see smiling faces. 'Hello again,' said the landlord as Hannah approached the bar.

Hannah nodded, glancing at the taps to see what was on offer. 'Hi,' she said and her eyes turned to the optics on the back wall.

'What can I get you?' prompted the landlord, his smile genuine.

'Erm... I'll have a vodka and orange please?'

'Ice?' The publican turned, arm raised, to press her glass to the optic.

'Please,' she said.

'Settling in okay?' he asked, placing the glass down on

the bar.

'Not too bad,' she answered, trying to figure out whether or not he was fishing for information, or just being friendly.

'Good, good,' he said. 'That'll be three pounds thirty please?'

She had hoped to be able to quiz him about the house, but there were customers waiting to be served. After she'd counted out some change and paid for the drink, Hannah turned back towards the room, looking for a seat, when the door opened and the man who'd been on the step came towards the bar. They each nodded their acquaintance again and Hannah side-stepped to let him pass. He smelled of freshly extinguished cigarette and although Hannah had intended to wait a while, she decided to follow his example and go out the front for a smoke before getting comfortable. Besides, it didn't appear there were too many empty seats for her to choose from and so, even before the heavy, oak pub door had swung shut, she'd caught hold of the edge and pulled it open again.

Outside, the breeze had strengthened further, carrying the first bite of winter on its breath. Silver edged clouds scudded overhead, backlit by a moon which was just a smidgeon off full. Hannah tilted her head back to watch. When she lifted it again to light her cigarette, she went giddy and had to momentarily stay very still until she'd recovered enough to take a gulp from her drink, which was chilling nicely on the small metal and glass table just outside the pub door. She was reminded of the odd sensation she'd felt in the cellar, and the mirror was brought back to the fore of her thoughts. She took a deep drag of her hand-rolled cigarette, before blowing the smoke out slowly.

She wished again that Jake was with her, but there was nothing to be done about it. Looking up at the moon once again she wondered if he was doing the same, standing outside some bar. She didn't know why she even had her phone in her pocket, habit maybe, but she already knew there would be no signal. She fetched it out and glanced at it anyway, to see if there were any messages.

When Hannah went back into the warmth of the tap-room a voice called, 'Hi.'

She turned to see a mismatched group of people tucked away near the bay windows. She struggled for a moment to remember if she'd seen any of them before. The man who'd spoken was dressed in tweed, a curved pipe sat on the table in front of him. She glanced over his companions. They seemed unlikely company.

'Made your viewing then?' he asked.

'Eh?'

'I gave you directions, a couple of months back. I'm taking it you bought the cottage?'

'Yes, we did. Thank you,' she said, relieved she might have some company and a possible source of information.

The man was sitting at the far side of the table, his back to the window and flanked on either side by two couples. 'Won't you come and join us?' he asked beckoning to the chair opposite.

'Love to,' she said with a smile, her cheeks rosy from the chill outdoors. The chair scraped across the floor with a screech when she pulled it out from under the table.

'What'll it be?' he asked, working his way from behind the table so he could get to the bar.

Hannah glanced at her drink before tipping it back and draining the glass. 'Vodka and orange please?' The man's friends were looking at her rather quizzically. In turn, she was even more perplexed by them. 'Hi,' she said as she placed her glass back on the wooden table. Something about the man's companions put her on edge. Their smiles didn't feel quite genuine. 'I'm Hannah.'

'Oh, how rude of me,' said the man. 'I'm Vincent. I'll fetch the drinks while you all get acquainted.'

'I'm Danny,' said a blonde man who was difficult to put an age on. The skin of his face was riddled with pock scars, his hair was cut short and spiked. A leather jacket, hanging from the back of his chair completed the look, all he was missing was a toothpick twirling in the corner of his mouth.

Sat beside him was a slight woman, with shimmering shoulder length raven-black hair in a straight bob. Her skin was porcelain white. 'Hi,' she drawled, 'I'm Mel.' There was suspicion in her voice.

Hannah turned to the other couple. They couldn't have been more different. The man was dressed in a corduroy jacket and jeans, somehow managing not to look like the archetypal history teacher, despite having leather elbow-patches. 'Hi,' he said, thrusting out his hand in greeting. He appeared to be gazing at something over Hannah's shoulder. She glanced around but there was nothing there. 'I'm Stephen, with a PH -' He nodded towards the woman next to him, '- and this is Susan.'

'Hello,' said the woman, her voice bubbling from between painted lips. 'Charmed.'

'Don't mind them, Danny and Melissa.' Stephen beckoned across the table. 'Danny's a miserable bastard and Mel's just... Well Mel's just Mel.'

Melissa shot him a look while Danny sneered. Susan giggled and Hannah wanted the uneven floor to open up and swallow her. She studied the grain of the table-top, wishing she hadn't downed her vodka. After a pause of about fifteen seconds too long Danny asked, 'So, how's the house?' His voice held a Northern twang, possibly Lancashire. All the others leaned in, almost imperceptibly, taking a collective breath, waiting on her response.

'Erm.. Fine thanks.' There followed another moment of thumb twiddling before Vincent leaned across from behind to set Hannah's glass down. She felt his breath brush against the back of her neck.

After a bit of bustle while he fetched everyone's drinks to the table and squeezed round to his bench in between the couples, he asked, 'So, how's the house treating you?' The question itself was almost identical to Danny's, but without the loaded tension and she relaxed a little.

'It's good,' was still the best she could muster though. Not expecting much of a response, she asked, 'So, do you know anything about the house's history?'

Vincent smiled and leaned forwards, propping his elbows on the table, hands clasped beneath his chin. 'Do you believe in magic?' he asked.

Hannah leant in closer still, studying the iridescent pattern of Vincent's eyes. His reply had thrown her off guard. 'I guess so,' she said. 'Maybe.'

'Well, let me tell you,' he said. 'Five hundred years ago, there was a woman lived in your cottage, went by the name Ella Jameson. She was burned at the stake for being a witch. She was a powerful one too.'

'Really?'

'Really,' he said. 'Where do you think the name Picker's Bleed comes from?'

'I did wonder,' she said. 'I guessed it was something to do with a farmworker or something like that.' Hannah settled back in her chair.

'I'll tell you, it's derived from Wicca's Bleed. As in where they killed the witch, or rather where she lived, because they dragged her here and burned her on the village green.'

'So, what did she do, this witch?' Hannah shuddered with a sudden chill. Her own experience added an air of truth to his outlandish story.

'I don't know why they burnt her, probably one of the neighbours had their milk go sour or something, but I do know that by all accounts they dragged her from the cottage when she was partway through some sorcery. She'd opened up a portal to *somewhere else* and something came through. Trouble is, only she could close it. It's a curse which has blighted the village ever since.'

'What came through?' Hannah ventured to ask.

'Well, some say she was summoning a demon, but it's also the presence of this portal which has been left open and corrupts the land.'

'So, you're telling me there's a way to another dimension in my house?' If she hadn't seen the curious mirror with her own eyes, she would have thought Vincent was batshit crazy. 'How do you know all of this?'

'This land has been in my family since 1066, or thereabouts,' he said. 'For more than half of that time it's been cursed.'

Hannah shivered as if someone had walked over her grave and was compelled to change the subject. 'There was an old crib in the cottage. What happened to the people who lived there before us?'

He gave a small, mirthless chuckle. 'The place has been abandoned for nigh on thirty years now. I was only a young lad when it happened, but I remember all the fuss. The woman's name was Marie Hodges. They hadn't lived there long when her husband was found hacked to death after she ran onto the village green one Christmas Day, stark raving mad and covered head to toe in blood.'

'What happened?' Hannah shuddered.

'No one knows exactly, other than she had some kind of episode and killed her husband.'

'And the baby?'

He slowly shook his head. 'They never found the baby.

She might have killed him too.'

'Did they look?'

'Of course they did.'

'Then what happened to it?' She thought about the crying she'd heard and the apparitions in the mirror.

'Folks 'round here say it was the curse, and I for one am inclined to believe them,' he said quite matter-of-factly.

'Really?' she said, alarmed.

'Yes.'

'What about the woman, Marie?' asked Hannah.

'They carted her off to the loony bin,' said Vincent, making a twirling motion with his finger near his temple.

For a moment there was a contemplative silence around the table, where they listened to the hushed babble of other people's conversations around the barroom. A knot exploded in the fire.

'This is madness,' she said. 'I'm surprised the place hasn't been torn down.'

'There's a protection spell on it.' He tailed off, as if struck by a minor revelation. 'I guess no-one's ever thought of it.'

'A spell, you say?' For a moment she thought of Jake and his reaction to the cottage.

'Like I said, a protection spell. To stop people going there and snooping.'

'Then why doesn't it affect me?'

Vincent downed the remnants of his pint; 'I have a theory about that,' he said, his eyes darted from side to side, as if expecting eavesdroppers. Nearby, the man she'd seen outside was two tables away, intently staring at the crossword, while the landlord was polishing wine glasses with a tea-towel. 'Come 'round to mine in the morning and we'll discuss it further,' said Vincent.

'But...'

'It'll wait until tomorrow,' he said.

13

It was a brittle, crystalline morning of pale blue skies and sharp frost. Water dripped incessantly from where the weak sun struck golden-brown leaves and thawed the rime, leaving them hanging soggy and limp from threadbare branches, whereas already fallen leaves still glinted and crunched underfoot. Winter had arrived at Picker's Bleed. Overhead, the rooks wheeled and called to each other. Hannah could well imagine they were talking about her, a trespasser into their woods.

She was following a little winding path through the trees, taking time to think and to savour the fresh morning as best she could. Wrapped up in mittens and scarf, her coat collar pulled tight around her face, she was snug and warm. Her breath hung in plumes before her face.

After consulting a map, she was walking in the direction of Marsham Hall, where Vincent had told her he lived. She'd never known anyone who lived in a manor house before. Hannah's head was spinning. Curious about what she'd been told the night before, she was aching to know more.

As it happened, the Hall was an awful lot closer through the woods than by road. As the crow flies it couldn't have been much more than half a mile. Before she came upon any sign of habitation there was the inviting, warm smell of wood-smoke hanging in the air and not long after, she came upon an ancient red brick wall. Its edges were softened with time and crumbling, overgrown with ivy and buckled outwards as if the wall would split open and collapse at any moment, disgorging the earth which lay behind.

The path followed the course of the wall for some way. In places, trees had grown up against the dilapidated masonry, blocking the way, but at some length she made it through and was spat out onto a dirt track next to a set of old, rusted wrought iron gates. One of the gates was hanging limply from the lichen covered post, leaving a gap just wide enough to drive a car through. The other gate appeared as if it hadn't been used in decades.

It was more than a little different from what she'd been expecting, although what she had been expecting she couldn't say. However, Marsham Hall seemed in an even worse state of repair than the cottage had been when she and Jake had first moved to Picker's Bleed. Once upon a time it would have been a residence of the grandest order but, although still impressive, the driveway and grounds were in desperate need of tending.

As she walked in the tyre tracks, passing through shoulder high brambles and other sodden, brown unkempt herbage, dead and soft from frost, she looked up at the dismal building in front of her. The sun was low behind the manor and in the building's shadow the ground was still covered with frost. Hannah stood just on the edge of the freezing gloom, staring at the grimy façade, looking for movement behind any of the windows, which were set in three rows and too numerous for her to bother counting, but she guessed at least twenty. More than one of the windows were broken, leaving the rooms beyond open to the elements.

All was still, nothing stirred. For a moment Hannah thought she must have made a mistake, but how many other grand halls could there be in the area? Maybe Vincent lived in an annexe somewhere, but if he did, he hadn't said so.

As she got closer the state of dilapidation became even more apparent. The roof was sagging quite dramatically in places and peppered with dark holes where slates were missing, like a gap-toothed old fighting man. One of the four chimney stacks was leaning at an alarming angle. Hannah couldn't figure out why it hadn't already fallen over and severely doubted it could last another winter.

The tracks led around the side of the building, but Hannah left the driveway and went up three wide gritstone steps to the weathered portico and heavy oak front door. The worn, pitted knocker was freezing to the touch and when slammed it echoed long and loud inside the building, as if Marsham hall was empty, but only moments later there came a shuffling from inside and the clunk of heavy bolts being drawn.

Hannah was a little taken aback by the man who pulled open the door and it hadn't crossed her mind that anyone other than Vincent or one of his friends might have answered. But this man was old, in his early eighties at least, and most likely older. His body was crooked and stooped, with a slight hunch-back. The formal butler's suit he wore was too big for his withered form.

'Miss Hannah, I presume?' The butler's voice held the tremble of age and as he shuffled back a step to let her pass, her nose wrinkled at the slight odour of stale urine. 'Master Vincent has been expecting you.' He extended a bent arm. 'Would you like me to take your coat?'

'No. No thank you.' It seemed just as cold in the entrance

hall as it had outside, and thrice as gloomy. There were no windows and the walls were panelled with dark wood. Directly opposite the front door rose a wide staircase. A faded maroon carpet ran up the middle of it, worn threadbare by countless foot-traffic. Just to the left of the door was a full suit of armour. Gossamer sheets ran between it and the wall, all of the sheen gone from the beaten metal.

The heavy door closed behind them with a seeming air of finality as the cold daylight was shut out. 'If you'd care to follow me, Master Vincent will receive you in the dining room.' As he headed along the hallway ahead of her, the top of his liver-spotted head level with her eyes, Hannah wondered what she'd walked into and let out a small nervous laugh at the absurdity of it all. If the butler heard then he didn't give any indication of it and a moment later he swung open a heavy door which was set into a pointed arch and stepped aside for her to enter.

The difference of temperature as she went into the room brought a flush to her cheeks. The source of the heat was an imposing square fireplace at the far end of the room, possibly large enough to spit-roast a whole cow. The fire was burned down to a couple of blackened, smouldering logs and embers.

The room itself was of a good size, but not overly grand, designed more for eating than the kind of banquets that involved jesters and the like. The long table which ran up the middle of the dining room could comfortably seat eighteen in the high-backed chairs, without much in the way of elbow contact. A chandelier hung above the centre point of the table, full of candles which were all alight, but burned down to pustular nubs. A dozen dusty portraits hung on the walls, observing any feast that might have adorned the table, which at this present time bore the leftovers of decadence. Empty wine bottles littered the table-top along with a few dirty glasses, some of which were still half full. These were accompanied by the remnants of late-night cheeseboards, stuffed olives and a selection of half-eaten cold meats.

'Apologies for the mess.' Vincent appeared from a small door, hitherto unseen and gesticulated toward the detritus.

'Were you celebrating something?' Hannah asked.

Vincent gently touched the mouthpiece of his pipe to his temple. 'Yes.'

Hannah paused for a moment, unsure whether to press him to elaborate, and thought it not too impolite to make small talk. 'Anything special?'

'You,' he said.

'Pardon?' Not sure she'd heard correctly.

'Follow me,' he said, and turned to return back through the door from whence he'd just come.

She was led into a library of sorts, much smaller than the dining room but stacked floor to ceiling with books. Heavy sun-bleached curtains were pulled back from a narrow, lead lined lancet window that looked out onto a courtyard, where the Range Rover was parked, beyond which was a sizeable stables. The roof was half collapsed, leaving the exposed rafters to rot.

In front of the window were two high backed Winchester style chairs in oxblood and between them sat a small table, covered in velvet cloth that hung almost to the floor. A crystal ball was on the tabletop, its pedestal made from white marble and fashioned in the likeness of a pair of hands, which held the orb firm in a stony caress. Next to the crystal ball was a candelabra, evidently well used, and a heavy, ancient looking book which appeared remarkably similar to the one she'd found in the cellar of her own cottage.

'Please sit,' said Vincent, gesturing to one of the chairs while he took the other. The room was dominated by books and she saw most of the spines on display were blank or written in words she could not decipher. Whether this was due to linguistic or stylistic reasons she couldn't say, and decided it must be a bit of both. However, there were enough pentagrams on display to draw the conclusion that a good portion, if not all, of the books were concerned with matters of the occult.

'Do you know anything of your family history?' The question came abruptly, interrupting Hannah from her scrutiny of the library.

'Nothing,' she shrugged. Genealogy had never been a pastime of hers. She'd spent most of her adult life trying not to think about her family. 'Why?'

Vincent gave a slight shake of his head, dismissing her question but only because he was wrapped in his own thoughts. 'What about on your mother's side?'

'Nothing,' she replied. 'I didn't even know my gran. She died when I was little.'

'Sorry to hear it,' he said.

'That's okay. But what's with all the questions?'

Vincent rose from his seat and went to one of the shelves near the back of the room. From between two books, he fetched an old drawing on yellowing paper, that was curling at the edges. 'Do you recognise her?' he asked, placing the drawing face up on the table between them.

Apart from the hairstyle being of a different era, the resemblance was uncanny. 'Well,' she said, a little taken aback. 'It looks like me.'

'Exactly,' he said. 'And why do you think that is?'

'I have no idea.'

'This is supposedly a likeness of Ella Jameson; the witch I was telling you about.'

'The one who lived in my cottage, the witch who was burned?'

'Yes, one and the same.'

'And made a curse and summoned some kind of demon?'

Vincent nodded.

Hannah paused for a moment. 'So why does she look like me?' she asked.

'My theory is that you're directly related, through your mother's side.'

'Why would you think that?'

'From my research.' He indicated to the books which lined the walls.

'Okay,' she said, nodding slowly. 'So even if I am related to this Ella witch, how does it mean me being here is anything other than a spooky coincidence?'

'Don't you see?' he said, an edge of excitement crept into his voice. 'It's a chance to finally be free of this curse.' He paused for a moment before continuing with much fervour. 'That witch, Ella Jameson opened a gateway to the other side and brought something through. Unfortunately, when she died, it was set free. The genie was out of the bottle so to speak. And the bottle's been left open.'

'I still don't understand where I fit in.'

'We need to close the gateway and all of this will be made better.' He waved his hand.

'How?'

'Magic,' he said.

'So, I still don't get what I have to do with it?'

'I recognised you the instant I saw you. It's way more than mere coincidence. I believe there's enough of her DNA in you, enough of her spirit to do the job.' He practically jumped up from his chair and strode the couple of paces to one of the bookcases, enthusiastically pulled down a particularly large volume and flicked through the pages. 'It's all in here!' he said. 'Only Ella Jameson had the right spells. Only she can undo what's been cast.'

Hannah craned her neck to see the book. The writing was similar to the one she'd found under the cellar. 'What language is it in?' she asked.

'One of the ancient ones.'

She shook her head, but didn't press him further, the language wasn't really important. 'And what makes you think I'll be able to do anything?'

'I can feel it in my bones,' he said.

From above the door a small bell tinkled and they both looked up towards it. Vincent smiled a toothy grin, 'Breakfast is served,' he said and led her back through into the dining room.

14

Even though the window in the library was narrow and grimy, the dining room had no windows at all and was gloomy with candlelight. Someone, it seemed, had set the chandelier swinging, perhaps while replacing some of the spent candles. Thick shadows danced around the corners of the room, growing and shrinking as the candelabra moved back and forth.

All the detritus from the previous evening had been cleared away and in its place, evenly spaced around the table, places had been set with plates, knives and forks. Two steaming coffee pots sat at either end of the table along with toast in a rack and an assortment of pastries. The smell of bacon seeped into the room.

Spread around the table were Vincent's friends from the night before. In these surroundings, away from the pub, they seemed an even stranger mix of characters and Hannah wondered again how or why they were all friends of Vincent. She decided they were more likely to be acquaintances than proper friends.

Danny was already out of his seat and upon their entrance he approached, almost snake-like in his movements and appraisal of her. His lithe body contorted and craned, entering her personal space and making her uneasy. He was either wearing the same clothes as the night before or the leather trousers, jacket and white tee-shirt were his standard uniform. She suspected the latter as the white looked pristine. He smelled of leather and cosmetics and he started to circle around her and whether the effect was intentional or not, Hannah's discomfort was bordering on fear and so when he moved to pull something out of his pocket she flinched. 'Cigarette?' he asked, proffering an open packet of Lucky Strike.

'Please.' She took one gratefully, the tension suddenly gone from the room.

'Help yourself to coffee,' said Vincent, and Hannah poured herself a mug and joined the others at the table. Melissa nodded in her direction with a look of scrutiny about her. Stephen was buttering a croissant and Susan was sipping at her own coffee, looking like she felt awful with tangled curls and last night's makeup smeared across her face.

'Rough night?' enquired Hannah. In return she received a nod and a grunt from Susan, but they were friendly enough.

'You could say that.' Stephen looked up from his breakfast and smiled. Hannah noticed his one eye looking off towards a point on the wall behind her again. She resisted the urge to glance around and follow his gaze. 'It turned into quite a session when we got back here.'

Melissa gave one of her unnerving giggles.

'So I heard,' said Hannah, not really wanting to contemplate that they'd been celebrating her arrival. She wondered whether that was mutual amongst them or just Vincent's personal fantasy.

Just then the decrepit butler came back into the room,

walking backwards through the door and pulling a serving trolley through after him. On it were platters of bacon, eggs, tomatoes, sausages, hash browns and mushrooms.

Danny, who was still pacing the corners of the room, was at the trolley as soon as the butler shuffled away, piling his plate as if he hadn't eaten in weeks. The others were out of their seats and doing the same within seconds. 'Tuck in,' said Vincent with his mouth already full.

As far as Hannah was concerned, the conversation in the library had been left unfinished, but in the company of others she felt uneasy with the subject matter. Odd as they were, she did not know their beliefs and didn't want to appear foolish. Even then, she wasn't sure she wanted to share her secrets. 'I can't believe you have a butler,' she said as a conversation starter.

'Appleby – he came with the house.'

'Appleby?' she asked with a little laugh, 'Is that his first or last name?'

'It's the only one I know.'

'So, he lives here and you don't know his name?'

Vincent shuffled his feet slightly, and for a moment seemed to lose a touch of his extruded self-confidence. 'I'm afraid not,' he said.

'Have you never wanted to find out?' Up until now, even with all the oddities, talk of magic, and the trimmings, she had thought of Vincent essentially as a charming eccentric. However, with this revelation she found herself wary and distrustful. Some of the barriers which had been broken down by his charms were hurriedly thrown back up. How could a man who had no interest in even the name of a life-long acquaintance be interested anything other than himself?

It was Melissa who broke the moment's awkward silence.

'So, you're supposed to be Vincent's big hope, are you?' she asked.

Hannah glanced over to Vincent before answering. He was smiling, his composure returned. 'Go ahead,' he gestured with a wry smile and a waggle of his pipe. 'We have no secrets here.'

Like fuck you don't, she thought and shuffled in the chair and cleared her throat, 'apparently so.'

Susan leaned forward on her elbows, flashing cleavage from the top of her white blouse, resting her chin on her hands. 'So, you're the witch incarnate?'

'Apparently so,' she said again, quieter than before. Hannah was confused. Everything was moving too fast and she seemed caught up in madness.

Susan's eyes narrowed ever so slightly. 'So, what's it like living in the cottage then?' It was a simple and innocent sounding question, but one loaded with potential.

If not for Vincent's aloofness with the butler, Hannah could have told them everything. She felt a connection with Susan, as if they were on the same wavelength, but these were strangers and she held her tongue, for the most part. 'Interesting,' she said.

'Tell me what you mean by, *interesting*?'

'Well, there certainly is something about the place,' she said. 'But I quite like it.'

A look shot the table. 'But that's impossible!' said Danny. He was out of his chair, waving his hand, palm up, in her general direction.

'Unless...' mused Stephen, more for his own, rather than for anybody else's benefit, drumming his fingers on his chin, his jaw throwing a strong outline in swinging candlelight.

'I'm reserving judgement,' said Mel, continuing with her scrutiny, her eyes scrunching further as if trying to see into Hannah's mind.

Vincent, who'd been passively observing, all of a sudden loudly clapped twice, so that everyone stopped and looked at him. 'Well, there's only one way to find out isn't there.' And then he said, addressing Hannah directly. 'Will you help us? It's got to be worth a try, to find out if you can break this curse which has hung over the village and my family for half a millennia?'

'Of course. But...'

'Don't worry,' he cut her off, mid-sentence. 'That will do for now. If you are who I suspect -' he looked towards Danny, '- then we'll worry about the hows and whys later.'

'It's all bullshit,' said Danny and, turning on a heel, practically stormed from the hall.

'Don't worry about him,' said Vincent, as Melissa chased after her lover. 'Why don't I show you around?' he extended his elbow for Hannah to take and asked Stephen and Susan if they would like to accompany them on the tour. Both declined and stayed seated, refilling their coffee cups while the host and his guest left by the same door Danny had taken.

'What happened?' she asked as they peered into another decrepit and dusty room. Once, like the rest of the house, it had been opulent, but that was a very long time ago.

'It's the gateway I was telling you about. The portal,' he shrugged, sounding resigned. 'Death seeps out of it and has corrupted the land. Everything growing in it turns foul. No crops equals no tenant farmers, which in turn means no income.'

Hannah thought back to the rotten apples in her own garden and paused in the doorway, hands on hips. A wide tangle of spider-web dislodged from the doorframe and brushed against her cheek. 'So, how can I help with the whole business then?' she sighed.

'There's a ceremony to perform.'

'In which I have to take part?'

'Yes.'

'And what do I need to do?'

'Just be there, we'll take care of the rest.'

'So, what does it entail, this ceremony?'

'We form a circle, with you in the middle, and we recant the right spell. It really is nothing to worry about,' he said with a reassuring smile.

'Well,' she said. 'Shall we get it done then?'

'I'm afraid it's not that simple?'

'What do you mean?'

'We don't have the exact spell yet.'

'What?'

'The right spell will be in your book…'

'My book?' *How could he know?* she thought.

'Well,' Vincent continued, 'Ella Jameson's book was rumoured to be an exceptionally good one. Must have been to…' He paused a moment.

Hannah's heart was fluttering.

'You see,' he continued along a different tack. 'Good spells are rather like good recipes. They get passed down through the generations. Father to son, mother to daughter, parent to child. Whoever has the gift.' He looked away, into the dusty room, 'It's never been found, you know?' He paused a moment and his stare snapped back in her direction, as if probing for tell-tale signs. 'I presume to think it's still in the cottage somewhere.'

'Really?' she said, trying to put on her best poker face. 'How do you know someone's not already been in and taken it?'

'I'd know.'

'How?

'I just would.'

'What does it look like?'

'Old,' he said, continuing to look straight into her eyes, trying to read her.

She suspected he knew she was holding back. 'Anything else?' she asked.

'Do you think you might have found it?' he asked.

She shook her head. 'No.' She wasn't even sure why she had lied.

'Sure?'

'I'm sure.' The lie was well and truly cemented.

Vincent decided to let it go, her defensiveness had told him all he needed to know.

'How do you know all this?' asked Hannah.

'I'm not ignorant of the arts, you know. Quite the opposite. Magic has been passed down through my family too, and runs thick in my blood. Generations of knowledge fill my own grimoire.'

'Oh.' She thought for a moment. Under any other circumstances she would have laughed out loud at the absurdity of the conversation they were having, but instead she found herself contemplating. 'So,' she said. 'You need me to find the spell-book, read the spell, vanquish the demon and break the curse.'

'Something like that.'

'Wow.'

15

Tap Tap Tap. Rapping on the kitchen window.

'Shit the bed!' Hannah was startled almost out of her own skin. There was a face outside the window, heavy with stubble and smiling in. *What the fuck is he selling?*

She'd not been back in the house long after her visit to Marsham Hall and had just come into the kitchen to make a cup of tea before settling down to take a closer look at the curious book she'd brought up from under the house.

Once her initial surprise wore off, to say she was furious at having her peace broken would have been an understatement. She strode to the back door and yanked it open. 'Yes?' she asked, her voice sharp. She thought she recognised him and it took a few moments to realise it was the man she'd seen smoking outside the Bull's Head, only now he looked a little more dishevelled.

Father Geoffrey Hamilton loathed the cottage at Picker's Bleed. He'd only visited once before and that had almost cost him his life. The priest had spent the morning building himself up for the oncoming onslaught, preparing through prayer and meditation, but he could not have put the visit off any longer if he was going to get away before nightfall.

The pressure in his temples had been building from about a quarter of a mile away and now, standing outside the back door, he was trembling. For possibly five or ten minutes he'd been fighting the pain, steeling himself to go back into the house and trying to push memories of the past from his mind before fear managed to get a toehold on his psyche and made him run away.

Hannah had come into the kitchen while Father Hamilton was steadying himself with prayer, muttering. Not wanting to appear a peeping tom, as soon as he saw her enter the room he reflexively rapped on the window and forced a smile which he hoped looked genuine. He hoped she hadn't noticed the act. 'Hi,' he said in his most supplicating voice when she snatched open the door. 'I'm Father Geoffrey Hamilton.' He always preferred to stay fairly formal on first meetings, '*Hi, I'm Geoff,*' sounded cheesy. He extended his hand in greeting, but instead of taking it she stood in stony silence, waiting for him to make his intentions clear. 'May I come in?' he eventually asked.

'Who are you?'

'Father Geoffrey Hamilton, from St Augustine's.'

'Okay, you already said that. And what do you want?'

'Please could I come in, I need to speak to you?'

'No.' For all she knew the man at the door could be a thief or a pervert. Or both.

'Please? It's important!'

A desperate undertone in his voice caught Hannah off guard, and she also warmed a little to something she saw in the priest's pale blue eyes. She sensed no threat coming from him, and was inclined to believe he really was a priest; he had that way about him. 'Tell me what it's about?'

He sighed. 'It's a long story...'

'Then give me the short version,' she butted in.

'I'm worried you might be in danger.' He was fidgeting with his fingernails.

'I don't think so,' she said.

Father Hamilton raised an eyebrow. 'Are you sure about that?' he asked, 'because if that's what you truly believe, nothing would make me happier than to walk away right now and never bother you again.' And he meant it. Even standing on the doorstep, the throbbing in his head was becoming more intense by the second. He was sure the pain must be showing on his face.

He could sense ghosts, bubbling up from somewhere deep within the cottage, where the boundary between this world and whatever lay beyond was fractured. The murmurings of a multitude of lost souls threatened to overwhelm him. There were other, inhuman things wandering amongst the spirits, potent with malignancy. Metaphysical beings which had never been human and were wrong in every way. One in particular ruled this roost, he could feel its oppressive presence and prayed he could be away before dusk.

Hannah stood firmly for a moment longer before, mistaking Father Hamilton's inner struggle for something else, she stepped aside. 'You'd better come in then.'

Once over the threshold she beckoned him to sit at the pine dining table. The banging in his head multiplied tenfold and the ghostly chatter grew to a dull roar like a mountain river in spate. He needed to hold himself together. Father Hamilton took a few deep breaths, putting into practice some long learned techniques for keeping the pain at bay.

'Are you alright?' asked Hannah, finally becoming aware of his discomfort.

'Yes,' he said, touching two fingers to his temple. 'It's just this house, that's all.'

'What do you mean, this house?'

'I'm what you might call, *sensitive*, to certain... things.'

'What things?'

'There's a spell on the house; a curse if you like,' he said, raising an eyebrow. 'It's to keep people away.'

'Well, I'm here, and I'm okay.' She didn't mention Vincent had said the same.

'That's what worries me,' he said. 'It means whoever set the spell wants you here. Or did. The place has been protected a long time now.'

'What's special about me?'

'You were with Vincent Mandeville last night weren't you?' asked Geoffrey, keen to get to the point.

'Yes. Why? What's that got to do with anything?'

'What do you know of him?'

'I know he lives up in the hall, is a bit of an eccentric and, as I'm sure you know yourself, has hit on hard times.'

'Did you know he's a practitioner of the black arts?'

'He said he dabbles in magic, but I wouldn't presume to be so dramatic as to call it Black Arts.'

'Oh, rest assured, him and his cronies definitely err on the side of evil.'

'Wouldn't you say that of any magic, being a man of the cloth an' all?'

'No. Although I can see why you'd think so, and many of my faith would think like that. However, I've spent my whole career – and it's a long one – studying many types of magic, and I do believe that there are types which can work good, and there are others which are plain perverse and evil. Lord Mandeville's brand of sorcery definitely falls into the latter.'

'All he's trying to do is make everything right again.' Even by Hannah's standards she was having a weird day.

Father Hamilton raised an eyebrow. 'Did he tell you how the curse came to be?'

'Something to do with a witch, who lived here, in this cottage.'

'Ella Jameson,' he said.

'Yes, that's her,' she said, trying to sound casual, although her heart quickened at the name.

'Did he tell you how Lord Richard Mandeville, the then occupant of Marsham Hall, ordered her to be burned at the stake?'

'No,' she furrowed her eyebrows and leaned forward slightly on her elbows, wanting to hear the whole story.

'It was right at the beginning of the witch trials, before witchcraft was even officially outlawed in England, and a long time before suspects had to be tried by the crown. You won't find mention of it in any history book or legal record, although word – as it always does – reached the church.'

Hannah nodded for him to continue.

'There was no doubt Ella dabbled in magic, and more than likely openly admitted it at the time, but it was also recorded that Lord Mandeville was a schemer, and for some reason decided to be rid of her.'

'This doesn't say anything bad about Vincent's character. Isn't it what they did to witches back then?'

'It's just... I guess we'll never know the whole story,' he said.

'Anyway,' she said. 'You still haven't told me why I'm in danger.'

'There are ghosts here, I can't believe for a minute you haven't felt them. But there are worse things. There's a..' he seemed to be searching for the right words. 'There's some kind of entity.'

'Tell me?' She gave a small shudder.

'What do you know of the last occupants of this house?'

'Didn't she go mad and kill her husband?'

'Her name was Marie Hodges, and her husband was possessed.'

'Eh?'

'It was the middle of summer when she first came to me. I was tending roses in the rectory garden and I can still remember there was some strength to the sun. She came around to the rectory pushing a buggy. A skylark went chattering up from the fields, all a flutter of wingbeats and melody. It's odd, the details you remember when your life turns upside down.

'I dared to hope the day would never come, that the family would spend their lives in happiness and the curse would have been no more. But there's no stopping the inevitable and there she was, on that day, coming towards me with tears in her eyes. My heart skipped a beat and at the same time a lead weight landed in my gut.

'I pretended not to know why she'd come in such a state and at first she was hesitant to explain. We went into the rectory kitchen and I made a nice cup of tea while she took young Joshua from his buggy. Poor child. He's not the first to go missing from the village either...' Father Hamilton stared off vacantly for a moment before continuing. '...poor things. Anyway, she clutched the child to her bosom, rocking, and I waited patiently, listening to the steady tic-toc of the grandfather clock. After a while she started to speak.

'"I'm scared," she said.

'"What of?" I asked.

'The next pause was longer than the first and the clock seemed louder, until eventually she said. "There are things."

'"What sort of things?" Although I already knew what was coming; it's the reason I was sent to this Godforsaken village. I felt sick.

'"You'll think I'm mad," Marie said.

'I told her I wouldn't,' added Father Hamilton, 'but it took a while to coax anything more out of her.

'After a long silence she eventually spoke again. "There are strange things in the house. They're trying to take my son." She promptly burst into a fresh bout of sobbing. Tears gushed.

'I sat forward in my seat. Attentive. My initial dread remained, but I was also excited. This was my calling. The moment I'd been training most of my life for, and I was now eager to get on with the job. In a way I was arrogant, but I was young. I believed I could win out where all others before me had failed. I have my gift on my side, you see?'

'Gift?' asked Hannah.

'I see things, and sense things. It's why the church took me on in the first place.' He looked pained. 'But enough about me,' he continued. 'My arrogance was ill placed and foolish. We sat and I listened while Marie told her story. She started, naturally, at the beginning; about all the hopes and dreams the young family shared and about how happy they were to be embarking upon a new and exciting chapter in their lives. She then went on to tell how when they were decorating, things would go missing or move and how their happiness turned to bickering. She told how she started suffering with headaches and was becoming more irritable by the day, muttering curses about the house and about how she wished they'd never moved there, but Gary, although he knew there was something odd going on didn't think it was so bad that they couldn't live with it.' Father Hamilton must have seen something in Hannah's expression and he asked, 'sound familiar?'

'Eh?'

He decided not to press the point, satisfied a seed had been planted. 'By the time she realised her family was in real danger, it was too late. When she came to me she was in such a state, and me being eager, I agreed to drop everything and go with her to Picker's Bleed straight away.

'I'd not been to the cottage before. With hindsight it seems an utterly idiotic thing. I suspect the spells which are cast over the place had something to do with that particular oversight. Some magic can influence you in such a subtle way, make things which should be in plain sight invisible.

'But on that day, when I began to get close to the cottage, it felt like there was a crushing weight settling on my shoulders which was getting heavier with each step. Every breath had to be fought for. The sun, which half an hour before had been pleasantly warming my skin, now only served to parch me. I could feel the veins throbbing in my temple and my heart raced as we walked up the driveway to the front door. Even then the front garden was overgrown and it felt like the brambles were trying to cut me. I knew I should have taken the time to properly prepare, but I was eager and proud.

'When we came inside, she shouted to see if Gary was home. It was all I could muster to stay on my feet, clinging to the door frame. I was caught in the psychic equivalent of a rip tide. Marie was a few paces in front, standing in the murk of the hallway, in front of the open cellar door and still calling her husband.

'An unholy, miasmic darkness was being spewed out of the cellar, which billowed like ink in water. It had already practically swallowed the buggy. I'm not sure if Marie had even noticed. The baby began to scream. It was such an awful sound but at least it shocked me into action.

'I pushed my way into the hall, and it really was like trying to push through something thrice the thickness of treacle. On the walls the pictures were rattling. The lightbulb exploded when the dark cloud touched it and sent slivers of glass flying into my face. It's a wonder I wasn't blinded. When I opened my eyes, Gary was in the doorway, lurching towards Marie and the baby from below.

'I'm certain it was a genuine case of possession, because his face was so...' Father Hamilton shuddered at the memory.

'Marie retreated towards the kitchen, putting herself between the baby and it. I say *It*, because the thing there wasn't Gary Hodges. For a few panicked moments I forgot the incantations, but a lifetime of recital and practice served me well and I found my voice.

'Gary's head snapped around to stare at me. His eyes were vacant. The dark somehow swirled about him, like a throng of cobra. His face was a mess of welts and pus-distended boils, which split when he spoke; "Leave," said the voice, which was guttural and low, with an odd reverb to it, so it sounded loud, yet far away. "Leave and never come back." Dirty yellow globs of pus slowly rolled off his chin, splatting into pats when they hit the floorboards.

'I shouted the prayers, doubling down on my faith. Something was coming up the cellar steps. There was a rushing in my ears. I was being buffeted by a vile wind and needed to shout over the cacophony of banging doors and rattling window frames. Something, I assume pans, was clattering and smashing about in the kitchen, where Marie was hiding.

'I yelled until my throat was raw and the supernatural storm reached a sort of climax before, all of a sudden everything went still and all I could hear was the baby crying. That was a sound which filled me with the deepest sense of relief. Gary's vacant body stayed upright for a few moments before he crumpled in a faint. Marie rushed over to him, leaving little Joshua in the buggy and I collapsed to my knees, exhausted.

'I glanced up when Gary took a deep, short and rasping breath. His complexion was back to something like it should have been. He looked confused.

'Stupidly, I thought it was over. So, while husband and wife comforted each other, I made a quiet exit. That was without doubt the biggest mistake of my life.'

'What happened?' asked Hannah.

'After then I didn't see the Hodges' so often, but when our paths did happen to cross, we exchanged the normal nods and pleasantries. There was little in the way of conversation and while in some ways that suited me because I didn't want to dredge up bad memories, I remember being quite put out at the lack of gratitude on their part. I asked Marie how she was, but she always said she was fine.

'Over the next few weeks I watched her grow old, far too quickly. She'd become haggard; the bags under her eyes were purple and deep lines furrowed her brow. Her eyes had gone wild, and grey streaked through her lank hair. I don't recall seeing Gary at all. I did surreptitiously check the baby as best I could when we exchanged small talk and at least he didn't seem to be suffering, and even offered up plenty of smiles from his pushchair.

'I should have acted sooner, but what could I do? She said they were fine and while I didn't ask directly about whether they were suffering any supernatural issues, she didn't mention any either, and so I wrongly assumed that the problem had, for then, gone away. Deep down though, I knew. It was cowardice that kept me from intervening, and guilt has been my cross to bear ever since.

'It was Christmas Eve by the time I resolved to do anything about it, but in my line of work things tend to get a tad busy over Christmas. I had intended to go around there on Christmas morning, when the service was finished and I could slip away unnoticed.

'After the service the congregation were filing out of the church and heading across to the pub, like a string of ants across the square, when my questions about the fate of the Hodges' were answered. I was standing in the vestry, shaking hands and wishing merry Christmas to any who met my eye.

Old Mrs Jacobs was the last to leave, hobbling out on her two sticks, when we both saw her at the same time. Adam Jones and Roger Beauchamp were just in the pub doorway when they both stopped dead in their tracks.' Father Hamilton paused for a moment, reliving painful memories. 'She was inconsolable.'

'They declared her mad, didn't they?'

Father Hamilton nodded. 'After it all happened I wrote to the Church and begged them to find a replacement. I told them how I'd failed and was unworthy of their trust. I'd let them down.'

Father Hamilton bowed his head towards the tabletop, acutely aware of the pain building behind his eyes. The air became thick. Putrid. Hot with the slimy reek of decay. There was laughter; hollow, ill-tempered and malignant and again, he wasn't sure whether or not it was in his head. He looked across to where Hannah was sitting, and although his vision was blurred, it didn't seem as if she'd noticed.

Hannah realised something was wrong with the priest as soon as he looked up. A trail of blood trickled from his left nostril; already there was enough so when he opened his mouth his teeth were stained red. 'And now, we might have the opportunity to stop it,' he said, sending flecks of blood across the table.

Dusk had crept up unnoticed and caught Father Hamilton unawares. He was sure he hadn't been at Picker's Bleed that long. The kitchen was all of a sudden gloomy, whereas only minutes before, bright shafts of sunlight, divided by the trees outside, had been streaking through the window to land warm on his skin. Now, all of a sudden the temperature dropped, leaving him icy cold. His teeth were chattering. Father Hamilton looked across to Hannah, but she seemed completely unaffected. It was then he realised the error of his ways.

The cellar door slammed open and Hannah swore at the sound. However, she didn't see the enormous, black dog prowling towards the priest, who was now clutching at his temples. Likewise, she did not hear the low rumble of a growl which petrified Father Hamilton.

'Are you okay?' she asked again, reaching across the table and clasping Geoffrey's arm, which felt as cold and hard as iron. *Shit*, she thought. *He's having a seizure.* And as she thought it, Father Hamilton stiffened and jerked in a fit which sent him onto the kitchen floor with a crunch.

By now there was blood gushing from both nostrils and a trickle from the corner of each eye. His mouth worked but no sound other than a strangled gargle came out. Hannah rushed to his side, unsure of how she could help. She tried to hold his hand, but the spasms snatched it away again. It was then she ran into the living room to dial 999, leaving the priest fitting on the hard, cold floor.

It was no surprise there was still no dial tone on the landline. She hit the button a few times and checked the wire before slamming the receiver back down and frantically rummaging through her handbag for the mobile which she already knew would be useless. Clutching it in two shaking hands, she pushed the button to turn it on while making haste back to the kitchen.

Father Hamilton's condition had worsened. The priest lay on the kitchen floor, his back arched. His blood-filled eyes were staring at some point in the hallway, where Hannah had just come from, and his mouth was shaping words – prayers, Hannah imagined - but the only sound which came from him was a rich gargling wheeze. His expression was one of pure panic as if something were moving towards him; something which was going to do him great harm and which he was powerless to resist.

And then Father Hamilton exhaled his last rattling breath and a tangible silence fell over the room. His body went limp while blood trickled from his ears, forming rivulets that tracked down his neck and dripped onto the kitchen floor. The expression of terror remained on his face and Hannah reached forwards to close the priests bulging eyes. His eyelids were tight and she struggled with them while the corpse stared at her.

Hannah ran out into the freezing night.

16

The Fiat's door-seals had started to freeze shut and a good yank was needed to open the door. Once Hannah was in the car, she fumbled the keys in the ignition and almost dropped them into the foot-well before she forced herself to take a few deep breaths and calm the fuck down. Focussing on the task in hand, she managed to start the car and turn the heater blowers up full. Then she had to jump out and clear ice from the windscreen. She rummaged in her purse for a credit card and worked frantically to clear a patch she could see through. Her fingers ached with the cold, but any pain was insignificant relative to the panic of having a body lying on the kitchen floor.

She set off before the windscreen had fully demisted. Craned forward to peer through the small clear patch of glass, she drove as fast as she dared. Light from the head-lamps made the trees on either side dance, their slender limbs reached out to snatch at the car and slow her progress.

Then a terrible thought struck her. *What if Father Hamilton isn't dead, and I've left him alone?* She hadn't checked his pulse, neither had she held a mirror to his mouth to see if it steamed with breath, like she'd seen on TV. But then, what else was she to do with no way of communicating with the outside world? Driving into Marsham was her only option, regardless of the priest's mortal condition.

When the scant, orange streetlights of the village flickered into view Hannah exhaled a sigh of relief. Her knuckles were white on the wheel as she pulled into one of the spaces in front of the church. Frost glittered atop the headstones, glinting in the harsh light of the car's headlamps. She stared at the imposing building of the church itself and up at gargoyles in the eaves, just about discernible in the night, and imagined sadness in their immobile and weathered stares. Then, she flung open the car door and ran across the empty square and into the Bull's Head.

Hannah burst into the bar and hushed talk from the few drinkers fell away to silence as they all turned to look at her. The pub wasn't busy; a couple sat on a cowhide two-seater sofa near the end of the bar and another couple were sitting in a nook. There was a pair of old locals sitting on bar stools in front of the taps, talking to the landlord. One of them was Les, who'd helped cut up the tree. Tom rested the pint he'd been pulling and leaned across the pumps.

'Call an ambulance,' said Hannah.

'Why? What's happened?'

'It's the priest. I think the priest's dead.'

Around the pub there was a collective intake of breath.

'Dead?' asked Tom.

'I think so. He's had some kind of fit.'

'I'll get on it.' In a flash the landlord was back behind the bar, dialling 999.

While he spoke to the operator he kept relaying questions to Hannah, but she was in shock and to her it felt like an interrogation. Too much was happening at once and it was all too much to handle. She sat in a daze and let the voices wash over her. Hannah was aware she should have been concentrating, but the landlord's voice phased out of her conscious hearing and she became mesmerised by the dancing, crackling fire.

A brandy was pressed into her hand and she glanced up to see Tom, having finished the emergency call. And then, as the brandy trickled warm down her oesophagus, her senses snapped back into place and she stood up. 'Could I use your phone please?' she asked. She needed to call Jake.

'I'm sorry, but the number you have dialled is temporarily unavailable. Please leave a message after the tone...' the automated voice was saying.

'Jake, it's me,' she said. 'Give me a call as soon as you get this message.' She hung up and muttered, 'Fucking shitting bastard,' under her breath. 'I'd better be going,' she said to the landlord, making her way back into the bar. 'The ambulance will be there soon.'

'I don't think you should be going anywhere,' he said, placing a gentle hand on her shoulder and guiding her back to the couch.

'But...' she started.

'But nothing,' he said. 'Is it open?'

'What?'

'Is the cottage unlocked, or do I need to send someone up there with a key?' Tom really hoped the door was unlocked, especially as he knew there'd be no volunteers and he'd end up going to the cottage himself. A prospect he didn't much relish.

'I...' She thought for a moment, chewing on her lip. 'I left it unlocked. But won't they need me there?'

'I can't see why, and I told them on the phone where you are.' He turned his back for a moment to measure two more brandies from the optic, one for him and another for Hannah.

Several brandies later a policeman walked into the bar, looking furtively into all the nooks before his eyes finally settled on Hannah and the landlord getting drunk and melancholic on the sofa. She'd almost managed to forget the fact there was the body of a priest on her kitchen floor, but the sight of the constable straightened her back and made some of the rosiness drain from her cheeks. She looked at him expectantly, absentmindedly chewing her bottom lip.
'Miss Jenkins?'

She confirmed with a nod, rising unsteadily to her feet. 'Any idea what happened to him?' she asked.

'It's a bit early to say, but we're not treating it as suspicious -,' he reassured her and then, with a pause for thought, '-for now. But please let us know if you're planning on going anywhere.'

Hannah's jaw went slack. 'Wha...'

'Don't worry,' the policeman said. 'Do you have somewhere to spend the night?' His concern seemed genuine.

'Well,' she looked at Tom, and then back to the policeman; 'I was planning on going back to the cottage.'

The policeman and Tom exchanged a look and asked, 'Are you sure?'

'Yes. Why?' Despite all that had happened, she still felt no great threat from the house. 'I don't suppose I could get a lift, could I?' she asked the policeman. 'Only, I'm well over the limit with all this brandy.'

'Are you sure it's a good idea?' the constable asked again.

'There's a spare room upstairs,' Tom offered. 'You're more than welcome to stay. In fact, I insist.'

'Really, it's fine,' she said. 'I want to go home.'

'If you're sure?' said the policeman.

A smile touched her lips when Hannah remembered the last time she'd been in a police car, but no sooner had she started reminiscing then they'd arrived. The young constable held the car door open while she slithered out. 'Now, are you quite sure you'll be okay?' he asked.

'Positive,' she slurred and began to walk up the drive.

The policeman stayed with the car until she'd opened the front door and was safely inside. With a wave, she shut the door and the constable shuddered, but not with the chill of the night. Without waiting a second longer than he needed to, he was back in his car and moving, afraid to look in his rear-view mirror.

When the front door clicked shut the first thing Hannah noticed was a steady drip from the kitchen tap, into a pan which sat unwashed in the sink. The cottage was eerily quiet. It felt different. The fire in the sitting room had burned out and a chill had settled into the house. Hannah continued along the hall, past the open cellar door, from which a cold draught blew, and into the kitchen where she flicked on the bare lightbulb hanging from the ceiling. Until now the lack of a shade hadn't overly bothered her, but now the cold incandescent light only served to further flatten her mood. It was as if the edges were sanded off her senses, like a world in watercolour.

She stood in the doorway, staring at blood smeared across the floor and realised she was exhausted, drunk, and in need of a lie down. Too tired to scrub the floor, she turned the light back off and made her way up the stairs and to bed.

Upstairs was colder still. The sight of her reflection in the bathroom cabinet, while making short work of brushing her teeth, shocked her. *No wonder things feel a bit flat,* she thought, looking at the saggy, purple bags under her eyes and sallow skin. *You need to get some sleep, woman.* She went to bed in a tee shirt and pants and pulled the duvet up over her head for a short while until she needed fresh air, and then she only poked out her nose.

It took a while, but eventually she managed to get warm. However, insomnia had taken over and the sleep her body and mind craved eluded her. For an indeterminate length of time, Hannah lay and stared up at the ceiling. Moonlight made a bright rectangle of the window that lit the room, casting shadows of branches across the ceiling and walls from the trees outside, which were swaying on a stiff breeze. From downstairs came the constant dripping of the kitchen tap.

Eventually boredom and mounting irritation at the drip drove her back out of bed. She wished she'd taken time to relight the fire before she'd gone upstairs, but then remembered how exhausted she'd been when she'd got home. The beginnings of a hangover were coagulating in her head. A floorboard creaked when she put weight on it.

Somewhere in the house something scuttled and Hannah cocked her head to one side, listening intently, but she couldn't hear anything over the incessant dripping of the kitchen tap. She went downstairs irritated, but stopped dead in her tracks at the cellar door. The draught which had blown chill before was now freezing. Her breath spread out in front of her, wafting and billowing slowly like smoke. The portrait of the little girl, hanging opposite the open door, had a thin rime of frost on the frame.

The lights flickered, which prompted Hannah to fetch a torch from the kitchen before she ventured down the steps. Although the kitchen tap must surely have still been dripping, it went forgotten and unheard as she rummaged through the kitchen drawers. While she thought about it, Hannah grabbed a cardigan from the back of the chair and shoved the torch into one of the pockets before heading down into the cellar.

The overhead light stayed on, but it was gently pulsing, as if about to expire at any moment. The temperature dropped further as Hannah descended and when she stepped off the bottom step, she immediately saw the trapdoor was open. The strange radiance rolled up from the square hole in the floor, just a shade lighter than the shadows around it, but noticeable.

Her heart cantered as she made her way through the clutter towards the trapdoor. Her toe caught something and sent it skidding across the floor. Hannah looked to see what she'd kicked and saw it was a child's doll, the old-fashioned sort, with a ceramic head and painted features. *Strange,* she thought. She hadn't seen it before, but there must have been plenty of things in the cellar yet undiscovered and so she paid it little mind.

The rope bindings creaked as she put weight onto each rung and descended into the strange grotto beneath the house. The same, eerie glow lit the room, but the mirror was black, as if devouring light. It was to this void she was drawn, and to the certain knowledge that something otherworldly lay behind the glass. She glid across the floor in a trance, focussing solely on the mirror without noticing ice beneath her feet. The ends of her fingers began to turn blue. And then she was standing directly in front of the ornate mirror, reaching out an arm to touch the inky black glass. The thought of Father Hamilton came into her head and she stayed her hand, unsure of why.

As Hannah's senses cleared, she heard the pitiful sound of crying. Her first thought was there must be a child in the house. It slowly dawned on Hannah that the sobbing was coming from inside the mirror. Hannah thought about Jake and the things he'd mutter about when waking from his nightmares. The cries were the saddest thing she'd ever heard.

It was then Hannah began to shiver, until her knees gave way and she collapsed onto the frozen earth floor. Her fingers hurt like long needles were being shoved under her nails. An instinct for self-preservation kicked into action and it was all Hannah could do to crawl to the bottom of the ladder. For a moment the short climb seemed it would prove impossible but somehow she forced herself upwards.

Hannah clambered out into the cellar, but just before she slammed the trapdoor shut the crying came again, drifting up through the hole in the floor. It was a wretched sound. But there was something else; a guttural growling and grunting.

Every surface was frosted and glinting in the pulsing yellow electric light, before the bulb guttered out and Hannah was plunged into complete darkness.

The panic was instant. All recollection of the torch in her pocket eluded her and she bolted towards where she thought the cellar steps were. She was sure she'd left the door at the top of the steps open, but it must have been closed because there was no light coming down from above. She trod on something which rolled away beneath her feet, turning her ankle and pitching her headlong to the floor. By chance, her fingers caught the bottom step and by feel alone she crawled up the brick steps to make good her escape.

Oddly, she saw the door into the hallway was open after all, but she could only see the rectangle of light from three or four steps down. When she reached the hall, she slammed the door closed behind her and fastened the flimsy latch.

She missed Jake.

Lacking the energy to go upstairs, Hannah made for the sitting room, which at least had a comfortable couch or rug to lie on. Her mind was whirring, she paced the room, drinking vodka from the bottle and chain-smoking. She thought about everything she'd been told, about kids going missing. She thought about the priest. She thought about Jake's dreams, and she thought about the strange mirror under the cottage. All of it going round and round and round in her head. With utter conviction, Hannah knew the children she heard were the same ones the mirror showed her in the black room with the crone. It was all real. She also knew they were in need of saving and she was the only one who could do it. Call it intuition, but Hannah knew the children who'd gone missing weren't dead.

She passed out on the sitting room floor, unable to get any warmth back into her bones and wishing again that she'd taken the time to light a fire.

17

The cottage was quiet when Hannah woke. Shafts of weak sunlight shone down to where she lay on the thick maroon rug in front of a cold hearth, curled into a tight ball, reluctant to open up and expose herself to the chill air.

But nature called and eventually she relented and made her way upstairs. All her joints ached. Whatever had changed about the cottage the night before, stayed changed. Every creak of the stairs put her on edge, too loud in the quiet house. It was as if the cottage were some giant entity which had taken a deep breath and at some point would exhale with violent gusto. But for now, she felt something was playing a waiting game with her.

Without unnecessary delay, Hannah snatched the ancient spell-book off the coffee table and left the cottage with it under her arm. When she was out of the gate and standing in the middle of the lane, she paused and glanced back. The cottage seemed to be mocking her. The rooks adorning the roof laughed at her plight. One or two wheeled overhead, flying from cottage to forest and back again and she almost expected to be dive-bombed, but it didn't happen.

Her unease began to lift when she was approaching the gates of Marsham Hall, and for a moment she wondered whether she was being foolish. She paused for a moment, weighing up what she knew and what she felt. And then, giving herself no time to change her mind, she strode up the driveway and banged on the door of the dilapidated mansion.

The decrepit butler looked Hannah up and down with some intensity before stepping aside for her to enter. 'Third door on the left,' he said with a touch of resignation in his voice, as if somehow disappointed to see her. As she went along the dingy hallway, she heard the front door close with a heavy clunk. The corridor was plunged into deep gloom. Looking back over her shoulder she could see no sign of Appleby. In the quiet it was easy to imagine he'd never existed at all and she was the only living thing in an otherwise derelict building.

Hannah knocked, but opened the door before waiting for a reply.

Vincent looked up from where he was sitting in a high-backed chair, poring over some ancient book on a large writing desk. 'Good morning,' he said. 'To what do I owe the pleasure?' His tone was welcoming and he didn't sound at all surprised to see her.

'I need your help,' she blurted and slammed her own book down on the desk. Vincent's eyes passed over it and he looked like he'd started to salivate.

'Oh,' he said, clasping his hands and peering over the rims of his wire-framed spectacles before he removed them altogether, his attention shifting from the book to fully concentrate on Hannah. 'So, you decided to take me up on my offer'

When Hannah gazed at the floor, shuffling her feet and

floundering for the correct words, he broke the awkward silence. 'Drink?'

'Please?'

'You'd better sit down.' Vincent gestured towards a battered Winchester chaise longue before he rose, went to the other wall and pressed a spot in the wooden panelling. A concealed door opened with a soft, well-oiled click. The secret door must have been the most rigorously maintained part of the house.

After Vincent slipped through and Hannah had stopped gawking at the small gap where he'd left the door ajar, her fidgety eyes moved to study the desk and chair. Like the rest of the mansion, they had once been grandiose, but had now gone shabby, devoid of any chic. The heavy maroon curtains, piebald in places, were drawn across the narrow window, blocking out the morning sun. Light shone instead from an incandescent bulb, encased within the bejewelled but dusty shade of a tall standard lamp which stood just behind the chair. It appeared to be carved from the same wood as the other furniture, possibly mahogany, so as to make a matching set.

A large patch of mould filled one corner of the ceiling, spreading out across bumpy and blistered plaster. The other corners were filled with cobwebs, but presumably spiders did not like mould. The room smelled of stale incense, pipe tobacco and damp.

While she was taking all of this in Hannah didn't see Vincent, out of sight in his small antechamber, unfolding a small square of paper and carefully emptying its contents into the tumbler of gin and tonic he'd poured. Only into the one he'd poured for Hannah, of course. He stirred the drink with his finger and held the glass up in front of his face to check no traces of the powder were visible before returning to the study.

'What are you smiling at?' Hannah asked when he handed her the drink.

'I knew you'd come,' he said with an air of self-assurance.

'Really, how?'

'I saw it.'

'Saw it?'

'Yes.' He gestured to the crystal ball, in its stone-claw stand.

'So, you already know why I'm here?'

'Not exactly, no. You see, the crystal can sometimes be a little hazy, like glimpsing a silhouette in the fog. Some interpretation is required.' He took a sip of gin and tipped his glass towards Hannah.

She took his cue and took a large gulp, swallowing down about a third of a tumbler full. 'I'm really glad you believe in stuff like that...'

'Like what?' he said, reclining in his chair and taking another sip of gin

'Paranormal stuff,' she said. 'Like your crystal ball and the supernatural.'

'Yes', he said appreciatively, once again tipping his glass, a subtle gesture this time.

'It makes it much easier to speak about...'

'Go on?' he encouraged.

'It might sound stupid but...' she took a deep breath before blurting out, 'There's a kind of mirror in my cellar, which isn't a mirror and shows things which aren't there and... I'm sure there are some children somehow trapped on the other side, in the reflection, like I can see them and hear them, but they're not really there but I know they are. I know they're real.' She paused a moment, reflecting on her own words then, slightly flushed in the cheeks, she looked up at Vincent. 'I'm not mad. Am I?'

'No darling,' he said. 'You are not mad. Now drink up and I'll pour another.'

While he was gone, Hannah was left perched on the end of the chaise-longue feeling slightly foolish. The gin brought a flush to her cheeks and she thought it strange how just one glass had made her fuzzy in the head.

The drink he handed over this time was not spiked with any magic potions, as the drug she'd already ingested would already be taking hold, freeing her of inhibitions and better judgement. Vincent was gleeful that she'd come to him willingly, needing his help as much as he needed hers. He mused that the drug might not have even been necessary, although it would help ensure she was malleable to his plans. His heart quickened at the prospect of the ceremonies to follow. He might have even got a little stiff. 'These children...' he said, not quite believing his good fortune, '...where do you think they are?'

'I don't know,' she said, once again questioning her own sanity and suspecting Vincent may be humouring her; something about his facial expressions didn't quite fit the situation she was describing.

'Shall I tell you what I think?' he asked.

Here we go, she thought, *this is where he tells me it's in my head.* She nodded in the affirmative, not really wanting an answer.

'I think they're trapped on the other side.'

'The other side of what?'

'The portal I was telling you about. If you imagine it as two worlds existing in the same space, but out of *phase* with each other, so the two are always separated...'

She nodded in the small pause he'd left, although not really following what he was saying; instead wondering how much alcohol he'd poured into her glass for her to be feeling so woozy. Her attention was starting to drift. She tried to concentrate on understanding his words, rather than simply hearing noises with no meaning.

'...one of those worlds is ours, home to the living, while the other is home to the dead.' He paused again, for effect. 'And although these realms are generally invisible to each other, there are some places where the fabric between the two is thin, like they are touching through lace. Very rarely, a hole can be made in this lace and travel between the two worlds becomes possible. Now, I know there is one such tear at Picker's Bleed, and I've already told you about the curse; whereby as well as the earth being barren, the children disappear.'

'So they're dead?'

'I didn't say they were dead, did I? I said they vanished. Now, I think they've slipped, or been taken, through this hole and into the other world. The world of the dead.'

'Poor things must be terrified,' she said dreamily, from far away.

'Right,' he agreed. 'But thanks to you I think we can help them.' And then he added, 'if you're willing?'

'How?'

'We open up a hole-between-worlds of our own, now we have the spell.'

'From the book I found?'

'Exactly,' he said.

'If you can do that?' her words were becoming slurred. 'Why has no-one done it before?'

'As I said before, we needed the right words, so we can connect to the right place on the other side, where those poor, poor children are. We need you. You know how you're hardly affected by the magic around Picker's Bleed; How it sends others mad, but not you? You're the discoverer of the book and the *gateway*. I think it's destiny. You were supposed to find them.'

'The mirror,' she said.

'Exactly!' replied Vincent with a small flourish with his pipe.

'So, what do I need to do?' she asked.

'Leave that to me,' he said, trying to sound sincere. 'You wait here and I'll make the preparations.'

'What? Now?'

'I can't think of any good reason why not?' he said, but he could think of one good reason to hurry, and that was to get the ceremony over and done with before the drugs wore off and she had a change of heart. Hannah would not be the first person they'd lured down into his private temple, but none had meant quite so much. The stakes had never been higher, and he wanted nothing left to chance.

He tugged on an old, frayed cord hanging next to the door. Somewhere in the house a bell rang and moments later, Appleby appeared. 'Could you gather the others?' Vincent asked and the butler, with a discreet bow, ducked back out of the door to comply. Vincent turned his attention back to Hannah, 'And while we're waiting, would you like another drink?' he asked, and downed the last of his gin.

'Thank you,' she said in almost a whisper.

18

Danny and Melissa arrived first, their voices could be heard in animated conversation coming down the hallway, but they stopped speaking just shy of the open door and entered the study in heated silence. The atmosphere was awkward; Danny's piercing blue eyes were scrutinising Hannah while Mel's gaze didn't stray far from Danny, apart from when she shot daggers across the room. Hannah wanted to ask the reason for their disdain, but found she lacked both the will and the energy, and so she sat on the edge of the chaise-lounge, hands on knees, staring at the floor.

It wasn't long before Stephen sauntered in and looked about the room with his one good eye. The other stared vacantly off towards some distant spot beyond the wall. *It must be glass,* thought Hannah. 'Well, it's mighty jolly in here,' he said.

'Sarcastic bastard,' muttered Mel.

Even in her drowsy state, Hannah was baffled as to why these people kept each other's company when it was quite apparent they hated each other's guts. Her train of thought was interrupted, however, by the arrival of Susan, oozing vintage glamour even though she was wearing only a fleecy dressing gown.

Do they live here all the time?' Hannah briefly wondered, before Vincent re-entered the room. In the time he'd been absent, he'd changed his clothes from corduroys and woolly jumper to a long black robe, the hem of which brushed the floor around his feet. The significance was not lost on those gathered and any questions they might have had fell away before leaving their lips.

This is some weird shit, was all Hannah's addled brain could muster, as Vincent placed a hand on the small of her back and ushered her through the secret door. *But everything about this is weird.*

They'd entered a cloakroom, of sorts, in the sense that it was a small, rectangular room, literally with cloaks hanging along one wall; black, monk-like robes, all like the one Vincent was wearing. There were four hanging up, and an empty peg near the end, next to the top of a flight of stairs, which disappeared into darkness below. There was also a door on the other wall, although this one was closed, and she expected it led to a larder, or something similar, where Vincent had poured the gin. She watched in a state of befuddlement as the others, besides Vincent, stripped naked and changed into the robes which were hanging up. *Whatever floats your boat,* she thought.

'You have to get undressed now,' Vincent was saying.

For a moment the request jogged back her senses. 'What did you say?' She wondered whether she'd heard him correctly.

'You can't wear those clothes down there,' he pointed towards the staircase.

'But there aren't any robes left.'

'I know,' he said. 'You don't need one.'

Mel snorted. 'Don't worry, you have great tits.'

Vincent shot her a look and turned back slowly to reassure Hannah. He gently cupped her hand in both of his. 'I know it's difficult, and not what you're used to, but you have to trust me. You do trust me, right?' he asked, using his most sincere tone of voice.

'Uh-huh,' she nodded. It was no use, the drugs which were running thick in her system robbed her of reason, leaving behind a skull full of fluffy confusion. She was swaying, unsure if she could still feel her legs.

'They might contaminate the...' he was saying.

Although Hannah was trying, she couldn't really absorb Vincent's words, he sounded far away.

'And in any case, you can't *cross over* with any material possessions. That includes clothes.'

'Uh-huh.'

'So, let's get you undressed shall we,' he sounded like a priest or some other professional in whom one should have implicit trust. But at the same time, he was unbuttoning her jeans.

When any argument against what was happening failed to form in her head, she meekly said, 'okay.'

Hannah allowed herself to be led down the staircase, into a basement where all traces of natural light were lost. She followed in a daze, seeing her surroundings but not understanding what her eyes were telling her. They'd descended into a large, vaulted space which, unlike the rest of the mansion, was immaculate. The floor was tiled with black marble and polished to such a sheen the fires, which were lit in four large iron braziers, appeared to be floating in mid-air. The room was thick with incense-fragranced smoke, which served to further cloud her senses as it blurred her vision and filled her lungs. The braziers were positioned around a circle of brilliant white marble laid into the black, within which was a pentagram. Hannah was all too aware of her vulnerability and far away, in the deepest recesses of her mind, alarm bells were clanging at her to run, but she'd been rendered incapable of action.

Vincent and his accomplices spread themselves evenly around the circle with Vincent taking a position at the head of the pentagram. 'Step inside,' he said, his voice soothing.

Despite her drug induced fugue, she was hesitant. The alarm bells were increasing in volume like a speeding fire engine. Her heart was racing.

'It's time,' said Vincent, gesturing towards the circle, the cuffs of his robe hanging low off his wrists. 'It's the only way to save those poor children.'

Hannah took a deep breath and stepped inside. A small thrill passed through her as if she'd let go of some final taboo, cast her inhibitions aside and taken the plunge. Her naked skin prickled with goosebumps and she let out a small gasp. She looked around and saw Vincent had her book resting in one hand while he traced letters on the open page with a finger.

He started to read in a language Hannah had never heard before. His voice was vaguely musical, starting soft and low, almost a rhythmic hum, and in parts the others joined in, so she was immersed in a polyphonic drone which, as it got louder, reverberated through her body and sent a tingling to her extremities. Tension was building in the air and the thrum grew stronger.

An impossible, ill and swirling wind made the braziers grow angry and flare up. Flames were being whipped in all directions. Smoke whirled about the room. At the edge of the circle, Susan looked shocked and stumbled over her lines. However, it was only a momentarily lapse of control and she quickly regained her composure.

The tepid wind, that reeked of rotting animals, vomit and faeces, wrapped around Hannah, whipping her long hair. The effect of whatever concoction Vincent had given her wore off all of a sudden as if it had been nothing at all and Hannah was overcome with an immense and primal terror. The suddenness and intensity of her dread left her feeling like every part of her body was filled with rocks. The urge to close her eyes and crumple to the ground was overwhelming but she knew that if she did, then she would be committing to something worse than death. It might well be a way to cross to the other side, but no matter how noble her cause, she didn't want to go through with it anymore.

The chanting became louder and the smoke blew thicker than it possibly could from the braziers alone, whirling into a vortex within the pentagram, until it began to coagulate and take on substance. Hannah became aware of a presence in the circle with her.

All of a sudden her instinct for flight kicked into action, but she was unable to leave the circle of smoke. It was not the case there was a force holding her back or barring her way, but rather that she herself had lost mass and turned to vapour, unable to move while the foul smoke continued to coalesce into something bigger. Something sentient.

As the thing took on form, she could see that whatever it was didn't stand as tall as she did, but it was heavy-set and down on all fours. The darkness became more solid until she could discern a large canine head, lolling beneath the muscular shoulders of its forelegs. Hot, fetid breath smothered her face, which was worse than the foul wind that whipped all about. There were no features she could discern other than its eyes. The thing appeared to absorb light, so it was nothing more than a black animation, cut from the fabric of reality, but the eyes were swirling pools of molten copper; round black flecks in their centres seemed miles away in the burning heat, floating in timeless depths of hellfire.

Around the edge of the circle, Vincent and the others were struggling to keep their feet as their robes flapped in the violent wind. Their chanting needed to be shouted to be heard. But nonetheless, Vincent's face was a vision of rapture. Dan and Mel also were in the throes of ecstasy, while Susan had paled somewhat and showed a tinge of fear. Stephen too, had taken half a step back and looked on with a touch of trepidation, although he still returned the chants. They all did; whatever was unfolding now it was too late for a change of heart, they were past the point of no return.

The thing moved closer, ears pricked, its eyes mesmerising. A deep growl, which was felt deep in the gut, came from it and the hound's maw gaped to reveal filthy, dripping teeth. Hannah knew that once in the grip of those fangs, there'd be no escape. And yet she was powerless to resist.

She spun around, meeting the eyes of all those around the circle, in a vain plea for help, before she too realised the awful truth. In a last-ditch effort, she kicked and punched and struggled, but none of her blows connected. The dog let go a low, rumbling snarl. Hannah felt cold, then nothing. She was becoming insubstantial. It felt like the ill wind was tugging and stretching her being. She peered down at her arms and saw them spiralling away into tendrils of colourful smoke, before being absorbed by the maelstrom.

There was less of her with every passing moment until the wind died. When the smoke cleared, the circle was empty.

19

They went to Picker's Bleed the morning after the ceremony. It was clear as day something had gone terribly wrong although, with all their combined knowledge and experience, they couldn't figure out what and were in search of answers.

Vincent's lips were curled into a grim half-smile as the Range Rover wound through the woods. Stephen was sat in the back, staring out of the window trying to glimpse the interior of the forest, but they were travelling too quickly and he couldn't see past the blur of trunks and branches. The effect was somewhat hypnotic when coupled with the drone of the engine and the steady swish and rumble of tires ploughing through the layer of damp leaves surfacing the lane. He could hear Susan breathing beside him, eliciting the occasional quiet sigh. He could feel her leg, warm against his. Danny was sitting in the front passenger seat peering intently out of the front window as Vincent steered them though the forest. Mel was sitting on the other side of Susan, fidgeting with her fingernails.

A twig slapped against the outside of the window, right

in front of Stephen's face, bringing him back to his senses. There was a tangible, yet undefinable change in the atmosphere. What had been anticipation was now pure anxiety. A quick glance around the cabin confirmed the others felt it too. Vincent's gaze was fixed firmly forwards. Danny was sitting stock still, wringing his hands. Susan was biting her nails. 'We're getting close aren't we?' asked Mel.

'Yup,' replied Vincent without taking his eyes off the road.

'Nothing's changed,' she muttered with an air of crushing disappointment. 'Fuck.' She slammed her hand against the inside of the car-door.

No-one responded. Stephen returned his gaze back out of the window. The Range Rover slowed. They were not racing to their destination anymore and the trees didn't rush past so quickly, although he wished they would. The woods were claustrophobic and menacing, closing in and bearing down on them. The familiar feelings of spiralling despair and nauseating dread had returned and he wondered how close to the cottage they would be able to get before one of them begged to turn around and drive the fuck out of there. The spell was always worse for those with an aptitude for magic.

At some point they had pulled up outside the front gate, but Stephen could not say whether they'd been parked for seconds or for hours, or even when they'd arrived. An excruciating pain shot through his head, ricocheting from temple to temple. In a blur - as if drunk almost to the point of comatose - Stephen watched Vincent wrap his hand around the doorhandle as if to open it. He tried to scream 'No', but the warning left his mouth as a short grunt, but at the same time he saw Danny put out a hand to stop him.

They all knew nothing had changed. Whatever they had been trying to achieve, they'd failed.

Vincent floored the accelerator and they sped off, almost

taking flight when the Range Rover crossed the small humpbacked bridge which spanned the stream, crashing back down onto creaking suspension and jarring Stephen's teeth. All the passengers were being tossed about as the car hurtled down the lane with reckless abandon, perilously close to hitting trees more often than not on some of the tighter bends. The pain in Stephen's head subsided with distance from the cottage to leave a residual dull, ache. Next to him, Susan had turned pale and vacant, her head flopped from side to side with the jolting of the car. He half-heartedly tried to bring her to her senses.

After driving the long way around, the Range Rover juddered to a halt in the village square, opposite the Bull's Head and following a moment's pause they clambered out on shaky legs. The air was fresh and the sun was bright. The contrast between the crisp autumnal morning and their experience was unreal. It was then they noticed the Bull's Head was closed and there was still an hour until opening time. Undeterred, Vincent strode across the empty square, the long taint of his shadow following close behind. Danny and Mel were close on his heels while Stephen tried to coax Susan from the car. Eventually he took her hand and she followed without resistance. Docile, he led her towards the pub.

Vincent was hammering the door with the butt of his fist, knocking in rapid bursts. 'Fuck me, I need a drink,' he muttered when the bolts slid back on the other side of the door.

'What the...?' Tom Stour looked like he'd been roused from his bed.

'Let us in, Tom,' Vincent said and made to walk straight into the pub, but the landlord's burly frame barred the way and wasn't moving.

'We're closed,' he started to say, but realising their

need was dire Tom stepped aside, ushering them in with a begrudging expression. After the group were in the pub, he shrugged and wedged the front door open for the day, before following them into the taproom.

'What'll it be?' asked Tom, manoeuvring himself behind the bar.

'Five brandies,' replied Vincent before adding, 'Make them doubles.'

'Everything okay?'

'Yes,' said Vincent, in an, *it's none of your business,* kind of way.

Tom didn't push the matter, but set about polishing the bar while Vincent and Danny carried the glasses to the snug within which the group had ensconced themselves. The bar didn't particularly need polishing, but Tom was a practiced listener. It never failed to amaze him how invisible he could become while people shared their confidences, with tongues loosened by ale. Most of what he heard was village gossip and tittle-tattle, but occasionally there were far more interesting things to learn. Something told him this was one of those times. And so, duster in hand, he set to work and made himself unobtrusive.

20

The following morning, breakfast at Marsham Hall found tensions running high. Appleby brought out sausages and hash browns and placed them on the table while managing to remain largely unnoticed in the silent room. Only Susan said thank you.

'This is shit,' mumbled Danny, not referring to breakfast.

Vincent looked up at him from across the table without raising his head but didn't answer. Melissa glared back at him from Danny's side, trembling with anger, fists balled by her sides. She stayed like that for a few moments before, with a sigh she shook her head and asked, 'What do we do now?' She looked to the others for answers, only to find blank expressions. 'What the fuck do we do?'

Vincent gave a minute shrug. 'I really don't know.' His tone was matter of fact and resigned.

There was a moment of collective inward and morose contemplation before Stephen, until now quiet at one end of the table, said 'I'm going to check the cottage again.'

The collective gasp was audible and all eyes turned to

him.

'I'm serious,' he said. 'We did something. It might not have gone how we expected, but I want to find out what was accomplished.'

So it was, that not long after breakfast, Stephen found himself tentatively wandering alone through dense fog along the winding deer-track towards Picker's Bleed. Most of the trees were bare and the woods were damp. Skeletal branches wove through the fog above his head, dripping with condensation. Apart from the occasional cawing of a rook and the swish of Stephen's feet though moist litter, the forest was silent.

Despite the oppressive weather the sensation of dread was not as bad as he might have expected, which gave him some hope, but nevertheless Stephen was brimming with apprehension as he picked his way amongst the trees and over roots towards the cottage.

After a while he heard the babbling of the stream which ran on the far side of Picker's Bleed and knew he must have missed the cottage in the fog. He decided to continue down to the river, for a brief glance about and to gather his thoughts before doubling back. For a while he watched the stream as it tumbled over rocks and fallen trees, between verdant banks dripping with mosses and ferns.

The air temperature dropped suddenly. Fog crystallised into fine snowflakes, that glinted as they floated earthward. Hoarfrost materialised on twigs and branches and with the cold came a profound and debilitating dread. Something was behind him; he was certain of its presence. Stiffly and slowly Stephen swivelled on his feet.

Standing on the path he'd just walked down, not twenty paces from where he now stood, was Hannah. She was corpse-like. Her skin was grey and moist with a half-rotted sheen. Something was very wrong, and for a short time he stood there while his brain tried to make sense of what his eyes were telling him, but well before he reached any kind of comprehension, instinct took over and he bolted into the forest at a right angle to the path.

More afraid than he could ever remember being, Stephen sprinted through the woods until his breathing was enormous and ragged and he had a stitch. Twigs raked and gouged his face into a hodgepodge of scratches and welts.

He ran full pelt into the bough of an ancient oak, hitting the tree with left side of his forehead. The blow slammed his teeth together and sent him abruptly to the forest floor, where he floundered, virtually blind from the blood which was trickling down into his good eye.

Almost as quickly as he fell though, he was back on his feet and running again, blinking away not only blood, but also a concussion. Fog seeped through the woods, winding long, wispy tendrils around tree trunks and Stephen couldn't help but think the world was slipping away from him.

Long after he'd become exhausted and his sprint had slowed to a crooked lurch, Stephen could go no further. The noise of his own breathing was by far the loudest thing in the forest. Holding onto the tree next to him with one hand and the other braced against his knee, he bent double. Gradually his heart began to slow and his breathing became more relaxed. 'What the fuck have we done,' he said out loud and his next thought was that he must let the others know. It was then he realised he had no idea where he was, or in which direction he'd been running.

For a while he studied the mulch beneath his feet while contemplating what had gone so terribly wrong and what it might mean. A bead of sweat popped from his brow and trickled along his temple. It fell to the floor and Stephen watched it land with audible plop onto frosted leaves where it sat, lightly steaming.

He looked up slowly. The thing inhabiting the girl's body was standing naked in front of him. Her pupils were utterly black, like devourers of light. The thing smiled. Stephen didn't have the energy to scream but his automatic instinct for survival burst into action and, without conscious will on his part, he was running again.

It wasn't a particularly large twig that cut short Stephen's flight, being roughly the diameter of his little finger, but it was long enough to drive itself unhindered through his eye socket and into the mush of brain beyond. His glass eye spun through the air and ricocheted off a neighbouring tree. Stephen slid off the twig and twitched a few times on the ground while Hannah loomed over him, watching the spark of his life sputter out.

21

His nightmare was filled with nothing but sound. No up. No down. There was nothing beneath his feet and yet he was not falling, or at least Jake didn't think so. There was no way of telling even if there was air, or indeed, if he was breathing. Did he possess substance and mass, or was he merely a floating ball of consciousness?

The noise that was all around was without end, a cacophony stretching to the aural horizon, and beyond to infinity. At first he couldn't decipher what the racket was, until from nearby came a person's voice, a woman crying. Whoever it was sounded lost and alone. Afraid and begging to be rescued.

Jake concentrated, to try and pinpoint the voice and isolate it within the voluminous static. With no other senses to stimulate his floating brain the din began to resolve into a billion individual voices, spread out like stars in an acoustic universe, each crying their own terrors.

The noise was vertiginous and Jake quickly succumbed to panic, adding his own pleas to the others. 'Help,' he cried.

'Over here.' He was being drawn into the madness, in danger of losing himself.

Somewhere over his left shoulder there was a horrible, toe-curling scream from a child, and what could only be described as a dog panting. Were the noises together, was someone being savaged? Jake couldn't tell. His panic deepened. He tried to flee but had no way of knowing if he was indeed moving at all. 'Help!' He forced out the scream with as much power as he could muster. His voice, high pitched and throaty, was ultimately lost in the cosmic babble.

And as he began to sob, there came a soothing voice in his ear. 'Jake,' it said. 'Calm down.'

Jake snivelled, trying to catch his breath like a toddler emerging from a tantrum, but his fear was almost absolute and the tears weren't to be stopped.

'Calm down,' said the disembodied voice. 'You're hysterical.'

After a small pause, where his mind made no sense of what was happening, he screamed louder for help.

'I'm here Jake. Please don't panic.'

Slowly, he forced himself to exercise a little self-control, and for a while he concentrated solely on calming himself and focussing on the friendly voice, trying not to hear the others.

Vision slowly came to him and a monochrome world faded into view. Jake felt detached from the scene, as if watching on an old black and white TV and unable to interact. The cottage was in front of him, looking like something from a Grimm fairy-tale. The garden had been cleared of weeds and the front door was freshly painted, but the roof still sagged and leaves were dropping from the gnarly apple trees. A thin wisp of smoke was rising from the chimney into a bleak winter sky.

In the middle of the garden, beneath one of the trees was an enormous black dog. Its head was down and facing the other way so Jake could only see its back. Nevertheless, he could tell it was eating and as he peered on, with mounting unease, the dog looked up towards him. It bore some resemblance to a labrador, but was three times the size and a whole lot meaner looking. The only things of colour in the scene were dog's flaming eyes and the crimson blood dripping from its muzzle. And then he noticed what the dog was eating.

Hannah lay sprawled at the creature's feet, a gaping, ragged hole in her midriff where the dog had been feasting on her offal. Her eyes were glassy, but she blinked and her lower jaw began to work feverishly as life ran away from her. And as the dog fixed Jake with its molten stare, it seemed to grin, although nothing about its features had changed.

He sat bolt upright in his bunk, gasping for air and slick with sweat. All was quiet apart from the constant drone of the bus's engine and muted snores of his bandmates and crew. Dave rolled over and Jake hoped he would wake up, because he could do with somebody to talk to. *It was only a dream,* he told himself, but it had felt like much more. He closed his eyes again, still sitting up, sweaty palms clutching the side of the bunk, while the bus gently rocked as they trundled along some motorway.

'Go,' said a voice over his shoulder and Jake spun around, expecting somebody to be there, although he knew there was only the bus's grey, corduroy interior panelling behind him. It was the voice from his dream. His heart pounded. The voice had sounded real, like there was a person right there, even though it was impossible.

He might have been hallucinating, listening to imaginary voices, but Jake knew with unwavering certainty there was something terribly wrong at Picker's Bleed and he needed to return without delay.

Clad only in his boxers, Jake lowered himself out of the bunk, keeping his movements careful so as not to wake anyone, and tentatively made his way down the bus's steps, holding tightly to the chrome handrail in case of any sharp braking, and made his way forwards to the driver. 'Alright Burt?' he said.

'Can't sleep?' asked the driver, without taking his eyes off the road.

Jake peered out of the windscreen, looking for a blue motorway sign or any other clue as to their whereabouts. 'I need to get off,' he said, matter-of-factly.

'Eh?' asked Burt, raising an eyebrow. He'd been a tour-bus driver for over twenty years and had seen it all. It wouldn't be the first time someone had been the victim of a bad trip while on the road. 'Just calm down a bit,' he said. 'Why don't you tell me what's bothering you?'

Jake felt panic rising again. 'I really need to get off.' For a moment he didn't know how to explain himself, floundering for words. 'There's an emergency at home.'

'Oh shit. Sorry,' said Burt. 'What kind of emergency?'

'Erm. Well,' said Jake. 'I don't exactly know.'

'What do you mean, you don't know?'

For long moments, Jake didn't answer, instead he stared out at the rain-soaked motorway, the swish of wipers filled the silence. Again, he contemplated whether he was losing his mind and concluded that although he probably was, there was no chance of respite from the crippling anxiety he was now feeling until he'd gone back to Picker's Bleed and seen Hannah with his own eyes. If only he could get hold of her on the phone to put his mind at rest.

He'd tried calling her dozens of times from borrowed phones, since the incident with the crossed lines, but every time there had been no reply. *She'd better be fucking dying*, he thought. He took a breath and said, 'I just have a terrible feeling something's wrong. I need to get home.'

'She still not answering?'

'No.'

'I'm sure everything's fine,' said Burt, 'But if you really need to go, I'll drop you at a station first thing, you can't do anything 'till then.'

Jake nodded in reluctant agreement. 'Thanks.'

'Do they know?' Burt asked with a small movement of his head to indicate he meant the remaining members of *Dead Man's Handle*.

Jake shook his head, knowing he'd be letting them down badly by cancelling any gigs.

'You've only got one more night to do,' said Burt. 'Then we're heading home for a bit.'

'Thanks,' said Jake and turned to head back up to his bunk, thinking how much easier everything would be if he hadn't moved to the middle of nowhere.

'Do you still need me to drop you off?' asked Burt.

'Nah, I'll get tonight out the way first. Where is it we're going again?'

'Newcastle.'

'Cheers.'

'Okay. Try to get some sleep and I'll drop you at a station early-doors tomorrow.'

That night's gig was horrendous, Jake's mind was elsewhere and his heart wasn't in it. Technically he'd played okay, but the performance was lacking and he knew he'd let the side down. Jake trashed his second favourite guitar before leaving the stage and went straight to the tour-bus before the inevitable post-gig autopsy and in-band fighting began.

Now it was four in the morning and sleep eluded him like a greasy eel. In the dark he could hear the quiet grunts and snores of his bandmates. Someone farted. The gentle rocking of the bus would usually lull him into sweet oblivion, but not this time. A knot of anxiety lay heavy in his belly and the urge to leave and go to Picker's Bleed was overwhelming. He could tell by the movements of the bus they weren't on the motorway anymore, and were stopping at roundabouts and traffic lights. Before long, with a hiss of the airbrakes they came to a stop.

A few minutes later Jake was stepping out into the cold rain, saying goodbye to Burt in hushed tones. 'Have a good Christmas,' he said.

'Yeah, you too,' said Burt. 'And good luck.'

22

Sometime in the early hours, well before sunrise, the rain stopped and a thick fog rolled in and nestled into all the nooks and crannies, making everywhere glisten with damp. All was still. Jake pulled his coat even tighter around his shoulders, wishing it had a hood, and fumbled in the pockets for the crumpled packet of cigarettes he'd put away only ten minutes before. He lit his cigarette and stared back at the digital arrivals board hanging from the canopied roof above the platform; new technology bolted onto Victorian design. His train was due at six twenty-two. The little digital clock in the bottom corner of the sign read four fifty-seven. Jake yawned.

There was a dull throb in his temples, his eyes were drooping and yet his mind raced with all manner of possibilities that might be waiting for him at Picker's Bleed, few of them good. He knew Hannah had no mobile reception at the cottage and it had only been a few days since their last call, although the crossed line and abrupt ending had freaked him out.

Despite all his efforts to see logic and reason, Jake was afraid. His dream, which should have faded away shortly after waking, replayed over and over in his mind's eye. Floating aimlessly in the void with a myriad of other lost souls, the greyscale vision of the cottage, the dog, and the voice telling him to go home. His mind kept returning from there to the crossed line on the phone. The hell-sounds he'd heard in the background of the call shared many qualities with the disembodied and lost cacophony of voices from his dream.

Who then, was the vile old woman who'd shrieked down the line, whose voice was so different to the kindly, warm voice which told him to go home? It had been the sound of lunacy. Irrational or not, he'd never been more afraid.

It had been a long and fidgety wait by the time the train arrived; a high-pitched hum from the tracks announced its arrival long before the solitary headlamp appeared from the fog at the far end of the platform. Jake groaned and stood up, trying to coax some life back into his legs. A handful of early commuters had joined him on the platform and he envied the sleep they'd probably all had. With a sigh, he followed them onto the train and walked through two carriages until he eventually found an unreserved seat.

With a low rumble from the locomotive and a steady vibration through the seats they were moving. As the train built speed, Jake tried peering out of the window, but it was too dark to see anything other than the inside of the carriage reflected back at him. He wished he'd thought to grab his book from the bus, but instead he had to content himself looking at reflections in the window.

The station was ten miles or so from Marsham and a relic from a bygone age. Made of red brick, there was an open canopy above the platform and hanging from one end, suspended from iron scrollwork, was what appeared to be the original, round clock. The ticket office was permanently closed and had been replaced by a vending machine. Jake was amazed there was a station at all, so far in the middle of nowhere, but he was glad there was as he wandered through a recently painted wooden gate to the old-fashioned red phone-box at the end of the station building.

Only one taxi firm had a card behind the Perspex display case and so he had little difficulty in deciding which company to call. When the cab was booked he headed back out into the fog, which seemed to be thickening into a peasouper, and sat on a bench, which was sandwiched between the phone-box and a large, round wooden planter. The day seemed even gloomier than it had at first light and as he waited, the knot of apprehension thickened in his gut.

There was silence in the taxi as it crept along the deserted lane, forced to a crawl because of abysmal visibility. The driver could have been concentrating too hard to make idle chit-chat, but he could have easily caught some of Jake's creeping fear. They spoke in hushed tones when money changed hands and Jake said his thanks. The taxi door swung shut with a deadened thud, which set the rooks cawing from the roof. The car's tyres briefly spun and soon the noise of its engine faded from earshot, leaving Jake standing in the empty lane, looking at the muted shadow of the cottage and twisted fruit trees.

The forest held its breath as Jake went through the limp gate and crunched up the drive, avoiding the trailing brambles that threatened to reclaim what was theirs. The rooks had settled back onto the roof and even they seemed to be watching and waiting. He caught his reflection in a water droplet hanging from the tip of a twisted apple twig. It only added to the rapidly building and surreal tension.

The scene before him was horribly familiar from his nightmares and part of him almost expected to see the black dog come skulking around the side of the cottage, which appeared deserted. No lights were burning in the windows and no smoke was rising from the chimney.

A few withered, red hips clung to the otherwise barren roses framing the front-door, their thorny stalks tangled up within the small vestibule overhead. The door wasn't locked and creaked open when Jake rested his hand upon the brass knocker.

A nauseating stench of excrement, vomit, sulphur and other equally foul but unidentifiable ingredients hit him before he'd fully crossed the threshold. In an instant, his fears that something was dreadfully wrong were realised. Blood drained from his cheeks and his knees trembled and almost buckled beneath him. As he steeled himself to step into the dark, damp hallway, Jake cocked his head, listening for signs of life, but none were forthcoming.

When he opened the door to the sitting room Jake more than half-expected to find Hannah's body inside. The room was empty and as gloomy and damp as the hallway. The curtains were open, but the fog filtered any vibrancy from the light coming in through the window. The ash in the grate was cold as bone. Mats of cobwebs gently wafted against the ceiling, disturbed by the eddies of his entrance.

It was with mounting dread he went back into the hallway and peered for a moment at the open cellar door. He could feel a chill coming up the steps, from out of the earth. He shouted Hannah's name down into the dark. His voice sounded small and feeble. He shouted again but there was only silence and so he decided to search the rest of the cottage before he ventured into the space beneath it.

It took long moments for his brain to process the scene

he found in the kitchen. Walls, which he'd only painted a few of weeks before, were smeared brown. Dried blood was spattered across the ceiling, that most probably came from the headless carcass of bone, cartilage and decaying flesh which was heaped next to the sink. And as he stared aghast, grief started to well inside him but as his reeling mind processed what he was seeing he realised there were scraps of brown fur clinging to the meat and his tears turned to those of relief, however temporary and misplaced. He briefly wondered where - what he now assumed was a deer's - head was.

The backdoor was slightly ajar. Fog seeped in through the gap, depositing moisture on all the surfaces and turning the carcass slimy. Overwhelmed and confused, Jake opened the door further to get some fresh-air and to peer into the back-garden.

Now his shock was greater still. Right outside the backdoor and at the same level as his face was a pig's head, eyeless, ragged and impaled on a stake. A rook flapped away, and its sudden movement caused Jake to finally shriek. The rook carried a small morsel of pork back to the roof.

The garden was a boneyard. Animal remains lay piled in several discrete heaps, none of them quite picked clean, although the rooks which cawed and flapped were having a good go at tugging the last scraps off the bone. Amongst the remains, more stakes had been driven into the ground. On them were impaled the heads of more animals. He counted three deer, two sheep, a badger and another pig, although there could have been many more close by, obscured by fog. He could see the outlying branches and silhouettes of two trees and tied to the branches were small animals and birds; mice, robins and even an owl, which was slowly and randomly beating its wings as it hung upside-down by one foot. Little care had been given to their arrangement as they hung, crooked from broken backs and wings.

While Jake stood, trying to absorb the scene and struggling to comprehend the sheer weirdness of what he was seeing, Hannah came walking, naked, out of the fog. She threw something into the undergrowth, then for an eon they stood motionless, staring at each other through the haze. Her head lolled to one side, hair matted, with skin that was stretched taut; mottled and greyer than the fog she'd walked out of. The way she studied him was more animal than human. There was no recognition in her eyes.

He fought to catch his breath and the urge to flee kicked in. But before him stood the woman he loved, although he could tell it wasn't really her. She must have lost her mind and he hoped more than anything he'd be able to help her find it again. The effort it took for him not to run away buckled his knees and he might have blacked out for a moment, because all of a sudden he was on his hands and knees, staring at Hannah's legs. They were filthy, bloody and covered in festering sores and gouges. He raised his head and found his face almost in her crotch. She stank of death and decay. Before he knew what was happening her free hand had shot out and was wrapped around the back of his head. Pulling him in. Her grip was strong, but he managed to break free and spring to his feet. 'My God,' he said. 'What's happened to you?'

He knew she didn't comprehend what he was saying and even as he spoke he was throwing his arms around her shoulders and pulling her close. She was slack in his embrace.

23

The rank thing which had been Hannah Jenkins compliantly followed him into the house. Jake had no idea what to do and although he tried to appear calm, he was in the breathless throes of a massive panic attack. The stench coming off her body was possibly worse than when he'd very first set foot in the cottage. Twice, as they went back past the mounted heads, he dry retched.

Guiding her with a hand in the small of her back, he gently led Hannah towards the sitting room. As they passed the open cellar door, he felt a twinge of the same despair others had felt in proximity to the cottage, carried up on the icy draught coming up from the dark below. With a shudder, he pushed the door closed and bustled Hannah into the other room, where he manoeuvred her to sit on the edge of the sofa. The telephone was on the windowsill. The curtains were open and a twig gently tapped and scraped the outside of the glass. It briefly registered that there was no breeze outside to sway branches, but this was something his mind squirrelled away for later processing, in order to preserve his already diminishing sanity. For Hannah's sake, he needed to keep his shit together.

When he lifted the telephone, on the off-chance it might be working, there came a screech from the earpiece, loud enough to distort the small speaker. Jake slammed down the receiver and looked back to Hannah, who was watching him fixedly with empty, black eyes.

Gingerly he lifted the handset again, to see if there was a dial tone and at first he heard nothing, but then, faintly at first, he heard Hannah's voice through the earpiece. She sounded broken by fear: 'Please God,' she was sniffling. 'God, get me out of here. Please.'

He slowly turned his head to look at the corpse-like thing on the sofa. A vague, taunting smile decorated Hannah's grey lips. He lifted the receiver back to his ear. 'Please?' the voice was whimpering. Jake let the receiver drop. He had no explanation for the voice on the phone, apart from it being a figment of his imagination.

What was clear however, was that the Hannah who was in the room with him was ill and needed taking to hospital as quickly as possible. It was evident he wouldn't be able to call an ambulance. 'Hannah, where are the car keys?' he asked.

There was only a vacant, empty stare in response.

'Stay here a minute,' he said and left her where she was while he went on a cursory search for the keys. To his dismay – if not surprise – the keys were not on the small occasional table by the front door and so he readied himself to go back into the kitchen.

As he passed, he pushed closed the cellar door, shuddering in the ice-ridden draught coming up the stairs. Another two steps along the hall towards the kitchen and he pulled up short, realising he'd already closed the door once. He went back and gave the handle a tug, rattling the door in its frame, to make sure the small catch he'd fitted was securely fastened. True fear had him firmly gripped as he went, bewildered, to the kitchen.

The deer carcass was pulsing with maggots, which writhed all over it, dropping onto the kitchen floor. Despite the cold, damp weather, flies buzzed lazily amongst the remains and bumped along the walls. He cursed about what a bitch cleaning the kitchen was going to be; his mind reverting to the mundane to protect itself from further damage.

'You okay?' he shouted through to the other room. Despite the silence, his voice came out muted and weak, almost lost to the thick atmosphere inside the cottage.

There was no reply from Hannah, just the steady drip-drip of moisture falling from the eaves outside. He had a quick rummage about the room and couldn't find the keys in any of the obvious places, and so he quickly moved back along the corridor, past the cellar door, (which was still closed) and briefly looked in on Hannah. She hadn't moved and was staring vacantly at a spot on the wall. Jake didn't bother trying to speak and carried on up the stairs two at a time.

Apart from the disgusting reek permeating everywhere, and cobwebs that fluttered against the corners of the ceilings, upstairs had escaped relatively unscathed. Unlike downstairs, the dirt was just a product of disuse and neglect. In the bedroom the bed was unmade and there was a pile of dirty laundry on the floor, which he rummaged through but there was still no sign of the car keys. Likewise, despite some serious discolouration of the toilet bowl, the bathroom was relatively clean. Still, he couldn't find the keys and so he found himself standing outside what they'd called the nursery. Jake shuddered before he opened the door.

The room was just as it had been left, fresh plaster on the walls and exposed floorboards. A couple of guitars were on stands next to his practice amp. Something in the air however, was stale and repulsive and so he quickly pulled the door closed again.

Now he was standing on the landing, trying, and failing, to think. It was obvious help wouldn't be a matter of minutes, or even hours away and so he needed a plan. With a deep breath he composed himself and headed back downstairs. The cellar door was wide open. 'Fuck you,' he grunted and kicked the door shut again. He paused, exhaled and fixed a smile before going back into the sitting room.

Hannah hadn't moved from where he'd left her on the sofa. Her head swivelled stiffly to follow his movements around the room with dead eyes.

'We need to get you cleaned up,' he said, trying to put on a vaguely jovial tone in a poor attempt to sound reassuring.

She just stared, so he took her hand and led her upstairs where she perched on the edge of their double bed in just the same way she had on the sofa. He left her there while he went to run a bath and as the bathroom filled with scented steam, fogging the mirrors, he could almost believe everything was normal.

When the bath was full and he was coaxing Hannah into the water he uttered; 'Jesus Christ, what happened to you?'

She sat with the same vacant passiveness she'd shown all along, arms wrapped around her knees and following Jake's movements with her eyes, while he scrubbed at the filth until the bathwater turned brown and scummy. He let the water out and showered her off where she sat, getting rid of the last traces of grime.

After he'd bathed, dried and dressed her clumsily in jeans and jumper, he led Hannah back downstairs and, ignoring the kitchen and the open cellar door, led her out into the dreary day.

As they came outside the rooks on the roof fell silent as if watching their departure with a sense of anticipation. When Jake and Hannah went out of the front gate and into the lane, they once again took up their cawing with fresh gusto; a great ruckus coming from out of the grey fog.

If anything, the fog had thickened throughout the day and Jake couldn't see more than fifteen paces along the lane ahead. Amongst the trees the shadows were already black as if twilight was upon them, but Jake figured there were at least a couple of hours' worth of light left in the day and they would have ample time to walk into the village to call an ambulance.

However, his hopes for assistance were dashed when, with the cottage out of sight behind them, Hannah abruptly stopped in the middle of the lane. He tried to cajole her along, but she was immovable and cocked her head to one side as if listening. Then she gave him a look which was purely alien before turning and starting to walk back in the direction from which they'd come.

'Shit,' Jake muttered then 'Hannah!' he shouted a little louder, his voice small in the miserable day.

Within a few strides he'd caught up with her and placed a hand on her shoulder, but she didn't seem to notice and carried on as if he wasn't there. Almost trotting to keep up, Jake grabbed her shoulders with both hands and with a little more force than intended.

Quick as a flash she turned, snarling, and shoved him onto his backside. Then, as if nothing had happened, she turned and continued back towards the cottage.

After a brief pause for contemplation Jake clambered to his feet and followed her, knowing he would not be summoning help that day, unless he left her alone in the state she was in, which was something he didn't want to entertain.

She'd already disappeared into the fog and so he trotted back up the lane to at least try and get her in his sights.

By the time he reached the cottage, Hannah was standing a little way off from the door, amongst the stunted fruit trees of the neglected orchard. It looked like she was sniffing the air, like a pointer. 'Hannah,' he called cautiously. She didn't seem to notice and certainly didn't pay him any attention. Her face held an eerie, vacant smile and she seemed to be listening with her head cocked again.

Suddenly she took off into the woods at a speed he would not have thought possible, and certainly at a pace far greater than he'd be able to give chase. Within two seconds her footfalls had faded to nothing and he was alone by the front gate.

Jake called after her but his voice was swallowed by the fog and he knew it was pointless. For a moment he stood still, not knowing what to do. The rooks began to kick up a fuss on the roof. Jake turned to them and swore. 'Fuck this shit,' he muttered before going inside to begin the unenviable task of cleaning the cottage while he waited on Hannah's return.

24

The insides of the cupboards appeared untouched and Jake had no problem finding all the cleaning products he needed. Donning a pair of Marigolds, the first task was to remove the animal remains from the corner. After a few moments to psyche himself up, he grabbed a leg and pulled. The decomposing animal came apart with a squelch, spilling a glut of maggots onto the floor. The stench was as if it had come straight from Hell and Jake was forced to stop and take some fresh air from the open door while he battled down nausea, trying to ignore the impaled remains in the garden. Eventually though, with much heaving, he managed to heap the carcass outside, where no doubt it would remain until scavengers had done their bit.

It was with single minded determination he set about the rest of the kitchen and it soon resembled something like its former state. Outside, the light was fading fast and he flicked the light-switch, simultaneously worried the bulb might not work, and relieved that it did.

After firing up the Aga and lighting a fire in the living

room grate he headed upstairs to run a bath and wash away the clinging filth with which he was covered. Before he did though, Jake took a few minutes to wash away the tidemark of scum left from when he'd bathed Hannah.

While he was doing so, he fretted about where she might have gone and when she might return; what had happened to her and whether her insanity was a temporary one, or whether her mind was lost forever. But as the taps ran and the bathroom once more filled with warm steam he told himself not to worry about that just yet. *One thing at a time.* To some extent, he'd managed to calm down a little by the time he gently lowered himself into the soothing hot water.

After a while of listening to the steady drip from the hot tap and irregular settling creaks of the cottage, there came the sudden crash of a door slamming downstairs. Threadbare nerves cracked and Jake jumped up, spilling out onto the bathmat. He only gave himself a cursory rub with the towel before hastily pulling on his jeans and tee-shirt; a task made difficult owing to wet skin. His difficulty caused him to panic. His breathing was rapid and he began to hyperventilate and so he forced himself to take long, slow breaths. The temperature had dropped again since he'd got into the bath. His breath plumed with the rise and fall of his chest and he began to shiver. *She must have left the door open,* he thought.

Footsteps were coming up the stairs, yet he hesitated with his hand on the knob before opening the bathroom door, unsure of what might be waiting for him on the other side. The footsteps drew nearer, the soft, slow padding of bare feet and the creak of floorboards, and as they got closer the temperature dropped further still, until the doorhandle was painfully cold to touch.

The footsteps stopped right outside the door and something in the air made it feel like the world was holding its breath.

Shivering, with chill tears in his eyes, unable to stand the tension any longer, Jake threw open the bathroom door to confront whatever was on the other side.

The hallway was empty. A little tension had gone out of the air, but Jake was left confused and frightened. He shuffled along the landing and peered back into the nursery. The light from the bathroom was dim and didn't penetrate deep into the corners of the room where, in the thick shadows, he thought he caught a hint of movement, but an instant later when he flicked on the light he was looking at an empty room, damp, full of shadows and bare plaster. 'Hello,' he called.

Nothing.

He left the light on and quickly made his way back to the top of the stairs, glancing over his shoulder. The lightbulb blew, which must have tripped the electric at the fuse box because all the lights went out, plunging him into darkness.

From somewhere along the landing there came another single footstep. Jake flew down the stairs, his overriding thought was he hoped the downstairs lights were on a different circuit.

To his relief, the light came on, but he almost wished it hadn't because for the briefest of moments, in the first instant of illumination, individual shadows with the distinct forms of humans, or creatures, vanished before his eyes, as if caught by surprise. He tried to bolt directly out of the front door, but found it locked and the key absent. He turned and faced down the hallway. Cold sweat filmed his brow. The cellar door was wide open. Shadows danced in the open doorway and there was a faint hiss from below, like a bait-box full of writhing maggots. The space between and beyond the shadows was completely devoid of light. Jake was struck by such despair he dropped, weeping, to his knees.

At the other end of the hallway was the open kitchen door. It seemed an impossibly long distance past the seething pit of darkness that was the cellar, but he knew that if he stayed where he was, he would not survive the night with his mind intact. And so, without further ado he steeled himself, put his head down and ran. When he passed the cellar, the air became frozen and viscous, like a black slushy. For an instant he thought he didn't have the strength to pass through and was trapped, struggling like an insect caught in a web. He heard all the screams, agonies, baying and barking of his dreams. But there was also the kindly voice floating up from somewhere deep in his psyche, telling him '...Go!' Jake was sure he felt a shove in the small of his back and then he was free and tumbling into the kitchen, slamming the door behind him.

His intention was to run straight out of the back door and into the night, but through the glass he could see the silhouettes of dark, looming trees and he convinced himself they would pull him limb from limb, or worse. Like ending up with his head on a stake. The thought of going out into the dark was more terrifying than being holed up in the kitchen, which now it was clean, appeared vaguely normal and a little haven of sanity. There was a low mumbling from the hallway, like a hundred voices just out of earshot and he skittishly eyed up the backdoor to make sure, should he need it, that his escape route was clear.

With tattered nerves, Jake repeatedly considered all his options. For now at least, the kitchen seemed relatively quiet and tempting as it was to run, there were miles of pitch-black woods between him and civilisation. Even if he did make it to Marsham he didn't know anybody there who he could wake up to ask for help without them thinking him mad. And so, he decided his best course of action was to stay where he was.

All night there was movement all about the house. The hissing, whispering, writhing sound which started way down the cellar steps spread throughout the cottage, separating into distinct sounds as it spread from the epicentre. There were more footsteps upstairs, the scampering of children across the landing and through the bedrooms. Doors were slammed. There was the occasional bestial grunt and snuffling from the other side of the door.

Jake grabbed the biggest knife from the drawer and clutched it to his chest until his knuckles were white around the handle. Even though he doubted the blade would offer any purposeful protection, it served as a talisman to hold up against his fear. Jake saw the keys in plain view on the worktop. *What the fuck?* He put them in his pocket for safe keeping.

In the early hours, just before daybreak, the commotion died down and the house fell quiet. The silence was more unnerving than the cacophony which had been raging all night. When the back door flew open, bringing with it a blast of icy air, Jake squealed.

Hannah was in the doorway, more vile and filthy than before. She was wearing an odd expression which, although vacant, contained a certain glee. A gaping tear ran down the flesh of her ribcage, opening and closing like a whale's mouth as she moved, oozing blood which looked unnaturally dark and greasy. She fixed him with a stare and – if it wasn't already apparent – he knew there was not a shred of Hannah left in the grotesque thing in the kitchen. Empty black eyes held his while she took a step forwards, squatted and defecated on the freshly scrubbed floor. A harsh cackle escaped through her dry lips and Jake knew he was being mocked.

The knife slipped from his fingers and clattered harmlessly to the floor. 'What the actual fuck!' he managed to utter.

A handful of shit was flung into his face. The harsh, grating laughter made him want to cover his ears. Of all he'd endured, this was the worst and now he was no longer afraid of the woods. The thing to be scared of was in the kitchen with him, blocking his escape.

It took a step towards him and Jake realised he was backed up against the kitchen door, the knob was digging into his back. Without realising, he'd pulled the house keys from his pocket. Whatever lay in the hallway couldn't be any worse than this. And so, as the thing that was Hannah got another step closer he reached behind his back with his free hand and had the door open before he'd even turned around.

The hallway was pitch black and freezing cold. He felt the skin on his face freezing and pain in his fingers, but he ran blind in the direction of the front door. Hannah made no move to give chase, but continued the frenzied laughter at his back. Shadows jumped out at him and he imagined frozen hands, claws; tentacles, reaching out to snare him. Jake thrust the key into the lock at full stretch. He felt a rush of relief when it turned without resistance and he burst out into the dark morning.

25

Dawn arrived at some point during his journey through the woods and other than a few wisps of low mist curled around the churchyard, the fog had lifted to leave Marsham bathed in the watery sunshine and long shadows of an early winter's morning. Wood-smoke hung in the air. The village square was deserted.

The shop door was closed, but the sign in the window read 'open.' Jake rushed straight past it and across the square, shooting a glance over to the red phone-box as he clunked through the lichgate and up to the church doors. To his dismay the church was locked. He banged on the door a few times, and gave the handle a rattle before, in a panic, he rushed around the side of the church to the rectory.

In the garden a man was sweeping leaves and throwing them onto a smouldering heap in a corner by the wall. The smoke was rising in a dirty column into the crystal sky. At Jake's approach the man looked up and rested his chin on both hands, which were cupped over the end of the rake-handle. The man was difficult to put an age on, but his hair had gone silver, as had the stubble on his chin. His eyes were a piercing shade of blue which matched the winter sky and he held Jake's gaze, asking questions without the need to speak.

'I was wondering if the vicar was about?' asked Jake.

'Priest,' replied the man, whose eyes might have been hard, but not unfriendly and neither was his smile, which bore no hint of mockery and put Jake immediately at ease. 'And that would be me.'

'Sorry,' mumbled Jake, thinking there was something familiar about the priest's voice. With a great deal more urgency he said, 'I need to speak to you.'

'You'd better come in then,' said the priest, leaning his rake against the wall and starting towards the rectory. 'I'm Father Geoffrey Hamilton.'

The kitchen had a homely warm glow about it. On the chunky pine table, bread rolls were cooling on a wire rack, but before Jake could sit down, Father Hamilton gestured towards a small downstairs bathroom. With the hot tap running, Jake tried to rinse away some of the filth which had been flung at him. Blood came back into his fingers with an intense ache. Perspiration sprang afresh from his temple and he found he was shaking uncontrollably. The cold receded into memory as he went back through to the kitchen and the priest motioned him to sit. The chair scraped across the tiles when he pulled it out from under the table, but it wasn't a harsh sound.

'Drink?' offered Father Hamilton after he'd already flicked on the kettle. Unhurriedly he made the tea, in no rush for answers. 'Right,' he said when they were both seated at opposite ends of the table, each with a steaming mug of sweet tea in front of them. Jake didn't usually take sugar, but this time it was welcome. Father Hamilton once again used the power of his gaze to ask the questions.

'I think my house is haunted,' started Jake, thinking there was no point beating about the bush.

'No shit.'

'Say what?' Jake was a little taken aback.

'Ha.' The priest gave a small chuckle. 'Everybody knows that place is haunted.'

'But I haven't told you where I live.'

'You're from the cottage up at Picker's Bleed, aren't you?'

'Yes.'

'It's my job to look out for my flock,' he said.

Jake shrugged. 'And,' he continued. 'You'll think I'm crackers, but I'm pretty sure my girlfriend's possessed.' He found he was shaking as he spoke.

'I know,' said Father Hamilton.

'If you know, then why haven't you done anything?'

'It's not that simple I'm afraid. Biscuit?' He pushed his chair back with another scrape and went to fetch a large ceramic jar from the counter. He pulled off the lid and offered it across the table. Jake took two custard creams and left the jar open halfway between the two men.

There were a few moments of quiet, while they dunked biscuits and sipped tea. The kitchen clock ticked away the seconds. 'What's going on?' asked Jake eventually.

'It's complicated.'

'Try me.'

'Well,' began the priest. 'You're right, she is possessed by something ancient and evil, which was brought into this world hundreds of years ago, by a witch who lived in your cottage.'

'This doesn't make any sense,' said Jake, then after another pause he quietly said, 'I don't know what to do.'

'All you can do for now I'm afraid, is to be brave and stay strong.'

'But I really need your help.'

'And you'll get it.'

'When?'

'I'm already trying to help.'

'I don't understand?'

'You will,' said the priest.

Jake shook his head. 'Are you telling me I've got to just go back up to the house and look after her like she's got a cold? You have no idea what she's like.'

'I think I do.'

'With all due respect, how could you? You haven't seen her.'

Father Hamilton cocked a cheerless smirk.

'Have you seen her?'

The priest nodded. 'In a fashion.'

'In a fashion. In a fashion, what's that supposed to mean? Either you've seen her, or you haven't?'

'I've seen her somewhere else. Not the possessed thing which is running around the woods, but the real Hannah. She's trapped in... in another place.'

Jake looked at him, confused.

'You see,' continued the priest, 'the vile thing which has taken over Hannah's body has forced out her essence, her soul if you will, and taken its place. She, in turn, has gone there.'

'Which is...?'

'Truth is, I don't rightly know.'

'Oh?'

'Well, it might be hell, but if it is, it isn't as I imagined,' he said, pondering. 'And it's definitely not heaven.' He scratched his nose; the first time the priest had appeared nervous. 'It could be purgatory I suppose.' He seemed to be talking to himself, rather than for anyone else's benefit. 'But at the end of the day,' he said, regaining his composure, 'it's just another place, occupying a different existence. I know none of this makes sense, but it's difficult to explain. The crux of the matter is, it just so happens that there's a way *between worlds* beneath your cottage and this thing, this demon came through. It uses it at will, and has done for centuries, along with all the other spirits which may have chanced upon the gateway.'

'So, this has happened before?'

'It started about five hundred years ago,' started the priest. 'There was a witch in the village, a local woman called Ella Jameson. She lived at your house.' He paused a moment and his brow furrowed. 'She was the first we know of and...'

'We?' interrupted Jake.

'The church.'

'Ah.'

Father Hamilton adjusted himself in his chair. '... and we have to assume she had something to do with opening this rift between life and the afterlife, whatever that may be.'

'You're not like other priests, are you?' asked Jake, scrabbling to inject a small amount of normality into the conversation.

'No.'

'Thought not.' Jake didn't want to believe what he'd heard; it was ludicrous, but hadn't he already arrived at the same conclusion, which was why he'd run past the phone box and straight to the church? 'I should just call an ambulance,' he said longing for sense. 'She needs professional help.'

'If you do that, you'll risk losing her forever.'

'What!?'

'Her body needs to be near the rift, so, with guidance, she might be able to find her way back.'

'This is insane.'

'Yes. Yes it is,' said Father Hamilton. 'I know it doesn't make a lot of sense, but please, you have to trust me.'

'In the cellar,' uttered Jake.

'Probably beneath even there.'

'And this *rift* is why the house is haunted?'

'Precisely. The evil thing which has possessed Hannah is only one of many things that have come through. Although this one was invited.'

'And why does she need to be close?'

'Because the only way to reach her, which I know of, is through that gateway.'

He seized onto the glimmer of hope. 'How?'

'Well,' Geoffrey Hamilton shifted in his seat. 'Usually it involves dying,' he said, 'but I've been having some thoughts about that. It's an ethereal place, of the soul rather than body. No, your body can't travel there, but your mind can. You have to be dead to get to that place, or sometimes, I'm thinking, you could do it in your sleep?' He locked gazes with Jake across the table, his intense eyes probing.

Jake immediately thought about his nightmares, floating in the void. He thought about seeing the cottage in monochrome and the huge dog on the lawn. He looked back at Father Hamilton and pondered the kindly, guiding voice he'd heard. He kept all these things to himself however and sighed. 'And you can help me?' he asked.

'As best I can,' replied Father Hamilton. 'I just hope it's enough.'

'So, what do I do now?' he asked.

'Go back to the cottage. Get some sleep and try to look out for Hannah, take care of her as best you can and hopefully, soon enough, she'll be back in her rightful place.'

'I don't think I can do it. She... It'll kill me,' he said, shuddering and on the verge of tears now the adrenaline had worn off.

'I know it seems terrifying, but try to keep strong and have faith. I'll be praying for you.'

Jake looked up at the kitchen clock; a large, ceramic plate decorated with brightly painted fruit; orange apple, pear and banana. He was shocked to see it had gone eleven. 'Thanks for the tea,' he said and stood up, once again scraping the chair across the floor.

20

26

The difference between the welcoming warmth inside the rectory and the chill outside seemed more profound than simply a matter of temperature. Icy water dripped from the lichgate in the late morning sun. A drop splashed onto the back of Jake's head and dribbled down his neck. He made his way directly across the village square to the Bull's Head to see if it was open. To his great satisfaction, the door was unbolted and he clunked open the latch and went directly to the bar.

The landlord looked up from where he was piling logs in the fireplace. 'Be right with you,' he said, and with his hands on his knees and letting out a small groan, he pushed himself to his feet and replaced the fireguard. Jake moved to the stool closest to the kindling fire while the landlord stood waiting for the flames to take hold. 'You're the lad from up Picker's Bleed?'

'Jake,' he said. 'Yes.'

The landlord clicked his tongue and gave a small shake of his head. 'How's the missus bearing up?' he asked.

'Why?'

'After all that business with the priest and wot not.'

'What do you mean?'

'Eh?'

'What business with the priest?'

Tom's brow furrowed, 'You mean you don't know?'

'Know what?' more resigned than worried.

'About Father Hamilton dropping dead in your kitchen, that's what.'

'But I've just been speaking to Father Hamilton. Unless that was another priest by the same name?'

Tom poured two large brandies and handed one to Jake while draining his own and refilling the glass. 'That one's on the house, anything else?'

'Please. I'll have a pint of Stella, and another brandy.'

'As far as I know,' the landlord spoke at the same time as serving. 'No replacement has arrived from the church yet.' He put the brandy bottle between them and only charged for the beer. 'So you must be mistaken,' he said. 'Are you sure it was Father Hamilton?'

'Yes, quite.'

He went to the back wall and took down a framed photograph. The picture was of a cricket-match on the green and Jake recognised a man in the background, standing slightly away from the team, as the priest. 'It was him I was speaking to,' he said, pointing.

'Well, that's our Geoff alright,' said Tom. 'And he's most definitely dead.' He paused, 'And what's more, he died in your house and you didn't even know about it? What's all that about then?'

'What? You're taking the piss.' Jake downed his pint and the dregs of his brandy and ran back through the door in a state of confusion.

The instant he rounded the end of the church he knew the rectory lay empty. There was no smoke rising from a pile of smouldering leaves and as he neared it was clear there hadn't been for some time, for there was only a small heap of sodden char. There were also other, less tangible differences which his senses drew on. The rectory seemed colder and less inviting than it had, almost as if before it had held some warm hue, which was now lost. He tried knocking the door anyway and heard the empty reverberation of his knocks from inside. He walked around and cupped his hands to peer through the window. The glass was wet and cold. There were no freshly baked rolls on the table and just a general sense the place was uninhabited. He noticed the kitchen clock had stopped at quarter to eight. For all Jake knew, it could have read the same time for weeks. Dumbfounded, his mind reeling, he wandered back across to the Bull's Head, leaving the church gate ajar as he passed back through.

His brandy glass had been refilled and was waiting for him on the bar. He also ordered another pint of Stella.

'So, what happened?'

'I think your missus should really be the one to tell you,' he said but then, reading the pained look on Jake's face asked, 'She is alright isn't she? I mean, something like that's going knock her about a bit.'

'Something like *what*?'

'Well...' The landlord proceeded to recount the story of the evening Hannah had come running into the pub.

And as he spoke, Jake heard the voice of reason he'd been longing for. *Poor thing,* he thought. *It's some kind of post-traumatic stress disorder.* 'Can I use your phone?' he asked, interrupting the landlord mid-sentence.

'Sure.'

'I've been such a fucking idiot,' he mumbled as he rushed

to where the phone was perched on the end of the bar, picked up the receiver and dialled 999.

With the ambulance called, Jake downed what remained of his drinks and headed for the door. If he were to make it home before the ambulance arrived he would need to run.

'Before you go,' called the landlord.

Jake paused with one leg already across the threshold. 'Yes?'

'You didn't hear it from me, but she's been spending a bit of time with Vincent Mandeville.'

'Who?'

'Lord of the manor,' he said.

'And?' asked Jake.

'Just in case you wanted to piece things together.'

'Thanks.'

The fresh air and sunlight hit him simultaneously and brought on a heady beer-buzz which usually he would have enjoyed, but on this occasion he battled to straighten his senses and broke into a jog back along the lane towards the cottage. Whether tired from the earlier run into the village, or whether he was simply just drunk, every couple of minutes he needed to stop and rest and it was during one of these short walking breaks, when he was wheezing heavily, that the ambulance came racing up behind him, giving a small blast of the siren for him to get out of the way as it sailed past. Jake tried to flag it down, but the ambulance showed no sign of slowing. He sighed and forced himself back to a slow trot.

By the time he arrived at Picker's Bleed the ambulance was parked outside the front gate, blocking the lane completely. The engine was off and making quiet ticking sounds as it cooled. To all outward appearances, the ambulance was empty. He paused for a moment, catching his breath and listening for movement. When he heard nothing, he made for the house. By now he'd regained his breath, but his heart continued to pound through anticipation. The loudest thing as he walked up the garden path was the sound of his feet swishing through the mulch that carpeted the ground.

When he went inside, Jake was bewildered to be hearing soft conversation from the kitchen. He paused for a moment before opening the door. Two paramedics, dressed in green overalls, were sitting at the kitchen table drinking mugs of tea with Hannah, who was clean, fully clothed and coherent. She was wearing a white and red floral dress, her hair was tied into a ponytail with a ribbon. A bottle of nail polish was on the tablecloth next to her steaming mug of tea. He glanced at her nails to see they were immaculate and red. Under the table, her bare toes were drying with cotton wool between them.

They all turned to face him and Jake came to a stop, stumbling over his words, utterly unsure of himself and feeling guilty for wasting the ambulance's time. 'What the...?'

'You okay honey?' asked Hannah. The mockery in her tone was so subtle as to only be detectable by him.

'Of course,' he said. 'But you, you?' He gestured with his hand.

'What do you mean?' She asked. Her confusion was almost genuine. 'Why did you call an ambulance?' she asked, shaking her head. 'I was worried.'

'Because...' He looked at her and no one had ever seemed saner and more level-headed. 'Because of how you were acting.'

'How was I acting?' she asked with a slight shrug.

'Like a fucking lunatic.' Both paramedics looked up at his tone of voice. Jake noticed, 'Sorry,' he said. 'But that's the truth. She was filthy, covered in mud and blood...' And then he remembered the pig heads on sticks in the garden and rushed over to the back door.

Hannah's eyes followed him, sharp and alert. The paramedics thought he was going to make a run for it and looked at each other, silently communicating that neither of them was quite sure what to do.

The garden, although still a winter mess, was clear of any hint of animal remains.

He turned to Hannah. 'What..? But..?'

She gave a subtle, mocking raise of an eyebrow. 'Seriously, what's got into you?'

'How?' asked Jake.

'How what? You're frightening me now,' she said.

'How,' he mumbled. 'I don't understand.' He felt a comforting hand on his shoulder and realised it was one of the paramedics, who'd come over without his noticing. When the hand applied a little reassuring pressure and tried to guide him forwards, Jake took a step before realising they were planning on taking him into hospital. 'I'm okay,' he said. 'Seriously.' He looked around the room. 'I think I must be overtired.'

The paramedics looked at each other, and then at Hannah, clearly trying to work out whether they needed to convince Jake to accompany them, or if they needed to call the police to get him sectioned. 'I'll be able to take care of him,' said Hannah after apparent consideration.

'Are you sure?'

Jake stayed silent.

'Yes,' she said. 'And I'm terribly sorry for wasting your time.'

Jake, stunned into a kind of paralysis, didn't move while she saw them out of the front door. All three were talking quietly in the hallway before the door closed and Hannah came back into the kitchen.

He opened his mouth to speak but saw Hannah's face

was a contorted mask of devilment and his jaw clamped shut. She came right up to his face, her movements fast and fluid and said, in Hannah's voice although he knew it wasn't her, 'Try anything like that again and the bitch dies.'

'How the..?' He was thinking about the animal heads in the garden.

A horrible laugh came out of Hannah's mouth. It sounded like it might be damaging her throat lining.

'They're still there, moron.' She tapped a finger to her temple. 'They see what I *want* them to see.'

He turned around. The door was still open and just outside was the pig's head, glistening with putrefaction. The stake was now leaning slightly, so it seemed as if the pig was staring back into the kitchen through empty eyeholes. Its jaw sagged open on a moist thread of tattered cartilage and the same laugh came from it that he'd just heard from Hannah's mouth, which started up again.

Behind Hannah, in the hallway, the cellar door flew open. All the doors in the house began to slam open and closed, the kitchen door jerked back and forth, back and forth, back and forth. Jake heard wood splintering. A cuckoo clock started to chime, adding to the cacophony. He didn't even know they owned a cuckoo clock. It must have been something Hannah had bought before she had fallen ill.

For the second time that day, Jake stumbled from Picker's Bleed with his sanity in tatters.

27

Vincent was in his study, intently reading from the leather-bound book on the desk. There was something slightly frantic about his mannerisms as he searched for answers within the stiff pages.

Danny entered without knocking, wearing a grey tee-shirt and jeans. He looked like he hadn't slept. There were huge, dark bags under his eyes while the rest of his face was ashen and drawn. 'Stephen's been gone for days,' he said. All the confidence had gone out of Danny's swagger and he stood fumbling like a naughty schoolboy.

Vincent looked up over the rim of his reading glasses and tapped his pipe out into a heavy glass ashtray on the table between them. 'What can we do?' he said. 'He chose to go back.'

Danny stood, shuffling and looking at the open book between them. The pages were meticulously filled with tiny scrawl.

Vincent saw him looking and put an intricate leather bookmark in the page and closed the journal. 'Go and look for him, if you want.'

'Pardon?' The thought made him blanch.

'Well, I don't know what you expect me to do about it?' Vincent snapped. 'But you certainly don't need my permission to go looking, if that's what you want to do?' The last part was a challenge and he held his eye steady for a few moments. 'Sorry,' said Vincent after Danny dropped his stare. 'But this whole thing's a bit puzzling.'

'Yes,' said Danny. 'Yes it is.'

'How're the others?'

'Mel's a bit tetchy, but okay, I think. Susan hasn't left her room, so I wouldn't know.'

'Oh. I suppose I'd better go and check on her,' said Vincent.

'Before you do,' said Danny, 'have you managed to find any answers in there at all?' He nodded towards the book on the desk.

Vincent gave a small involuntary expression, almost a wince. 'Not yet I haven't.'

'Do you think you might?'

'I do,' he said, then he mused; 'I'm missing something. I know I am.'

'I thought the old lord said we'd be able to bring her back if we found the right vessel?'

'He did.'

'But the host vanished.'

'She did.'

'So, what do you think happened?'

'I'm not sure what we expected, but I didn't bank on her completely disappearing into thin air. I didn't think the corporeal body could pass through. I'm guessing she was dragged back across. Fascinating really.'

Danny slapped his hand on the desk, snapping Vincent out of his musings. 'So, what do you think will happen now?'

'Honestly?' he fixed Danny with his stare again, his eyes intent, 'I haven't a cunting clue.' he pushed back his chair and stood up, making it clear he wasn't comfortable with any further questions about something which he claimed to know so much, but apparently knew remarkably little.

Just then there came a discreet tap at the door, before Appleby popped his head around. 'There's somebody here to see you,' he said.

'Tell them to go away,' said Vincent, irritated.

'I really think you'd like to see this gentleman.'

'Do you now?'

'Yes, sir,' he said, unperturbed by Vincent's temper. 'It's Jake Evans, sir.' He paused a moment, to see if Vincent recognised the name. Vincent simply stared an angry stare and so Appleby continued. 'From the house at Picker's Bleed, Sir.'

Danny and Vincent looked at each other, then back to Appleby. 'You're quite right Appleby,' said Vincent. 'You must show him in at once,' before adding, 'and then make yourself scarce.'

Danny's unuttered protest came as sharp intake of breath as he held his tongue in front of Appleby. While Vincent had unerring faith in his butler to keep the family secrets, Danny did not.

'I must warn you,' said Appleby before leaving the room.

'Yes?'

'He seems quite... upset.'

'Thank you Appleby. Now show him in.'

'This way, sir?'

Jake was somewhat startled by the butler's reappearance. He'd been off in a world of his own, picking flakes of peeling paint off the doorframe while his mind made all efforts to supress madness. He followed the butler into the hallway, slightly awed at how grand the entrance hall must once have been. With damp, warped panels and a mouldy ceiling however, Marsham Hall was uninviting. The house was eerily quiet. His footfalls sounded dead and empty when he walked the floorboards, and silent when he was walking on the once opulent runner.

'Here we are, sir.' Appleby opened a door halfway along the hallway and showed Jake into the study. A pale man, with blond, spiked hair was just leaving. He looked Jake up and down before pulling the door closed behind him.

'Drink?' asked Vincent, who remained seated behind his desk.

'Please?' Now the situation had become less frantic and Jake's breathing had begun to slow, a headache like no other had started, doubtlessly aided by his earlier visit to the Bull's Head. Hair of the dog was worth a go, especially in a predicament such as his.

Vincent pushed his chair back and went to his antechamber to serve the drinks. This time he didn't spike the brandy. He was aching to know what reason had brought the visitor to him; what he might know and, more importantly, if he had any suspicions. Once he knew, *then* he might consider lacing the drinks, especially if this young man was onto something approaching the truth. However, the look of wild-eyed lunacy on Jake's face had Vincent intrigued almost to the point of trembling. For a short while he savoured the anticipation, knowing that whatever Hannah's partner had brought to the table would change the game entirely. As soon as he sat back down with the drinks he could wait no longer.

The two men scrutinised each other for a millisecond before Jake spoke. 'Apologies for the intrusion,' he began.

A good start.

'But am I right in thinking you've been spending time with Hannah in the last few weeks?'

'Hannah?'

'Yes,' he said, 'My Hannah, from the cottage.'

'Ah, yes. Of course. Lovely girl,' he said. 'How is she? I haven't seen her about in a while?'

'Not good, I'm afraid.'

It was not the answer Vincent had been expecting and his heart skipped a beat. As far as he was concerned, Hannah was missing, presumed dead or eternally damned. 'I'm sorry to hear it,' he said. 'May I enquire as to her ailment?'

Jake gazed into his eyes, and Vincent hoped the broiling energy of his racing heart wouldn't show through his calm exterior. 'She's either seriously ill,' answered Jake and then said, rather more quietly. 'Or possessed.'

'Possessed, you say?' enquired Vincent, absently rubbing his chin.

Jake shook his head and avoided the question. 'I need to know if you can shed any light on what might have happened to her?'

Vincent shrugged. 'Like what?'

'I don't know,' he said. 'Anything: How was she when you last saw her?'

'She seemed fine,' Vincent lied. 'I didn't notice anything out of the ordinary. We didn't know each other that well, really.'

'Oh,' said Jake, deflated. 'The landlord down at the Bull said you'd been spending time together.'

'Just a little, I'm afraid. She joined us for drinks the other night.'

'And how was she?'

'As I said, she seemed fine,' he continued. 'Now, if you could tell me whatever the matter is and maybe I could be of some assistance?'

'Really, how? I thought you didn't know anything?'

'You said she was possessed, correct?'

'Well... I said it's *like* she's possessed.'

'Balderdash. You said she was possessed.'
'Or ill.'
'It's happened before, you know. In that house.'
'What has?'
'Demonic possession.'
'Really?' he said. 'You're not the first person to say something along those lines.'
'Who else have you been speaking to?'
'The priest.'
'Isn't he deceased?' said Vincent.

There was a pause. Outside, the wind had started to pick up. A tear tracked down Jake's cheek. With a splutter, he broke down into an uncontrollable fit of sobbing. 'What's going on?' he managed to sniffle. Jake wiped his eyes with the back of his hand and didn't see Vincent smile.

'Don't worry,' he reassured, 'I'm sure I can help. But first you need to tell me what makes you think she's possessed.'

Jake recounted his story and while he did, Vincent listened intently, interjecting with the occasional "hu-huh", or "yes" and other sounds of approval and when Jake had finished, he declared 'You must bring her here.'

'What?'
'You must bring her here.'
'And what are you planning to do?'
'An exorcism of course.' He said it as if they were about to embark upon a fishing expedition.
'Don't we need a priest for that?'
'The priest's dead.'
'Well, yes. But we should send for another one.'
'There's no time for that. By the time the church has gone through its many bloated layers of bureaucracy to obtain the required permissions, it will be far too late. No,' he said, 'we

must act quickly.'

'I don't know,' said Jake. 'I think we ought to get professional help.'

'You've tried that already,' said Vincent. 'It didn't work.'

Jake thought for a moment. 'So why do I need to bring her here; wouldn't it be easier if you came back to the cottage with me?'

'There are many reasons why that would be a bad idea,' Vincent said, his tone verging on condescending. 'For starters, I can't go near the place.' Jake shot him a puzzled look but Vincent continued before he had a chance to ask. 'Also, I have all my apparatus and books here and I'll be able to better prepare the trap.'

'But how am I supposed to bring her back, I have zero influence over what she does.'

'I'm sure you'll find a way,' he said.

An hour-and-a-half later Jake found himself back at Picker's Bleed, standing in the dark outside the front gate, still wondering what to do for the best. Should he stay and try to help Hannah, like the priest had suggested? But the priest was dead. Had he spoken to a ghost, or was he going insane? Surely he'd have to be insane to take advice from a ghost, wouldn't he? Nothing made sense anymore.

Vincent claimed he could help, but something niggled at the back of Jake's mind. There was something about the man he didn't trust. Regardless, he steeled himself and started up the driveway, past the car, telling himself he'd play it by ear and make the rules up as he went along. It was a strategy that had served him well so far in life, he sincerely hoped it wouldn't let him down now.

The front door was ajar but before Jake went inside he went around the side of the cottage to the wood store and fetched the axe from where it was leaning against the wall. It felt reassuringly heavy in his hands. Then he went back to the front door and pushed it open. 'Hello,' he shouted from the hallway. There was no echo. 'You in?' No reply. He was quite relieved Hannah wasn't home, but he went upstairs to check, just in case.

All was quiet and still and so he went back downstairs and leaned the axe next to the cellar door before re-lighting the fire. Within half an hour he was warm, in a tee shirt and sipping coffee (black because the only milk they had was long curdled) on the sofa. All was quiet, none of the riotous action of the previous night was apparent. Before many minutes had passed, he succumbed to exhaustion and his eyes closed.

It was the version of the cottage from his dreams; monochrome, with an unreal edge about it. All of his senses were slightly muddled. He filled with terror at what he might encounter, but this time there was no dog on the front lawn and thankfully no body either. Thick exotic lichens dripped from the trees. Movement caught his eye, long and low in the undergrowth and as he stared an enormous millipede emerged from under a bush and snaked across the sodden wasteland which was once upon a time, a lawn. Its writhing movement made it difficult to tell the length of the thing, but it must have been eight inches in girth. Repulsion coursed through him and Jake didn't know whether he'd be able to venture any further.

The millipede disappeared back into the undergrowth, and Jake tore his eyes away from the point where it had gone under the bush and looked towards the cottage. Roses and brambles had completely grown up the house's façade, forming an impenetrable barrier of wicked hooked thorns and tangled branches three feet thick. Only one of the downstairs windows was left uncovered and at a glance it appeared there were bars across the glass.

Without conscious effort, Jake found himself moving through the front garden towards the cottage. He was aware the millipede or some other grisly apparition might appear but it did not stop his forwards motion, unaware of putting one foot in front of the other. It was a movement more like gliding, or even a slow version of teleportation because without realising, he was standing in front of the window, peering inside.

Now he was close-up, he could see the bars were made of thigh bones, thick and yellowing. Scraps of leathered meat hung in one or two places, forgotten by the rooks and with the texture of beef jerky.

Just like when he and Hannah had first gone to Picker's Bleed to view the cottage, the windows were brown with grime. However, he could clearly see Hannah through the glass, inside a grim version of their own sitting room.

The walls and floor were bare. Stained plaster was crumbling off the walls, revealing the lathes beneath. Growing through them, although it was an interior wall, were more brambles, but they seemed fluid, as if the mass of thorny tendrils were the appendages of a terrible monster that twitched and writhed. The plants looked to be covered in some kind of goo, which had the consistency of golden syrup but tinged red like blood. It was dripping in splats from the ends of the thorns onto the floorboards.

Hannah was meshed up in the tangle of thorns, suspended above the floor. Her arms were splayed out from her sides like a crucifixion. Her entire body was completely criss-crossed with long cuts where the wicked branches had her gripped. One of the tendrils, he saw, went diagonally up her face, tearing through her cheek. Thorns had stapled her lips together.

Jake hammered on the window through the bone-bars.

Unable to move her head, only Hannah's eyes flitted his way. They were wide with terror and pain, but they were the eyes of the real Hannah.

His heart almost burst at seeing her in agony. He beat the bars with his fists and tried to pull them loose. There was no hint of movement from the bones. Jake ran around the cottage, looking for another way in, but the brambles made an impenetrable barrier all the way around. What's more, when he reached the back of the cottage he saw, to his disgust, there were still heads impaled on spikes. Although this time they were not the heads of pigs and deer, they were human.

He thought he heard something in the garden, something lurking. It sounded like a low growl, but the noise was soon forgotten when all the heads (in varying states of decay) swivelled on their stakes to face him. The closest had dank, long, greasy black hair which hung down past where its shoulders should have been. And yet the empty, ragged eyeholes managed to hold his stare for a moment, before, in unison, the impaled heads started to laugh.

Jake screamed and ran back the way he'd come, until he was once again standing at the sitting room window, sporting more than a few cuts and scratches of his own. Hannah was no longer looking his way, and it seemed the thorny coils that bound her had pulled tighter still, cutting deep into her flesh. Jake banged on the window again, but she didn't respond.

He looked around for something he might be able to use as a tool and saw that a few paces away there was a fallen branch, about four feet long and sturdy, but narrow enough to fit between the bars. He wedged it into the gap and used it as a lever, really putting his back into it, but in the end it was the branch that broke first, sending him tumbling into the brambles. He panicked when he couldn't immediately pull free, thinking he too had become trapped, but he was only snagged and managed to tear himself away. Frustrated, he drove the broken end of the branch between the bars like a battering ram, shattering the glass behind. There was an implosion of sorts and Jake was engulfed in a blast of cold air.

He was back on the sofa in the living room, lying on his back and shivering in a cold wind. Confused at the merging of the worlds of dreams and of waking, it took a few moments for him to realise the sitting room window had been shattered inwards. A storm had come in while he'd slept and a stout apple branch must have snapped off one of the trees in the orchard, which was now poking in through a jagged hole in the glass.

28

Hannah could have been entangled in the thorns for eternity. She couldn't remember arriving, she was simply there. She hated Vincent for what he'd done to her, but hadn't he given her exactly what she'd asked for? Still, it was unlikely she'd have heeded his instruction had she not been drugged. She thought of the thing which came for her and the memory alone was almost enough to break her. Then there was the feeling of being torn apart on an atomic scale; every nerve disassembled molecule by agonising molecule, only to be re-assembled and plunged, raw, into the thorns.

I must be in some kind of drug-induced coma, she thought, *a really fucking bad trip*. Hope that the drug might at some point wear off was an anchor to cling to, a rational explanation because the kind of hell she found herself suffering couldn't possibly be real.

Thorns, both long and short, trawled in all directions across her skin, flaying her flesh bare, leaving her furrowed and bloody. It was torture without relief, but she found herself incapable of falling unconscious. Hannah yearned for death. She couldn't open her mouth to scream and wondered whether her voice box had been shredded. Was she even breathing?

There was movement from the floor above. Hannah tried to focus on listening hard, to distract herself from the pain. There were mumbles and whimpers. It was the children she'd come to find. There was no plan, she'd have to figure things out as she went along, but for now Hannah was given a sense of purpose.

There was a banging at the window and Hannah let her head lol as far as the thorns would allow. The glass was filthy and the figure on the other side appeared as little more than a silhouette. She recognised Jake in an instant.

She watched on, prone, while Jake's hammering became more frantic before he finally left. An indeterminate amount of time later she concluded he wasn't coming back to the window and that her vision of Jake was just that, a vision constructed by her ailing brain.

Hannah didn't feel the slivers of glass that peppered her when the window burst inwards, but she did hear the crash. Cold air gusted in, which soothed her skin and made her shiver at the same time.

Although it took all her effort, she slowly tried to raise her head again to look towards the window. It was then she saw the twinkle of broken glass from a shard that had caught in the brambles, not far from the fingers of her left hand. It was almost within touching distance and with determination she wriggled her hand to try and tear her fingers free from the thorns. The tip of her pointy finger touched the glass and it juddered in the brambles, almost tumbling out of reach.

Ever so carefully, so as not to create too much of a disturbance which might dislodge the shard, she tried to move her whole body sideways in an attempt to increase her reach.

Row upon row of hooked thorns bit deeper into her skin – as if actively tightening – but she pulled hard and pushed with her feet, aware of every new puncture to her soles. Her lips tore apart and she screamed. Something gave a few millimetres, it could have been the flesh over her ribcage, but it was enough that she could lightly grasp the sliver of glass between two fingers and carefully manoeuvre it until it was clutched tightly in the palm of her hand.

Gripping as hard as she dared – fearful of causing some major damage to her hand, thus rendering it useless – she began to saw at her bindings.

Progress was slow. Too many times the shard slipped, and every time it was almost lost from her grip she froze, heart thumping, trying to control her breathing while her fingers gripped the broken glass as hard as she could make them.

At times it seemed for every strand she cut there were two more to take its place, but eventually she had a little more wiggle room for her fingers and the task became progressively easier until eventually Hannah could move her hand at the wrist and cut enough slack to make a start on liberating the other arm.

'I'm coming,' she shouted, although her voice escaped as a hoarse mumble, somehow muffled even to her own ears. She tried again, but using her voice was exhausting and she gave up after the second attempt. *I'm coming*, she screamed in her mind. *I'm coming*.

Tears – which she thought she had no more to cry – were rolling down her cheeks as she chopped and sawed the briar, slashes of the glass shard grew increasingly frantic the more of herself she freed. Her hands were cut to the bone. All fear of damage had left her mind. Her skin was shredded and hanging in ribbons. The glass was so firmly embedded in her palm it was wedged between two small bones and she hardly needed to grip onto it at all. Which was just as well because most of the tendons needed to work her fingers were severed.

Eventually, Hannah fell face first onto the floorboards. Her ankles remained suspended a foot or so above the ground. In one final and manic effort she frenziedly chopped at the tendrils holding her legs until, with a thud, she was lying in a heap on the grubby floorboards.

For a moment she lay motionless in the foetal position and wanted nothing more than to close her eyes and slip into oblivion, but forlorn cries and whimpers from upstairs spurred her on to crawl, naked, across the debris-strewn floor. All her focus was now on the small brass doorknob – dented and worn from age – and trying to reach it. She didn't even know what was on the other side of that door. She presumed it was the hallway, but couldn't be entirely sure.

All around there was a surging noise. Wind and rain lashed in through the broken window. A storm had whipped up suddenly, raging as strongly inside the room as it was out. Climbing roses were being flung about and they cracked like bullwhips.

A stray runner snagged her foot, and then almost as if it had sensed the contact, quickly wrapped itself around her calf. Hannah's progress was halted. The thorns bit deep into her flesh and with sickening terror she realised she was being pulled back towards the swaying mass of brambles.

It was in a panic she clawed and scrabbled for something to cling to. The doorknob was only half a pace away and yet entirely out of her reach. Two fingernails were ripped from her right hand and in photographic freeze-frame clarity she saw them, bloody roots and all, poking upright from the floorboards like little keratin tombstones. Hannah's eyes flitted to her other hand and saw that the shard of glass had gone all the way through. Its jagged point protruded a good three inches from the back of her hand. The other end had jammed into the gap between two floorboards and it was this stopping her from being pulled backwards.

She felt something give as the glass ripped through the sinew of her hand towards the knuckles. Hannah screamed and kicked with ever increased urgency and abandon.

It was in every sense a last-ditch attempt to win her freedom, which thankfully paid off when Hannah lurched forwards and began scrabbling for the doorknob with her better hand. If she'd looked back, Hannah would have seen the skin of her foot dangling in the brambles like an abandoned Converse.

The doorknob was icy to the touch and slick with her blood. The wind whipped her rain sodden hair into her eyes and from behind there was a constant rustling. She knew without looking the brambles were coming to get her. Hannah grabbed her hair with her good hand and used it to try and wipe away some of the blood before she made another lunge for the doorknob.

All of a sudden she was plunged into silence so complete she could hear the beat of her own heart. Even the cacophony of the raging storm had vanished. She was in the hallway of the cottage, the door to the living room was closed behind her. An old-fashioned oil lamp burned on the occasional table, setting shadows dancing across the dingy walls. To her left, the front door was obscured behind a two feet thick wall of thorns. At the other end of the hall the kitchen door was closed, as was the door to the cellar. She looked at it and shuddered, before dragging herself to the foot of the stairs.

29

Six people were gathered in the back room of the Bull's Head, sitting around an old and worn dining table, on mis-matching folding chairs. Around the edge of the room were stacked cases of bottled beer and boxes of crisps. A layer of gunmetal tobacco smoke hung in the air just above their heads, lazily whirling with every gesture. The only window was small; wider than it was tall with bars running vertically across it, which had been glossed white a long time ago. Large rust spots were showing on their bumpy surface where the paint had cracked and warped. The frame was also made of painted iron and hinged in the middle. It had rusted shut years ago.

Tom Stour, the landlord, was there, as was Alan Wright who was the butcher. Lillian Harris was there too, puffing on a B&H. She was the keeper of the village store and the only woman present. Next to her was Old Les and so was Peter Norris who was postmaster until the post office closed for good. He still lived in the old post office building with his wife, Mary, but now it was just a house with a big bay window instead of a store front. There was also the decrepit butler, Appleby.

Between them they formed a sort of unofficial village council. Each of them could trace their family history back generations, and with their long lineage they saw themselves somewhat as guardians of Marsham. For all the good that had done.

For more than five hundred years the village had been cursed. By all accounts, even before the witch was burned Marsham had a queer taint to it, but history dictated that was the time it all began.

Marsham used to be much larger, way back when the soil had been fertile, but following the events of one fateful Christmas, the population had rapidly upped and left, leaving homes abandoned. Over the years, people had moved into the village, but they didn't tend to stay long. When Hannah and Jake moved into the cottage there was much trepidation. No tenancy of Picker's Bleed ever ended well, but this time seemed stranger than most, as if there was an air of finality to the whole affair.

Lillian was saying, 'Should have burned the place to the ground years ago.'

'Feel free to do it then?' retorted Alan, the butcher. That shut Lillian up. There had been many attempts to burn Picker's Bleed over the generations, but it was obvious the cottage was protected by witchcraft. Alan's own Grandfather had been the last to die trying, and there had been no attempts since, although each of the people around the table had relatives, some more distant than others, who'd come to some kind of misadventure trying to destroy the place.

'So,' started the old postmaster, 'we know from what Tom and Appleby are saying, that the game's now afoot.' He paused a moment, to gain consensus from the others before continuing. 'What are we going to do about it?'

There was silence. The situation they'd found themselves in was unprecedented, but they all understood it was their generation's call to action.

Alan Wright turned to Appleby, 'Do you think Mandeville will be able to break the curse?' he asked.

'I don't know,' replied the butler. 'Something's not right, that much's for sure.'

'Do we know what?'

'Well, I think they were trying to bring *Her* back.'

'And you really think he can do it? Do you think he can raise a five-hundred year old legend from the dead?'

'You have to remember,' said Appleby, 'this is his lifetime's work, and his father's before him and grandfather and so on and so forth.' He waved his hand to gesticulate. 'He truly believes bringing back the witch will end the curse.'

'How?'

'I don't know. I don't get involved in their rituals. It gives me the willies.' He made an exaggerated shudder.

'And so it should,' said Lillian, abruptly. 'So, is it this notorious witch who's gallivanting around the woods and sending our young friend stark raving mad?'

'Something's gone wrong,' said Tom. He was thinking about overheard conversations in the taproom.

'I agree,' said Appleby. 'They've been walking 'round with faces like smacked arses ever since the other night.'

'This is bad,' mumbled Alan, more to himself than anyone else, slowly shaking his head.

'Yes. Yes it is,' said Les. 'But it still begs the question, what are we going to do about it?'

'Can't we just let things run their course, and hope Vincent can somehow break the curse; turn a blind eye to his ways?'

'That's what got us into this mess in the first place.'

'It would also be tantamount to murder, I suspect,' said Appleby.

'We don't know that.'

'Please!'

'And who knows what he might be unleashing upon us. It might be worse than we've already got.'

'How could it be worse?'

'Come on, we've all heard the stories, ever since we were kids.'

'They're nothing but stories.'

'Of all people Lillian, you should know these things are real. We've all seen it, all been touched by it in our lives.'

'I don't understand,' said Peter. 'How could a dead witch end all of this? How do you even begin to resurrect a pile of ancient ashes that blew to the wind hundreds of years ago?'

'I don't want to know. It can't be good, whichever way you look at it.'

'So, what do we do?' asked Lillian.

'I'm not sure we're any further forward. Do we try to stop Vincent or what?' said Tom.

'Maybe we call the police?'

'And tell them what, exactly?'

'That the girl's been kidnapped, and Vincent has her.'

'Only by all accounts he hasn't. Her fella was saying she was up at the cottage. For all we know she's got her feet up, eating Garibaldis and drinking tea.'

'Her chap seemed worried.'

'Yes, we know there's definitely something afoot. That's well established.'

'Did he say what was wrong with her?'

'No, but from overhearing him on the phone, it sounded like some kind of psychotic episode,' said Tom.

'That figures.'

'But mind you, he didn't seem too hinged himself. Claimed to have had a conversation with Geoffrey, he did.'

Appleby looked thoughtful, perplexed. 'What's up?' Tom asked.

'I don't know how she got out without me knowing.'

'You must have just missed her.'

'Yes,' said Appleby, 'but I don't see how. I always know who comes and goes.'

'Secret door?'

'I know every inch of Marsham Hall. Better than anyone,' he added. 'The only way would be the old tunnel, but nobody's been down there in decades. I'm fairly certain I'm the only living person who knows of its existence. But there was a right old mess in the cellar,' he mused, fiddling with the collar of his Jacket.

'What do you mean?'

'Ay,' he sighed. 'They'd had one of their rituals, and they can be raucous affairs at the best of times, but this one must have been particularly bad. It looked like a cyclone had gone through the place. And the girl was involved somehow.'

'What did they do in this ritual? What's involved?'

'I don't know. I don't want to know.'

'So there really are tunnels beneath the hall?'

'One, that I know of.'

'Where does it go?'

'I don't know.'

'I thought you knew every inch of the place?' said Lillian.

He looked her square in the eye. 'You wouldn't want to go down there either.' His look and tone were enough to dispel any further questions on the matter. 'She must have disappeared into thin air,' he finished.

'It's not important how she got out.'

'Do we know what happened with the ambulance?'

'Evidently not a lot,' huffed Appleby. 'Or our young friend wouldn't have been banging down the door begging for help.'

'Are you sure that's what he was doing?'

'Certain.'

'So, it appears our fate lies in the hands of Mandeville?'

'Or our own. We need to stop him,' said Tom. 'No good can come of it. Before we get into this debate again.'

'So how do we do it?'

'Burn the cottage. Do that and the rest comes tumbling down. That place is the centre of it all.'

'We wait until his back's turned,' said Lillian with rising venom. 'And we have another attempt at burning the fucking nest to the ground.'

No one disagreed with her.

Of those gathered, Appleby had the longest walk home. After the meeting had concluded he remained in the public bar for a while, as he often did on his rare evenings off, but shortly after eleven Tom rang his bell for last orders. Appleby ordered a shot of single malt for the road, drank it in three sips and pulled on his heavy, woollen overcoat, pulling the collar up snug around his throat before saying his goodbyes and doddering out of the door.

The sky had cleared and the night was beginning to freeze beneath the stars, which glinted like flecks of shattered ice against the vastness of space. The wind was cutting and smelled of impending snow. The painted sign above the Bull's Head creaked on its gibbet.

Appleby's joints hurt with age. Every step felt like nails being driven into his ankles and the cold penetrated so deep he could well imagine his flesh freezing away from the bones inside his wizened body. He'd refused Tom's offer of a bed for the night on account of him wanting to walk, despite the pain in his joints. *Use them or lose them, Old Boy.*

The road to Marsham Hall was only about a mile and a half long and more of private driveway, since all of the farmsteads along it were long abandoned. Appleby found himself shuffling beneath a barren canopy of interwoven branches. His mind was reeling a little, trying to make sense of it all. Appleby never dreamed he'd live for a time when there might be some resolution to this god-forsaken curse. It was inevitable some change was fast approaching, but the outcome was a complete unknown. Had Master Vincent really found a way to rid them of their demon and make the land workable again? It was gut-wrenching they had to try and put a stop to him, but deep down he knew Tom was right, no good could come of it.

Bereft of leaves the branches felt like a cage. The feeling surprised him somewhat. *It's all this talk of witches got your head a fluster,* he told himself. He'd walked the same route countless times during his eighty-six years and passing amongst the trees at night often put him mildly on edge, but tonight he found himself glancing over his shoulder more and more the deeper into the woods he travelled. He thrust his old, arthritic hands deep into his pockets, fists clenched. And yet he could get no warmth into them. Suddenly he was more afraid than he'd ever been.

'Silly old fool,' he mumbled, 'letting your imagination run away with you.' His voice was lost to the susurrations of the forest. He quickened his step to a lop-sided half shuffle, moving as fast as he could. He was jumping at shadows and cast another glance over his shoulder.

When he turned back, she was in the middle of the road, hunched on all fours like an animal, feral in the moonlight. She appeared to be eating something, snout to the ground like a dog, but this only briefly registered on Appleby's senses and he had no interest on finding out what it was.

Her head slowly lifted and swivelled to look at him. Her grimy face split into a grimace. Her mouth was too wide, like a gash through her cheeks and filled with teeth which were too sharp and too plentiful. 'Ooh, if it isn't the pissy butler boy,' she said and Appleby could have sworn he saw a forked tongue dart in and out of her mouth, tasting his fear. Relishing it. 'I have a body now,' said the thing which used to be human, standing for a grotesque twirl. 'Look.' Its voice was raspy, as if the very act of speaking was shredding its host's voice-box.

Instinctively, Appleby knew this was the evil that had stalked Picker's Bleed for generations. Egbert Appleby wet himself and didn't notice. He stood, mouth agape, steam rising from his legs.

'What's up, cat got your tongue?' The thing was right up in his face, although he hadn't seen her move. Pain gripped his chest, like a belt being pulled rib-crushingly tight. The piss froze on his trousers and when the thing in Hannah's body kissed him, so did the moisture in his lungs.

30

'First Stephen and now Appleby.'

'We don't know what's happened to either of them.'

'Like fuck we don't,' said Mel.

'Seriously, we don't. Stephen could have lost his nerve and run.'

'We all know that's not true. His curiosity wouldn't allow it.'

'I think he lost his bottle when shit got real,' Danny said.

'No way. He wasn't like that.'

'And Appleby was an old man, who got too drunk and froze to death on his way home,' said Vincent.

'Bullshit.' Mel was tugging at her hair.

'I dunno, man. The look on his face.' Danny shuddered.

'Anyway, where's Susan?' asked Vincent.

'Still in her room.'

'Go and fetch her would you, Mel?'

'I'm not your slave.'

Vincent inhaled deeply. 'Sorry, I was only asking. I'll

go and fetch her myself.' The death of the butler had hit him harder than expected. Appleby had been a constant throughout the whole of his life, and before him, his father had served the family. And so it went, all the way back to the founding of the estate in Norman times.

Like so many things, it seemed he was the end of his line. On so many levels it was the end of an era. Being the last of his gene pool was a burden, but he also knew the fate of the village rested in his hands. With him died the knowledge to save them. *It's now or never, Old Chap,* he uttered to himself while climbing the stairs. For the first time in his life he felt like an old man.

'Susan.' Vincent rapped thrice on the bedroom door. There was no reply and for a brief moment he feared to find a body within. His heart quickened when he tried the doorknob.

'Hold on,' came Susan's voice from inside, much to Vincent's relief. He waited a few moments with his hand resting on the knob until she called him in.

The rickety sash window was propped open on a pile of books and shaking in the wind. Rain was beginning to puddle on the windowsill. The bed was made and a mug of coffee was steaming on the bedside table.

'We were beginning to worry about you.'

'I'm okay,' she said. 'I've had my little meltdown. I'm fine now.'

'Glad to hear it,' said Vincent. 'Appleby's dead.'

'Oh shit. What happened?'

'First thing this morning I noticed he hadn't come home, so I went a walk up the lane and, you know...' Vincent shrugged. 'He must have fallen over on his way back from the pub or something.'

'Poor old cunt,' said Susan. 'Still, at least he died drunk.

Talking of which,' she said. 'I'm parched.' She headed out into the hallway and Vincent followed.

They talked as they made their way downstairs to join the others. 'Is there any news of Stephen yet?' she asked.

'I'm afraid not.'

'Shame.' And then she asked, 'do you think *she* killed him?'

'Who?'

'*Her*. Do you think we managed to bring back Ella Jameson, like we planned?'

'I don't think it's her,' he said. 'We fucked up. I'm sure the girl's body is possessed by the thing she conjured.'

'So, what went wrong?' Susan asked

'I don't know.'

'Well, I don't know either,' she sighed. 'So what do we do, burn her and start again?'

'Out of the question. It's taken half a millennium to get to this point. Starting afresh isn't an option. We're committed now, past the point of no return, as they say, whatever the outcome. But I don't believe we'll fail. Perhaps *She's* become weaker over time, but I'm willing to bet the demon is emboldened and unwilling to leave. If so, we can drive it out and then I'm sure *She'll* take care of the rest.'

'What if she doesn't?'

'She will. Fate's on our side.'

'Seriously though, what if none of this can work? What if Ella Jameson's lost forever, beyond hope and we're foolishly attempting the impossible and in getting it so horribly wrong all we've done is given flesh to a monster?'

'Come on,' he said. 'That would mean everything we've worked for, everything we believe in, has been bullshit.'

'Yes,' she said.

'I won't accept that for a moment. After everything, it would be utter madness to start disbelieving now.'

'Or madness not to.'

'True,' he said with a slight nod and gnawing gently on the mouthpiece of his pipe.

By now they'd reached the dining room. Danny and Mel were having toast and coffee. The mood was glum.

'So,' said Susan, with a snap in her voice. 'It's time to stop fannying around with this thing.'

The others all looked up and gave her their undivided attention.

'It's obvious events are reaching their climax. This is the moment of reckoning. It's not supposed to be easy, or it would have been done long before we all came along.' She paused and looked about the room, a wild gleam in her eye. 'The things she could teach us. What sights she must have seen?'

"What if we're wrong?' asked Mel. 'What if she can't be brought back?'

'It's all in here,' Vincent rapped the journal he'd left on the table, which had been passed down through the generations, from the time of the ill-fated Richard Mandeville. 'They knew where she'd gone and that one day she'd be brought back.'

'But it's been five-hundred years.'

'Time has no meaning on the other side.'

'How do we know?'

'Have faith.'

'How do we know it's not all fiction? For all we know your great, great grandad, or whatever, could be playing one massive joke on all of us.'

'You're beginning to sound a lot like Stephen now, but at least his scepticism had an ounce of intellect behind it.'

Danny shrugged. 'I do believe,' he said. 'I wouldn't be here if I didn't.'

'I guess we're all a little rattled,' said Vincent.

'So, you think that whatever this thing is has possessed the girl? How do we go about getting it here?' asked Susan.

'I'm hoping the young man will help with that one.'

'You asked him to bring it here?'

'How?' interrupted Danny. 'From what I can gather, it won't want to come.'

'The old Lord Mandeville certainly has a lot to answer for,' said Susan, shaking her head.

'This is what happened the first time, according to the accounts. She was possessed when they burned her,' said Vincent.

'For all the good that did.'

'That was a mistake. It's clear from his writings-,' Vincent tapped the old journal, '-that they'd summoned something more powerful than they'd anticipated. They'd planned on something more easily controlled.'

'Well,' said Danny. 'If we want to get the gateway closed, we need to get on with it and bring her back.'

'We should have seen it coming.'

'Well, hindsight is always 20-20. The thought didn't occur to us that, whatever this thing is, might jump in. We were foolish. It was supposed to be her.'

'Well, we were wrong.'

'So it seems.'

'Well, having a burning isn't feasible; your namesake demonstrated that one quite well. So what do we do?'

'We trap it, and we try again,' said Vincent.

'Try again?'

'Yes, we exorcise the demon and invite her back.'

'You make it sound easy.'

'Nothing in this world, or the next, is easy, but we've been studying this for so long; gathering all the knowledge in existence and now we have *her* spell-book. I still believe we can reach her from here, without going to Picker's Bleed. Physical distance is irrelevant.'

Danny didn't seem so sure.

'I know,' conceded Vincent. 'I do share some of your reservations, but we can't get near the place, so this is our best chance. We know how to make the connection. Do we still have the artefacts?'

'Some of them. We used a lot of the blood last time. We didn't consider the prospect of failure. It was supposed to be all or nothing.'

'We've got a few drops left, I hope it's enough.'

'I wish Stephen were here.'

'I think we all do. For all his sceptical ways, his knowledge of necromancy was unparalleled.'

'What makes you think we can trap it now?' asked Susan, getting the subject back on topic again. 'No one's been able to yet.'

'We do it the old-fashioned way,' he said with a hint of a crafty grin showing on his face. 'Duct tape.'

31

The wind had built to gale force and seemed to be blowing just as strongly inside the cottage as it was out. Embers glowed hot in the grate, occasionally eliciting flabby wisps of flame that spat and sizzled in the rain which had started lashing in through the broken window. The door was being violently shaken in its frame, banging. Water was running off Jake's face and his hair was sodden. The hole in the glass didn't seem large enough for the amount of weather in the room. Jake didn't dwell on it however, instead he bolted to leave the sitting room, struggling to open the door against the buffeting. With one foot braced against the wall, he managed to wrestle the door open and slip through before it slammed shut behind him.

The hallway wasn't much quieter. Rolling thunder and howling wind shook the cottage, but at least he was no longer being pummelled by cold rain. Jake didn't think he could remember a fiercer storm, including the time they'd moved to Picker's Bleed. The outside of the cottage was being whipped all over by branches, and Jake hoped none of the larger trees would come crashing through the roof.

With his back to the door, he fumbled blindly for the light-switch. There were other sounds in the dark too, not dissimilar to the cacophony of his dreams. The voices were coming up through the open cellar door.

At first when he flicked the light-switch nothing happened and Jake assumed power had gone down in the storm, but just as is heart sank into deeper despair the bulb warmed into a dim yellow glow, which wavered as if to die out at any time. But at least now the hallway was lit, albeit dimly.

Icy mist spilled up the cellar steps. There was a bang from upstairs and the scraping of furniture across bare floorboards. Shadows writhed in the mist, detached from the utter blackness of the cellar doorway and sliding across the dimly lit walls of the hall.

'None of it's real,' he told himself. 'It's my house,' he said a little louder, 'and I'm not leaving. I won't run away again.'

'Glad to hear it,' came a reply, clear as day from along the hallway.

Jake jerked his head up to see the priest standing near the kitchen door, partially obscured by the fog which was lazily billowing up from the cellar.

'And you're not real either,' said Jake. It came out as a flat statement because he was too shell-shocked to register surprise.

'It depends how you define real.'

'You're dead.'

'I suppose I am,' he said. 'In body at least.'

'Then you're a ghost?'

'I suppose I am.'

'Why are you here?'

'To help.'

'I can't do it,' said Jake. 'I don't know what it is you want me to do. I don't even know if you're a symptom of some kind of mental illness?'

'You're doing brilliantly,' said the priest, his voice soothing. 'You've already done much more than you realise.'

Jake shrugged. 'I can't see how.'

'Just look to your dreams.'

'I couldn't help in those either.'

'But you did. Hannah's free now, and making progress.'

'Of the thorns?'

The priest nodded.

'That's real?'

'Of a fashion.'

'Oh dear God.' Jake rubbed his forehead, trying to clear away some of the confusion. 'So, why can't she just come back, like you have?'

'Do you want to marry a ghost?' he said. 'I could help her through the rift, but without her body, well.'

'Gateway?' he said. 'The thing you mentioned before? It didn't make a lot of sense then either.'

'Down there -' He pointed to the cellar door. '- is a doorway that was opened many, many years ago and has remained that way ever since.'

'And?'

'We, I mean you, must close it.'

'How?'

'I think when the time is right, you'll know. Until then you must continue to be brave.'

Jake took one look at the cellar door and shuddered. 'Is that why this place is so haunted?'

'A door can't be left open for long before something comes through.'

'Why can't I just go down there and do it now?' He was feigning courage. Just the thought of setting one foot near the steps filled him with profound dread.

'We need to get Hannah back.'

'Vincent Mandeville says I need to take her to him. He can exorcise this thing from her there.'

'Then Vincent Mandeville is a fool.'

'Really, because he's the best hope I have right now.'

'Maybe he can conjure up a portal, but the one here is fixed, more stable if you like. We need something Hannah can find.'

'But what choice do I have? Should I believe him, or you?'

'You have to trust your judgement on that one I'm afraid.' The priest stopped speaking. 'Go,' he said. 'Go now.' As he began to fade, Jake realised he'd been focussed entirely on the priest, to the exclusion of all his other senses. Now the apparition of Father Hamilton had disappeared the cottage was deathly still. Even the storm had gone quiet. From within the kitchen came the sound of the back door opening.

'I'm not leaving.' Without really thinking, Jake picked up the axe from where it was propped against the wall and took up a stance in the hall, waiting to meet whatever was coming to meet him. Whatever state Hannah was in now.

The thing looked surprised to see him, and maybe a little amused. What had once been his true love was now reduced to some kind of Gollum type creature. Emaciated ribs were prominent below her breasts, which had taken the appearance of half-deflated balloons. Loose skin hung from her belly and thighs. Her hair was falling out in chunks, exposing large patches of sore-encrusted scalp beneath. Her skin, beneath the dirt, had a greasy, yellow tinge to it. Her eyes were wild and her lips were split and pulled back into a snarl. 'Wanna fuck?' it rasped before lunging with a ferocity which left no doubt the thing intended to kill him.

It all happened in a heartbeat. Jake was uncannily aware of the weight of the axe as he swung it in a wide arc. G-force almost launched the axe from his hands before it connected with Hannah's leg, just a fraction below the hip.

There was a wet thud and a loud crack and Hannah went down with the scream of an animal. The axe was embedded into her now useless thigh and for a moment Jake froze, staring at it. The thing fixed him with a stare of pure malice before its face relaxed into a sheet of pain and the voice which came from it was the real Hannah's voice. 'What have you done, Jake,' it said. 'Why did you hurt me Jake? Help me, please. Oh, it hurts. Help me,' she whimpered.

He faltered, automatically going to where Hannah was crumpled on the hallway floor. Her shoulder was pressed up against the small occasional table opposite the cellar door, which she'd upended when she fell, knocking a vase to the floor.

'Help me,' she said again, her voice pathetic.

Jake thought it was odd there was no blood, he would have expected more from an axe wound the size of the one he'd just made in his partner's thigh.

Sensing his confusion, the thing couldn't help but sneer. The expression was fleeting, but Jake caught it and knew it was still the demon lying in the hallway.

The demon realised its mistake and dropped all pretence. It lunged forwards again, unable to get off the floor on its half-severed leg, its movements surprisingly quick. Jake jumped back, turned and fled to the front door. He would have been caught within two steps if the axe, still buried in Hannah's thigh, hadn't got tangled with the table legs. While the demon in Hannah's body freed itself, Jake fumbled the latch on the front door and was out into the night.

32

The storm was raging, but rain had given way to snow. Driven on gale-force winds, it slammed against the cottage in waves and broke around him in a vortex of swirling white. Almost straight away Jake's ears and face were raw, but there was no chance of returning to the cottage to fetch his coat, and so he went into the night wearing a damp, woollen jumper. Already the windward tree trunks and the side of the cottage were frosted and sodden leaves, which carpeted the front garden, were beginning to freeze.

Wind snatched the gate from his hand, slamming it shut before Jake chanced a backwards glance and saw Hannah pulling herself through the front door on her belly. She seemed to be moving fast and fixed him with a stare with wild, black eyes, wide like a cat stalking prey. The gap between them was closing far too quickly for him to stand gawping and so – wishing he'd had the foresight to close the front door on his way through – he ran off down the lane.

It must have been three or four o'clock in the morning and the night was dark. As soon as Jake was away from the watery light coming from the cottage he found himself stumbling along the lane, unable to see the road beneath his feet. Snow was pelting his face; small, sharp pellets that stung, so he had to raise a hand to shield his eyes. Now his hands were freezing and being blasted raw. He decided to move beneath the shelter of the trees, to protect himself from the worst of the weather, but between the dark and the fresh covering of snow he soon lost the road.

In the shelter of the woods the storm was less intense, although the trees above him groaned and cracked in the wind which blew loudly through their boughs. Jake could hardly see where he was going and so had to shuffle his feet and feel his way with one hand while holding his other out in front of his face to protect his eyes from low hanging branches. He briefly wondered whether he might be getting frostbite. The pain in his fingertips from the cold was unbearable and he was sure tears were freezing on his cheeks.

Jake was also aware that his progress was painfully slow and in his mind's eye he could see *it,* pulling itself along in Hannah's body, slithering over leaves and roots, through mud and half frozen puddles, clawing at the earth to propel itself with unnatural speed and he realised his imaginations were probably correct and so he forced himself to push on, more quickly than was safe. Panic was building again. He thought he heard movement, and whatever it was must have been big and close to be distinguishable from the storm. He hoped it was a badger or deer, but in his heart of hearts he knew that any animals would have fled at his crashing through the forest.

He heard the noise again, closer now and was sure he heard ragged breaths below the level of the wind. With an arm raised to protect his eyes from errant twigs, Jake staggered as fast as he could, bouncing off any trees in his way, but getting a feel for how the ground rose immediately around their trunks.

When the inevitable trip finally happened, Jake went sprawling, hands outstretched, onto the forest floor. His chin hit the ground hard. The impact was somewhat softened by mulch, but still delivered a jarring blow. He tasted blood and dirt. His nostrils were clogged with rotten vegetation. Something crawled away across his face.

There was a cackle from nearby, in the dark not far off to his left, and he knew for sure the demon was with him. Jake froze, hugging himself into the foetal position.

'Got you now, Loverboy.' The thing sounded like a crow, or a rook, gurgling and sputtering as if the act of talking was physically exhausting.

Jake shut his eyes and tensed, trembling, trying to muffle his own sorry sobs while waiting for the inevitable end. He could hear nothing above the storm surging through the treetops. All he could do was hope his dispatch was quick and painless and he developed a sudden empathy for the cow in the slaughterhouse. Only a second could have passed but into it was compressed his entire existence. All the key moments from his life were relived. He reflected on things he'd regretted, stupid things he'd done. He thought about good times and laughed. He cried and all of it, his whole life, slotted into place and contentment washed over him. He'd made his peace, so to speak.

There came a loud crack and the creaking, rushing sound of a tree succumbing to the storm and crashing through the canopy. It fell so close the outer branches raked Jake where he lay, like he was being swept with a witch's broom. He squeezed his eyes more tightly to protect them. The demon shrieked and Jake instantly knew Hannah's body had been hit. How badly he didn't know, but it was a big enough glimmer of hope for Jake's nervous system to dump a load more adrenaline into his bloodstream and get him up and running again, praising God for his good fortune.

By now he didn't know or care in which direction he ran. It didn't matter. He just needed to get away from the thing stalking him. There was certainly no guarantee of safety at the end of it, he was fleeing on impulse alone and the off-chance an opportunity to evade capture would present itself.

Lo and behold, he found himself hammering on the door of Marsham Hall.

The next thing Jake knew he was choking on brandy, which was being tipped into his unconscious mouth. He was lying on a couch, or rather a dusty chaise-longue. There were three, four people standing over him, appearing blurred in his slowly returning vision. One of them was saying his name. 'Jake,' it was saying, over and over again. 'Jake, can you hear us?'

Jake tried to reply. The brandy made him splutter and cough.

'See,' said the voice, addressing one of the others. 'Told you he'd be okay.'

'We don't know that yet,' said another, a woman.

As blood started to flow back into Jake's extremities, the pain was excruciating. He curled into a ball, tucking his hands as best he could into his armpits and gritting his teeth. He wondered whether he'd lose any fingers. He hurt too much to be bothered answering his rescuers and as snatches of his ordeal came back, he assumed they were Vincent and his acquaintances, because it didn't seem he was in a hospital, which was where he belonged. But he couldn't be angry, he'd sought out Vincent, it was he who had come for help, although he wasn't entirely sure what that help would be.

'Jake?' There was a hand shaking his shoulder, he grunted. 'Sorry,' said Vincent. 'What happened? Where's Hannah?'

'It's not Hannah,' Jake croaked.

'I know,' said Vincent, his voice reassuring, but firm. 'But it's important. Where is sh.. it?'

He remembered and started to sob, feeling somehow he was about to commit some great betrayal, but unsure how. His main emotion was confusion, but there was an urgency that overruled all else. 'In the forest,' he croaked, it was meant to be a shout. 'She's in the forest, in the dark.'

One of the others in the room sighed.

'I think a tree hit her.'

'A tree?'

'Yes, in the storm. It blew down, it was too dark for me to see, but I'm sure it hurt her more.'

'More?'

He was openly sobbing now. 'I hit her with an axe,' he gasped. 'God, what's happening? This is bad, this is bad.'

'You did what?' asked Vincent but spoke again without waiting for an answer. 'Where was this, could you show us?'

Jake paused, trying in vain to gather his thoughts.

'Sorry,' Vincent said. I feel bad about pushing you, but this is important. Really important.'

'She's in the woods,' said Jake.

'Yes, yes, we know that. But where in the woods? Could you take us there?'

'Take?' the notion filled him with dread. 'I'm not sure.'

'Please, Jake? We wouldn't ask if it wasn't a matter of life and death. For all of us.'

Jake groaned and slowly pushed himself to his feet. He

thought he was going to be sick and the pain in his extremities had become an intense, throbbing ache. Vincent got his shoulder under one of Jake's arms and Danny supported the other, while Mel and Susan left the room to fetch lights from the back of the Range Rover. They came back around the house shining an industrial strength lantern, which illuminated the night and a billion streaking snowflakes as they met up with Jake and the others, who were struggling down the wide steps from the front door.

They'd gathered thick coats before coming outside and were wrapped up in hats, gloves, and scarves, but it was by no exception, a dangerous storm. Jake's chest seemed to spasm in refusal to breathe any more of the icy air, but he pulled his hood tight and his scarf up over his face and tried not to cry. The ferocious wind made his eyes stream anyway as the group paused outside Marsham Hall and silently debated whether they should continue, or whether to leave it for another night. While they did, Jake listened to the whistling and creaking of the forest. A stable door was banging around the back of the hall somewhere. He could almost hear voices on the wind; unable to tell whether they were friend or foe, only that they sounded miserable.

33

Vincent moved first. *We might never have this chance again,* he thought and decided that if the others didn't follow then he'd go alone. But he was confident they would, and sure enough they fell into line to follow his footprints through the gathering snow. Jake put up his hand to say he could walk without help but Susan looped an arm though his anyway and Danny held his other elbow as they guided him towards the woods.

The lantern cast long shadows and lit up streaks of driving snow. Trees thrash-danced with elongated limbs, their wildly moving shadows registered with the mind as monsters rushing out of the dark to devour and destroy. All of them wanted to run away, but they were on a mission for a cause they were willing to die for. All apart from Jake that was, who had no choice in the matter and was now resigned to being pushed from pillar to post, accepting of his fate. 'This way,' he said, and they changed direction.

They heard her first, the sounds of her struggle distinct from the storm. She stopped moving when the lantern shone on her and all apart from Jake gasped at the inhuman thing before them. A tree had fallen across Hannah's midriff, pinning her body to the ground. It looked as though the tree had broken her back.

The demon eyed them calmly as they approached and gave a sorrowful smile. 'I knew you'd be back,' it said in its corvid-like voice.

'Oh God,' said Jake. 'We need to call an ambulance.'

'No ambulances,' said Vincent. His words were snatched away on the wind. 'It's not her.'

The thing glared at him.

'We are going to lift the tree off you though,' said Vincent. 'And then you're going to come with us.'

'How am I supposed to do that?' it asked, gesturing towards Hannah's broken body.

'Good point,' said Susan. 'How are we going to get it back?'

'First we tie it up,' said Danny, taking the coil of rope off his shoulder and casually walking over to the tree where Hannah's trapped body watched nonchalantly on. Mel shone her lantern into its face and the thing squinted and averted its big, black eyes from the light but still kept them fixed on Danny, who said. 'Are you going to put your hands out for me?'

'Why would I want to do that?'

'Because it would make things easier.'

'Not for me it wouldn't.'

'It'll stop you trying anything.'

'I can't try anything. This feeble body is broken; snapped in the middle like a twig.'

'But still, it would make us feel a little better,' said Vincent.

'And then what are you planning?'

'We're going to help.'

'Help? How? You've already said you won't call for help.'

'And would you have gone?'

'To fix this body, yes.'

'We can fix your body.'

'I think you forget what you're dealing with here,' it croaked. 'I know your limits.'

'And I know yours,' said Vincent, lowering down onto his haunches to look the creature square in the eyes, while keeping a respectable distance. 'And I suspect you're more powerful than you're letting on.'

It laughed, a disgusting rasping noise which set everyone's teeth on edge. The wind seemed to blow a little harder.

'What are you?'

'Well, that would be telling, wouldn't it?'

While the demon's attention was on Vincent, Danny moved in as quickly as he dared with the rope. As he stooped to bind its hands, the thing reached up with lightning speed and grabbed him at the crotch.

Danny screamed as he was pulled to his knees. Hannah's nails seemed to have grown into talons, which easily ripped through Danny's leather trousers. Blood ran down Hannah's arms, streaking through the dirt, while the thing which was occupying her body sneered. 'I said no ropes.'

Susan began to recite a spell, raising her voice against the storm and Danny's screams, throwing it towards the demon. Jake couldn't make out the words and it took a few moments for him to realise it wasn't English he was hearing. He didn't think it was Latin either, or any other language he might have recognised even the timbre of, but her words were undoubtedly ancient, thick with age and powerful.

Without relaxing its grip, the thing snapped its head around to look at her. 'You think to tame me with parlour tricks?!' it shrieked. Its face contorted with inhuman rage. But its anger told Susan she was having an effect and she raised her voice with conviction.

Danny was flung across the forest floor, into the trunk of an old beech tree, and with a dull thud his head split wide open like a pistachio, splattering the soft nut of his brains across the smooth bark before his lifeless body crashed to the ground, chunks of grey matter, the largest about the size of a crab-apple, slid and tumbled down the tree after him.

Danny's genitals were still in the demons clenched fist; cock and balls intact and connected to a huge, dripping chunk of flesh which had internal tubes hanging from the bloody end. Somehow the thing seemed to make eye contact with everyone at once as it bit off Danny's shrivelled penis.

Mel screamed. Jake wanted to vomit. But Susan's spell appeared to be working. Vincent joined in with the chanting, slipping easily into the rhythm. Steadily, Hannah's movement slowed and her eyes slid closed until she appeared, to all intents and purposes, asleep.

All around them the forest lashed under the ferocity of the blizzard.

Mel took a large hunting knife from her belt and raised it high above her head, making a lunge for Hannah's throat.

'No,' shouted Jake. With reactions which were sharpened through unrelenting fear he flying-tackled Mel to the ground before she managed to use the eight-inch blade. She only put up the briefest of struggles before going limp in his arms and letting the knife fall. 'We can still save her,' Jake was saying in her ear while stroking her head, although he had no idea how. Susan and Vincent continued to recite their spell while signalling for Jake to tie Hannah's hands.

He let go of Mel and tip-toed towards Hannah. When he reached her, he lifted one of her hands at arm's length, ready to spring back out of harm's way at the slightest hint of movement.

Vincent stopped chanting, while Susan continued. 'It's fine,' he said. Behind him, Mel was sobbing. 'It's trapped in there. As long as Susan's chanting, it can't do anything. But as soon as she stops...,' he said, with a grim half-smile, which didn't help Jake's fear, but he thought fuck it and went in boldly. The thing stayed asleep.

Vincent came over once Hannah's hands were tied, but she still didn't stir. 'That fool Danny, why couldn't he have waited?'

'I don't know,' said Jake, although it had been a rhetorical question.

'He got lax. We can't afford to get complacent now,' said Vincent. 'Let's make sure it doesn't wake up and we'll get this tree moved sharpish, shall we.' He pulled a syringe from his jacket pocket and removed the plastic cover from the needle. Jake didn't know what was in it, and neither did he want to know. He watched on while Vincent squeezed a bit of liquid from the needle, gave the syringe a flick and jabbed it into Hannah's arm. Even though the demon was still unconscious from the prayer, Hannah's body visibly sagged as the sedative took effect. Susan stopped chanting and came rushing over. 'Well, I'm glad that worked!' she said before shouting for Mel to help move the tree.

'It's no good,' said Mel, puffing and panting through clenched teeth. Despite their best efforts, they couldn't budge the tree an inch. 'Do you have a saw?' she asked, raising her voice above the storm. Snow was settling on the forest floor now and dropping from the trees in slabs.

'It's in the workshop,' said Vincent. 'I'd better come with you. Susan, can you stay and make sure it doesn't wake up?'

'Is there a chance it will?' asked Jake.

'I wouldn't have thought so,' Vincent said. 'But until we

know exactly what we're dealing with I'd rather not take any chances.' He turned back to Susan. 'So, do you think you'll be okay until we get back?'

'We'll be fine. I imagine you've put enough dope into that thing to fell an elephant.'

'We'll be back soon,' he said, and he and Mel headed back towards the house at a trot. Their footsteps were quickly lost to the noise of the night.

The silence between them was awkward and Jake stood with his hands tucked under his armpits, trying to coax some warmth into them while jigging up and down on the spot and wishing he couldn't feel the agonising cold in his toes. Susan stood on the other side of Hannah, her attention split between the unconscious demon pinned to the ground, and the surrounding woods. The ferocity of the storm might have dropped a little, but the trees still groaned and creaked, and the sibilations were loud from the bare branches above.

As bright as Susan's lantern was, it only illuminated a narrow sliver of the forest and Hannah under the tree. Jake was unnerved by the dark at his back and the knowledge Danny's corpse was slumped only a few paces away, invisible to him in the night. But despite his fear, now he had little to do but wait, the levels of adrenaline in his bloodstream began to recede. The rational part of his psyche whispered in his ear.

His attention was focussed on Hannah, lying pinned beneath the tree. She could have been asleep. Her chest was slowly rising and falling, venting vapour from her half open mouth into the freezing woodland air and he couldn't help but go to her, cradling her head in his arms.

'I wouldn't do that if I were you,' hissed Susan. Jake shot her a look and she shrugged. 'Don't say I didn't warn you if it wakes up.'

He looked at her, his fear was overwhelming but even to his own surprise his love was greater. *What if she is just ill?* He thought. *And I'm condemning her to death. Oh God! What can I do?*

There was a rustling and scraping from where Danny's body lay crumpled at the base of the tree. Susan swung the torch's beam, expecting to see a fox scavenging the corpse, but instead they both saw Danny very slowly lifting himself to his feet.

'Impossible,' whispered Susan, glancing back to the unconscious demon.

Jake almost vomited at the sight of Danny's smashed and deformed face, on which snow had already settled to form a brittle crust. One eye was completely destroyed and the other stared lifelessly at him. *He must have hit the tree with some right force,* he thought momentarily before flying into full-on panic mode. 'What do we do,' he repeated, over and over again, getting louder with each repetition until he was shouting more at the advancing corpse than Susan, who was immobile, her torch beam firmly fixed on Danny.

The cadaver moved slowly and awkwardly, almost like a marionette. Its smashed and useless jaw flopped open while a distended, black tongue poked in and out, trying to form words but lacking the required physiology. There was only a gargle. Sputum bubbles dribbled from its chin. And still it advanced.

Jake was on the brink of turning on his heels to flee when Susan took a wide circle, clambered over the fallen tree and came round to where Jake was. She took hold of his upper arm and pulled him to her. 'Stay close to me,' she said as they slowly backed away across the small clearing.

Danny stopped next to the crushed, unconscious form of Hannah, put his hands under the tree and tried to lift it, but although it appeared he might have more strength in death than in life, the reanimated corpse couldn't shift the tree. They watched Dead Danny struggle, seemingly paying them no heed.

Three or four minutes must have passed and Danny's body showed no sign of tiring when they caught the sound of movement further off into the woods. Jake breathed a sigh of relief, assuming it was Mel and Vincent returned with a saw. Instead, Stephen came shuffling into the clearing.

Susan tightened her grip on Jake's arm. 'No,' she whispered, her voice finally cracking with emotion. Stephen was blue and stiff with ice. His good eye had been scavenged and the flesh had been torn away in numerous places around his face, exposing cold bone. Snow had settled on all parts of him. Entrails spilled from a hole in his belly, trailing across the forest floor, snagging on branches and spilling the reeking contents of his digestive tract.

Jake clutched Susan's arm; they were mere observers, too afraid to intervene while the two corpses worked together to move the tree. Between them they showed strength beyond what could be considered natural and sure enough, the tree trunk moved grudgingly off the ground.

The putt-putt of a chainsaw starting split the night asunder as surely as the wood it was designed to cut, startling Jake and Susan out of their stupor. Vincent was brandishing the saw in a two-handed stabbing action, rushing across the clearing and screaming in anger. As if sensing the immediate threat, the corpses dropped the tree back onto Hannah's midriff and spun around to face him.

The whirring chain easily went through Stephen's breastbone and chewed its way out of his back. Vincent whipped the saw upwards and the chain ate vertically up Stephen's spine, cleaving his skull in a line from his neck to just above his right ear. There was no blood. In the glare of Mel's spotlight his body looked frozen through, like partially defrosted meat from the freezer.

With the blade free, Vincent wasted no time in revving it back up and swinging it in a wide arc to take what remained of Danny's head clean off.

The two bodies lay twitching on the forest floor and Vincent set about destroying their limbs as best he could.

When he was done and the chainsaw was idling by his side Vincent pointed at Hannah's body. 'That thing's still conscious in there,' he said. 'Let's get a move on shall we?' He gunned the chainsaw and went to work on the fallen tree.

They carried her back to Marsham Hall on a stretcher Mel had rigged from two poles and a blanket. 'Learnt how to do this in girl guides,' she said. Everyone seemed surprised it held Hannah's weight when they lifted her onto it. Vincent took the front of the stretcher and Susan the back, while Jake walked alongside as best he could. Mel had her torch pointing straight ahead and Jake had the other pointed at the ground so they could see where they were stepping.

In the brief glimpses he managed to get of Hannah's injuries when the torchlight strayed over her body, Jake could see she was bruised from neck to knee; ugly purple and black, from blood collecting and congealing beneath the skin. Her face was a twisted mask of horror and he knew the demon was still in her. He looked away, eyes fixed firmly forwards for the rest of the walk back to Marsham Hall in grim, resolute silence.

By the time they left the treeline the storm had blown itself out and snow was floating down in flakes the size of saucers. The ground was long covered over and the drifts were getting deeper. Snow was piled up the front of the building as high as the ground floor windowsills. The entire front of the house looked like it had been dusted with icing sugar. 'Fuck it,' muttered Vincent. They'd all reached their limit.

Snow buried the front steps and had drifted about a third of the way up the door. Without any more words they trudged across it, Vincent rested the front of the stretcher on the drift while he struggled to unlatch the door. The weight of snow must have been putting pressure on the lock but, after many profanities were uttered, the door eventually swung inwards, spilling snow into the entrance hall and making it impossible for them to shut the door behind themselves. With the lack of heating in Marsham hall, the pile of snow wasn't going to melt anytime soon and so the door stayed open while the sombre procession headed straight through Vincent's study, through the antechamber and down into the temple beneath.

The temple was warm. A fire still smouldered in the hearth set into the back wall. The same could be said of the medieval style torches flickering in sconces along the wall. Smoke hung in a pall below the ceiling. The air was thick and fragrant with incense. The stretcher was placed directly in the middle of the pentagram and circle design set into the floor, while Mel lit the candles which were arranged around it.

Now Jake could see Hannah properly, he wondered whether the shadows had played tricks with his eyes while they had been outdoors, because her injuries didn't look anywhere near as severe as they had. The bruises on her belly and below her knees were turning an ugly shade of yellow, which was a vast improvement on what he'd thought he'd seen. But even as he stared, her smashed legs seemed to be ever so slowly straightening. The crushed mess that was her pelvis undoubtedly was, before his very eyes, fixing itself back into shape.

He stood up, took a step back and tugged on Susan's

sleeve, not taking his eyes off the miracle happening in front of them. 'She's fixing herself,' he uttered.

'Fascinating,' she said. 'We don't have long,' addressing everyone in the room. 'Is everybody ready?'

'What are you going to do?' asked Jake.

'Stand here,' she said as way of reply and directed him to one of the star's five points. She glanced around the others, as if seeking approval but if anyone had reservations, they didn't voice them. After a brief nod and without answering Jake's question she began to speak out loud in the same language she'd chanted in the woods. There was a rhythm to the words and at intervals Vincent and Mel spoke a refrain. It wasn't long before Jake picked up on the timing and repetition so he too could join in, tentatively at first as his tongue wrapped around new and alien syllables, but his voice became more forceful as his confidence grew.

Hannah's body began to convulse. Foam bubbled from her mouth; white to begin with, but thickening and turning yellow as she hacked and coughed the demon out. Her whole body contorted with spasms, like she'd been hooked up to the mains. Her back bent double the wrong way. Jake faltered, afraid they were killing her. *In for a penny...*, he thought and picked up the rhythm again while Hannah writhed on the floor. There was a strangled gargling too, as it tried to form words. Everyone glanced to Susan, who gave a small shake of her head and carried on the chant while their efforts were renewed afresh.

This went on for hours while Jake's voice got painful, hoarse and croaky but at long last Hannah's body lay peaceful and bruised on the cool tiles. A tar-like substance oozed slowly from her eyes and ears but despite this the undefinable ugliness had left her and Jake knew the demon had gone away. Although this was a double-edged sword, because she was undoubtedly dead.

Jake fell to his knees, crushed.

34

It's a dream.

She knew it wasn't. There were certainly dream-like qualities, floating, missing time and a general obscure and surreal order to her consciousness. But it was subtly different to a dream in a way she could not define.

The stairwell was in darkness, but Hannah could see an oblong of gloomy light at the landing. Sounds of children came to her again, quietly though; little more than snuffling and some movement in one of the bedrooms.

Hannah had too little energy in reserve for stealth, and the thought she might find something other than children at the top of the stairs didn't cross her mind. She also hadn't planned on what she was going to do when she did reach them, although she suspected her means of escape would lie in the cellar. Going down there filled her with dread worse than she was already experiencing.

One agonising step at a time, Hannah dragged herself up the stairs. Splinters raked at her raw flesh and dug into her bloodied hands and knees. Eventually she reached the top, but couldn't say how long it had taken. It could have been weeks, for she could not have ascended at a rate any faster than a snail. The door to the nursery was closed and so was the bathroom. Through the tall window at the end of the upstairs hallway, spindly, snake-like branches thrashed in a wind she couldn't hear, backlit by a sickly moon. Near the window, the door to her bedroom stood ajar and as Hannah dragged herself along the corridor towards it, her jubilance at finally having the chance to save the children, turned to a dread of what she might discover.

Too late to turn back now.

The bedroom was back to how it had been when they'd first moved to Picker's Bleed; black. Hannah peered into the gloom and saw the whole room was painted with something like tar, even the windows were blacked out. It oozed from the walls. The fumes were eye-watering. The walls glistened. She took all of this in a fraction of a second while her attention was caught by the figures in the room.

Near the tarred window, an ancient and naked hag was hunched in a rocking chair, just as she'd appeared in the mirror. A child was feeding at each breast; a baby and an older boy, of about twelve who was standing on the greasy floor next to the rocker. He had to bend over to feed. There were other children in the room too, huddled in the corners where the dark was deepest, glimpsed as the movement of vague shapes. Several rooks were perched about the room, almost invisible, camouflaged as they were, against the tarry walls. They watched on silently through glinting eyes.

'Well, well, well,' said the hag as Hannah dragged herself into the black room. She shook off the children, like a dog sloughing off water, and shooed them into the corners of the room, where they once again blended into the shadows.

'Welcome to my Hell.'

Hannah could only gaze up from the floor. There were so many questions she found herself incapable of asking. They were all asked together with one word; 'What?'

The old woman ignored her enquiry. 'How did you get here?' she snapped, leaning forwards in her rocking chair. A string of drool hung from the corner of her mouth. Her teeth were sparse and rotten.

'Vincent,' Hannah mumbled through her torn face.

'Speak up girl,' she said, and then, in a less direct tone; 'Although, we do have all the time in the world, you and I.'

Hannah was filled with unease, wondering what the witch meant. 'Vincent,' she repeated as best she could. 'Vincent Mandeville.'

'Mandeville, you say? Of course.' For all her years, the witch's eyes were sharp. 'I know of none called Vincent though.' A curious look crossed her face, then was gone. 'What year are we in?'

Hannah told her and the hag let go a long, steady breath, which whistled across her gums. 'Well I'll be. It's felt longer. I've been waiting five-hundred years, just to be cheated at the last...' she tailed off.

'You're Ella Jameson!'

'And you've been snooping around my house. I've seen you, stood over you at night while you slept. We're kin, you and I. It's the only way the cottage would have let you in. You were supposed to be there, but some things never change and that imbecile, Mandeville, has made a right pig's ear out of things. It must run in the family.' She gave a wheezy laugh at that. 'And now we're both stuck here forever.'

Hannah looked frantically about the room, desperate but incapable of action as her own blood pooled on the black floorboards. She realised all hope had gone. Her mind had raced for so long it had run out of steam.

'That's right. An eternity to share my Hell, and yours now. That creature's bested me again. It'll be back though, when it's killed your body.'

Hannah's mind was still whirring like a centrifuge, trying to make sense of everything. 'What are you on about, killed my body?' She stammered.

The with gave a little snort. 'While you and I are here enjoying each other's company, your body is still in the material world. Now, seeing as that vile thing which keeps me here has gone, I think it's a pretty good guess to say it's enjoying the pleasures of your flesh for a while. I don't imagine it'll be too careful with it either.'

Hannah was dumbstruck at what she was hearing. Any notion of being on a bad trip had left her.

The witch continued, seeming to take merriment from Hannah's suffering. 'Thing is,' she said. 'The only one's it's brought back here before have been these brats, and I'm sure that's just to torment me.' She seemed to be talking to herself again but then tailed off. 'Do you feel that?' She sat forwards on the rocker, attentive.

Something was happening. The air had a shimmer to it, and the atmosphere was tinged with dread. Ice crystals formed mid-air and floated like dust. Rooks took to the wing, jittery.

'It's coming back already,' the witch said, animated. She leaped up and slapped the arm of the rocking chair, cackling. 'Looks like you've got company.' She swept her arm around the room. 'Enjoy.'

The black dog materialised. Its eyes were fire and its fangs were death. Muscles bunched on its shoulders and haunches. Hannah recognised it for the foul creature that stole her from Vincent's temple. It was enraged.

The witch was gone.

From her place on the floor, Hannah felt like prey. The rooks were going wild and the children were running for the door. The dog advanced, teeth barred and it was making a low, savage growl. Its tongue lolled from the corner of its mouth, dripping saliva. The beast loomed over Hannah where she cowered. Then it pounced, going for the instant kill.

More by luck than by judgement Hannah raised her hands to protect her head, just as the dog hit her with its full weight. One end of the shard of glass, which was still impaling her hand, hit the floor just beside Hannah's exposed neck. The pointed end deflected off the dog's snout and was driven solidly into the hound's eye-socket as it lunged for her throat. She felt, rather than heard, glass scrape against bone and Hannah smelt the devil's last breath when its maw dragged down the side of her cheek.

The beast's weight was squeezing the air out of her and as her vision began to falter, Hannah was also crushed by the realisation she'd failed. The last of her senses to go was her hearing, as the clamour of birds faded to nothing.

She welcomed oblivion and let it swallow her whole.

35

The air was charged with static and the temperature had plummeted. Candles sputtered, their flames guttering almost to extinction. Hannah's body twitched. With the skip of a heartbeat Jake's grief turned to hope. He sprang to his feet.

'No,' shouted Vincent, but he was too late to instil any caution into Jake and could only watch impotently, without having the foggiest idea what the outcome might be. He was sure whatever had possessed her had gone, not only because there was colour returned to her cheeks, but because much of the unadulterated malevolence had disappeared from her features. *Have I succeeded?* He dared hope. *Have I managed to return Ella Jameson from the grave? Or is it the girl regaining control of her own body, like her idiot boyfriend thinks?*

Hannah coughed twice and sat up. Jake recoiled while Vincent let out a long, steady breath and almost chortled. It was all in the eyes. True, the possession was bound to leave some scars on her psyche, but there was something unnerving about witnessing a stranger's soul peering out of a familiar body. Once again Jake's emotions were feeding him conflicting signals, the end result was him being returned to his usual state of confusion and fear.

Sitting cross legged on the floor, Hannah looked down at her hands, turning them over to study every line. 'Young again,' she said and smiled.

Vincent dropped to one knee and bowed his head in deference and the others followed suit. All apart from Jake, who was already on his knees and stayed there while Hannah rose to her feet. Fully healed.

'Hannah,' he said. 'It's me, Jake. Please tell me you're okay, Hannah. Please?' He raised a hand to touch her pale wrist.

'Stop snivelling.' She batted his hand away.

In the instant she swatted him, Jake felt as if she'd released an invisible tsunami from her fingertips, which bore him through the air and dashed him against the far wall of the vault. The crack of his skull against the brick sounded like a twenty-one-gun salute. Beneath it was the crunching of bone from elsewhere in his body, and possibly the tearing of cartilage in his shoulder. *Try not to scream.* He bit his lip. He wanted to be sick. *Play dead! For fuck's sake. This hurts.* He held his breath until the blackness came over him. Time stopped having meaning and his body relaxed into semi-consciousness.

'I like it,' Jake heard her say through befuddled ears. 'All those years patiently waiting, practicing and honing my skills seem to have paid off. The things I have learned.' She was talking to herself, or so it seemed to Jake, who could only hear in a detached way. He might even have been dreaming. 'Let's try...this.' There was a sudden rush of warmth from the middle of the room, which was immediately followed by a scream so pained it sounded animal in origin. The scream ended almost as abruptly as it had begun.

'Fucking hell.' The voice was Mel's and came out cracked through fear.

A maniacal cackle rose from Hannah. 'Come,' she said, 'we have work to do.'

'But...' Vincent was spluttering over his words.

So, thought Jake. *Susan's dead.* He was surprised at how little emotion he felt, and supposed it had all been battered out of him by now. His pain had subsided to a nagging ache, detached like his hearing. He wanted to give in completely, let go of his body and die. In that moment he believed it was a conscious decision whether he lived or not, and would have happily taken death, but he felt there was reason to stay alive, that he still had a role to play in proceedings, whatever that role might be.

'Quickly now!' he heard Hannah say. 'I said there's work to be done.'

'Work?' asked Mel. She was crying.

'Revenge!' she said. 'The best kind of work. I've been waiting a long time for this. I'm going to make them pay for what they did.'

'Who? Make who pay?' ventured Vincent, curiosity getting the better of his fear.

'I'm... No, we are going to do unto them...' Her voice trailed off, like she was thinking. 'They will burn.'

'But?'

'But what?' she asked. 'Surely I can count on your loyalty? Both of you.'

There were fearful acknowledgements from Vincent and Mel. 'Yes,' they both said, subdued.

I must warn someone, thought Jake. But first I must rest a little.

***

It was Christmas Eve and snow was still falling. Big fat flakes floated down like paper-ash and quickly covered any footprints dotted around the village square. An inch of fresh covering must have dropped within half an hour. Inside the Bull's Head the fire popped and roared as another fresh log was slung on. It was the middle of evening service. Plates and cutlery clinked. Conversation was sparse and muted.

Lillian Taylor was sitting at a small, round table for one, gazing out of a fogged-up bay window at the freshly building snowdrifts outside while she ate dinner. A glass of Asti was fizzing on the table in front of her, but the sweet wine failed to lighten her mood.

Lillian spent considerable time smothering one of her pigs in blankets with apple sauce and was just raising her fork to her lips when Tom came over and bent to speak quietly in her ear. With a begrudging sigh, she put down her fork and calmly made her way behind the bar and into the back room. Amanda Brookes, who worked the bar on busy nights, nodded in her direction when she passed, but Lillian ignored her.

Peter was laughing with his wife when Tom tapped him on the shoulder. 'Sorry to interrupt, Mary,' he said.

'Everything okay?' she asked.

'I'm sure it is,' said Tom. 'I just need to borrow your husband for a little while if that's okay?'

'Of course,' she said.

'I'll try to have him back before you know it.'

'I'll be fine.' She knocked back her large glass of red wine and looked her husband in the eye. 'Leave me some cash though won't you, Pete.'

'Yes dear,' said Pete and took two twenty-pound notes from his wallet, handing them over before he followed Tom into the back.

Alan Wright was already in there, caressing a large whisky with one hand while a cigarette trembled in the fingers of the other. When they were all seated he took another sip from the heavy cut-glass tumbler. 'Anyone heard from Egbert?' he asked.

A look was shared about the room, accompanied by a slow shaking of heads.

'First Father Hamilton and now Appleby. I think it's time for action.'

'Like what?' asked Alan.

'We all know what,' Lillian cut in. 'We know all too well what must be done to witches.'

'We don't know for certain it is her.'

'Well, that's what we have to find out.'

'Kidnapping?'

'If need be.' She looked grim.

'I wish we could just call the police.'

'And tell them what exactly? As I understand it, Geoffrey was put down to natural causes and we don't know what's happened to Appleby.'

'I don't like it, that's all.'

'I know. None of us do.'

'What do we do when we've got her?'

There was a moment of grim silence before Tom asked: 'Shall I round up some of the chaps?'

'They'll be wanting to be safe behind closed doors come midnight.'

'Then we'd better be quick,' said Lillian. 'And then maybe none of us will have to cower behind walls anymore.'

'Right.' Tom planted his two hefty hands on the table and rose to his feet.

36

Jake remained motionless for a few minutes after the others had left, scrunched up on the floor with his eyes closed, listening to the dull reverberation of footsteps receding away into the house. They were walking with purpose and with very little in the way of conversation. Soon enough he was alone and in silence. The room was filled with the foul stench of burnt hair and charred meat, but nothing stirred. He waited a few moments longer before opening his eyes.

The candles had been left burning and by their dim, yellow light he could make out the heap of Susan's remains, reduced to a blackened husk. Her clothes had completely burned away and the skin beneath was depleted like lumpwood charcoal. Deep cracks ran through her charred flesh and deep inside, her bones were glowing embers. Her scalp was smouldering, but her eyes were still moist, almost shining against her blackened, cracked face.

Impossibly, Jake realised she was still alive, trapped inside a crispy shell. It was obvious there was nothing that even the best medical professionals would be able to do for her, there was nothing left to save of her body, her torture had to be supernatural. The only thing he could think of was to fetch a shovel to put her out of her misery, but he didn't, and as he turned away to hobble up the steps, he could feel her eyes pleading at his back.

Jake didn't appear to be as badly hurt as he'd first feared. All down his left side was stiff, with the bulk of the pain coming from his shoulder and hip, but his arm moved a little and slowly, and his legs just about bore his weight. At least he thought nothing was broken, except maybe his skull. He thought his skull might be broken because it hurt like there was a work-gang in there going at it with jackhammers. He was also experiencing an odd state of detachment, even more so than his unending confusion.

Clinging to the wall for support, he went creeping up the stairs and through the antechamber into Vincent's study, grateful the lamps had been left burning. A wall clock ticked away the seconds. On the desk was Vincent's crystal ball, covered by a maroon-coloured velvet cloth, plain apart from two rows of cream stitching around the hem. Jake felt drawn to it and reached out to remove the cloth, feeling like he was about to do something shameful but exhilarating at the same time. His heart was beating fast again.

Just as his fingertips brushed against the velvet, there came the sound of the Range Rover's engine turning over a couple of times from the courtyard before it burst into life on full revs. Jake froze on the spot when the car's lights came on and swept across the window, as it pulled away into the night. He was thankful the drapes were closed and hoped they were thick enough to mask his silhouette from the outside.

The moment was broken and Jake's inquisitiveness left him. At the same time, he realised he didn't have any kind of plan, apart from follow Vincent to the village, although he'd certainly be too late to offer any warning.

The hallway was in semi-darkness, lit only by the ghostly light reflected off the snow outside the front door. Jake listened to the Range Rover chugging away down the lane until it was eventually as quiet as the snowflakes that floated down in the breathless night. When he was sure they were far enough away, Jake made his way around into the courtyard to see if there was another car or something else he could use. All he could see were derelict and empty stables, but he had a quick poke around anyway, on the off chance he might come across something useful. Amongst old garden tools and at least three rusty lawnmowers he saw a bicycle leaning against one of the stable walls. It was an old Raleigh racer. For the weather conditions he'd have preferred something sturdier, like a mountain bike, but it was all there was. After brushing away some of the snow, which had come in through the broken roof, Jake clambered aboard the bike and teetered off. The chain was rusted but just about turned and the steering was stiff. The thin tires cut a narrow track as they crunched through the snow, but Jake was pleasantly surprised he managed to stay upright.

After a few yards he tried riding in the smooth tracks left by the Range Rover, but as soon as he did the wheels slid out from under him and he fell. His landing was cushioned by freshly laid snow at the edge of the track, but the impact sent shooting pains down his injured side nonetheless. For the rest of the journey he stayed in the middle of the lane, between the car's tracks and didn't pedal much faster than jogging pace. His face and fingers hurt with the cold more and more with every passing second. His eyeballs stung when snowflakes landed on them.

Long before he reached the end of the lane there came a

succession of orange flashes from the direction of the village, which lit up the bottom of the snow-clouds, turning them apocalyptic. Dull percussive bangs followed moments later. Jake picked up the pace as much as he dared.

As he came upon the village he could see flames belching from broken windows at the Bull's Head. Other fires burned here and there, but the pub seemed to be bearing the brunt of the assault. The next thing he noticed was the Range Rover, parked outside the church gates. Mel and Vincent were standing by its open doors, looking like they wanted to run away. Hannah was standing at the back of the car, screeching something indiscernible at the top of her lungs, before launching a ball of flame at the pillar-box across the square. There was another explosion and for a moment the post box was engulfed in flames.

Someone had been hiding behind the pillar-box and came running out into the open, head to toe in fire, screaming and waving his arms. The man dropped to the floor and rolled, but instead of putting out the flames the tarmac began to bubble around him as the fire became magnesium hot, glowing white from his belly. Within seconds the heat burned out, leaving a pile of charred bones and ashes.

Jake leaned the bike against some railings, vaguely aware he had no feeling in his fingers. *Frostbite?* he thought before consciously deciding not to think about it anymore. He stuck to the shadows, trying to make his way unseen towards the action, although he still had no idea why, just some crazy notion he could still save Hannah. But to look at her now, full of hatred and rage, he was watching a lost cause. Perhaps the real reason he continued was that he no longer cared to live and if he were to die then he'd rather it be at her hand. There was something vaguely poetic about it.

None of the cottages had lights in their windows, and

no-one was fighting the fires either. As Jake neared the corner he could see two men taking cover in the lee of the building, their faces blackened with soot, save for where tears streaked their cheeks. Jake ducked through a garden gate and crouched behind the low wall before anyone saw him.

From his hiding place he could see Hannah and he watched on impotently as another fiery sphere formed in the palm of her hand, rotating like a miniature sun before she hurled it in their direction. Quick as a flash Jake ducked his head back behind the wall and squeezed his eyes shut. The fireball must have struck one of the houses near the corner, but the explosion left a ringing in his ears. Dry heat raced over his head while glass tinkled down from the cottage's windows.

When he dared look again the Range Rover was pulling out of its parking space and driving off in the direction of Picker's Bleed. *Strange,* he thought, how he couldn't hear anything other than buzzing in his ears.

As soon as the car disappeared from view people emerged from their hiding places and rushed to the Bull's Head, desperate to reach the doors, only to be beaten back by the intense heat which showed no signs of abating. It was clear from their panic there were friends and loved ones still inside. Their chances of survival were nil.

Slowly, the survivors, mainly men, abandoned their efforts and milled, shell-shocked about the snow covered square. Jake recognised the pub landlord amongst them, whom the others seemed to gravitate towards, as if seeking leadership, someone to tell them what to do and how to cope with the devastation they'd been dealt.

Jake stepped out from behind the wall and lurched to join them. He was halfway across the square when the shopkeeper woman saw him. 'That's him!' she screeched, pointing with a straight arm. Jake's hearing was returning. 'That's the whore's lover.'

He felt naked under the weight of their hostility. The mob advanced on him, hatred clear in the whites of their wild eyes. All he could do was raise his arms and submit to the inevitable beating and probable death.

But before the first blows rained down Tom Stour shouted 'STOP!' in a voice powerful enough to fill the village square. He strode over to Jake and laid a heavy hand on his shoulder while Lillian glared back at him. 'I know there's retribution to be had' he said, addressing everyone, 'but this chap's as innocent as the rest of us.'

'So you say,' said Lilian.

'So I know.'

'How?'

'Look at him, for pity's sake. The man's half dead.' And it was true. It was a wonder he'd got this far. At least with the fires raging all around he didn't feel quite so cold anymore.

The mob wanted blood, that much was clear. Their sudden, collective grief needed to vent. They crowded around, the steam on their breath gave the appearance of a herd of bulls, just like the one that had been painted on the now destroyed pub sign. There was almost a growl coming from them as they pressed closer, a building tension which resonated in their chests; a trembling which intensified to a vibration running through the mob while it waited on the next word or two. 'So, what do we do with him?' asked Lillian.

'Now that is a question,' Tom said. 'Well, we can't leave him here.'

Lillian harrumphed. The mob needed their outlet.

'He comes with us,' he said and grabbed Jake by the scruff of the neck with one of his meaty fists and briefly swept his eyes across the small crowd. 'Is everybody ready?'

There was an affirmative grunt.

'Then let's get this done,' he said, and Jake was manhandled across the square to an old, grey Citroën people-carrier, his feet leaving long skid-marks in the snow.

He was in the back seat, half sitting, half lying. The shopkeeper woman was in the front passenger seat, with a shotgun across her lap. The pub landlord was driving. The car was crawling along the snowy lane in convoy with four others. The forest pressed in from all sides, twigs occasionally scratched along the doors with a high-pitched scraping like fingernails on a blackboard. 'What are you going to do?' Jake managed to ask.

'There'll be no witches here,' was the reply from the shopkeeper while the landlord didn't say anything. Jake was too tired to ask again. He could feel hot air from the car's heater blowers, but it didn't seem to be having an effect on his temperature, and now he couldn't decide whether he was hot *or* cold.

The cars came to a halt in the lane and the occupants spilled out, briefly congregating outside the front gate before they descended upon the cottage. They worked together as one, unrehearsed but seamless, as a can of petrol was passed forwards. Les, the chainsaw guy, doused the front of the house. There was movement visible in one of the downstairs windows and from where Jake was, still in the car, he could tell it was Hannah's outline. There were others with her.

Les paid particular attention to that window and when he stepped back, the mob stepped back too. Someone launched a Molotov cocktail, sending it smashing into the side of the cottage. Jake fumbled at the car's doorhandle, finding a fresh lease of life, falling out into the snow as a great whoosh of flame engulfed the front of his house and immediately began to take hold.

37

'Wake up.'

'What?'

'It's time,' said the voice.

'Time for what?' She was fourteen again; her dad trying to get her up for school while she snuggled under the duvet.

When there was no reply she opened her eyes and remembered. The voice belonged to the dead priest. *How long has it been?* she thought. Just like a dream, she existed outside time and space. A thousand years might have passed and she would have been oblivious to it. Or she might have been asleep for just a few moments. What Hannah did know was she felt more at peace than she ever had before.

'Where are you?' she asked into the dark.

'Right here,' came the priest's soothing voice.

'Where? Where am I?'

'I've got you in a safe place.'

'It feels it,' she said dreamily. 'And what is it time for?'

'For you to return to the land of the living and make

things right'

Hannah groaned, knowing she'd have to leave the comfort and security of her metaphorical bed.

'You can't stay here,' he said. 'It's a temporary retreat.'

'I know,' she sighed, wanting nothing more than to slide back into oblivion. 'What do I need to do?'

'Go back to the cottage.'

'And then what?'

'You'll figure it out.'

'But I don't know how? What about those children. I know they're real and they need me.'

'They're beyond you, for now,' said the kindly voice. 'One thing at a time. First we must get you back.'

'But I can't leave without them.'

'You have to.'

'They're lost, I know it.'

'And you will be too, if you don't go now.'

Hannah felt a guiding hand on her shoulder. She felt like she should be crying and would have given anything to feel tears streaming down her face. Her overriding emotion was one of failure. Then she could see the grotto under her cellar. 'Go,' said the disembodied voice and the hand gave her a gentle nudge forward.

Hannah didn't want to, she hated letting people down at the best of times, and this felt like the ultimate cowardice, saving herself. Funny thing was, she didn't even know if the children were real. All she knew was that they felt real to her and that was enough to compound her distress. In the end though, the choice wasn't hers to make and she found herself in the rocky space below her cottage. *Is it all over?* She wondered with great sadness, but she had a feeling it wasn't.

Although certain she was back in the real world, Hannah felt an odd detachment from reality. *Not surprising,* she thought. It was with mixed emotions she put her weight on the bottom rung of the ladder to begin her climb up into the house. The ladder gave an almighty creak which filled the grotto and Hannah was reminded how deep the silence was. She held her breath and waited, but other than the creaking of ropes and the pulse in her ears, all was quiet and so she continued to climb, as slowly and light-footedly as she could manage. Each rung groaned as loudly as the first.

The climb up through the chiselled shaft felt long, but eventually her head was touching the underneath of the trapdoor. There were cobwebs in her hair, but they didn't bother her. The trapdoor was stiff and Hannah gave it a good shove with the heel of her hand. At first it didn't budge. She pushed harder before smacking the age-worn wood with both hands, quickly catching back hold of the ladder to save herself a fall. The trapdoor slammed open onto the packed earth floor above.

Dust floated up into the cellar proper, illuminated by a sickly, flickering glow from the overhead bulb. Hannah's elbows rested on the floor astride the hole and only her head and shoulders were poking up into the cellar. The dark was thick enough so she could only make out faint shapes of the things around her. She was clambering out of the hole when she heard animated conversation from above. There was a scream.

It was with mounting trepidation she made her way up into the house proper. Something wasn't right, she felt insubstantial. It wasn't until she stepped out into the hallway and came face to face with herself that she realised.

In an instant Hannah knew beyond doubt she was looking at her own body in the hall, rather than a doppelganger. There was an irresistible attraction, like her soul and her body were two poles of the same magnet, attracted by the natural order of things. She also knew her flesh was possessed and corrupted by the spirit of Ella Jameson. It was as if she could see through her skin and bones to what lay beneath the surface. It was jarring to see her own body being used by someone else, and horrific to see it so misused.

Hannah could hardly hear what the witch was saying. She saw Vincent and Mel come out of the sitting room, they were shouting and waving their arms, but she didn't hear them either. She was only aware of her body, almost within touching distance and she wanted it back.

The witch turned around to look directly at Hannah. 'As for you,' she said. 'I don't know how you've done it, but I applaud your *skill*.' The last word was spoken with a hefty dose of sarcasm. 'But you should have stayed dead.'

Hannah found herself drifting closer, unaware of moving. She felt prickled all over, as if she'd come up against a barricade of barbed wire.

'Oh no you don't,' said the witch and Hannah noted she looked strained, as if it was taking substantial effort to keep her at bay and she pushed harder against the invisible barrier in the hope something would give. But eventually a point was reached where, even in corporeal form, she felt she'd be torn apart by the pressure and had to retreat, fighting the pull between her physical and spiritual halves.

There was a crash from outside, the dull smashing of a bottle, the tinkling of glass. For a long moment they were frozen in time as everyone tried to figure out what was happening. The witch pushed past Mel and Vincent into the sitting room and Hannah followed, passing right through Mel as if she wasn't there. But it was Hannah who wasn't there, and time wasn't on her side for she saw, through the window, the cottage was engulfed in flames. Black smoke billowed up beyond a curtain of fire and was seeping under the windowsill. The air was getting hot.

'You blithering idiots,' screamed the witch. 'In five-hundred years could you not get rid of that accursed bunch of yokels?' She spun to glare at Vincent and Mel, who were huddled in the doorway like frightened schoolchildren. Then they both turned and fled towards the back door. The witch screeched, turning her back on Hannah and tearing at her hair. 'Come back here, you dim-witted worms.'

In the confusion Hannah sensed the witch's guard drop and seized on the opportunity she'd been given. It was a chance which might not come again and she lunged, in a metaphysical way, towards her own body, letting herself get swept up in the current, feeling every ripple and eddy as she flowed around the witch's weakened defences. When Hannah made contact with her own back it was like sinking into warm molasses. The spark of life spread from her heart and radiated out to her extremities. She could feel the witch inside her, writhing like a snake beneath her skin and through muscle, becoming intertwined around sinew and bone, powerless to prevent the natural order of things, but with nowhere to flee, lest she return to an eternity of solitude in the void.

Vincent ran through the kitchen and yanked open the back door. A tongue of flame licked the ceiling. There came the bang of a shotgun and he flew backwards in a spray of gore as lead shot exploded from his back, narrowly missing Hannah and peppering the doorframe and wall close to her left.

She could see the woman from the shop just beyond the flames, raising the gun after reloading and Hannah ducked out of the way as Lillian shouted, 'die bitch!' and let go again with both barrels. The cuckoo-clock smashed as the back wall was filled with more holes. Before the woman could load again Hannah darted back into the hall, slamming the kitchen door behind her. Mel was still in the kitchen, hysterical. The smoke was thick now, hanging below the ceiling in a choking layer. Flames were guttering around the front door and the wallpaper was beginning to blacken and curl.

The front door burst inwards, splintering at the lock and Jake came spilling into the hallway in a state of wild-eyed panic, to end up sprawled at Hannah's feet. Along with him came fire, roaring along the ceiling with the backdraft. He looked up at her, helpless, and Hannah paused a moment, gazing back down at him with bewilderment. In that moment she loved him more than she ever had.

But there was no time to think, let alone get all soppy because the kitchen door was flung open and there was another crack of gunfire. Mel came staggering into the hallway and hot air raced through the cottage like the afterburner on a fighter jet. Mel's hair ignited. Hannah grabbed Jake by the back of his jumper and dragged him down the cellar steps. Cold air was being sucked up the stairs and despite its foul stench it was welcome.

The bulb had been extinguished, but by the dim phosphorescence seeping up from the open trapdoor they could see that the cellar was empty. The breeze blew stronger here and set cobwebs rippling across the ceiling.

'Wait,' he called. 'The fire's sucking all the air out.' But it was too late, Hannah was already halfway down the rickety ladder and all he could do was follow, not knowing if he was doing the right thing. *What the hell's going on?* he thought.

Seeing the grotto for the first time, Jake couldn't believe his eyes. 'What the fuck, man,' he muttered. Shadows flitted across the hewn rock walls and he seemed to be filled with every conceivable emotion at the same time. There was an enormous pressure in his head. The mirror caught his attention most of all, radiating grey, directionless light.

Hannah could still feel the witch writhing inside her.

Unwilling to let go and be damned, Ella Jameson clung on, entangling her essence with Hannah's until, like old, discarded cotton in the bottom of a sewing box, their threads would be impossible to separate. Within moments they'd become two people sharing one body, one brain, thoughts and memories. And what a vile and wicked creature Ella Jameson had become. Five-hundred years of solitude in the void had wrung all the humanity out of her. All she longed for was revenge and to inflict pain on the world. Hannah didn't have chance to ponder this as there came a deafening rumble and a crash from above, a sound that could have only been the roof caving in. Jake screamed at the same time as a cloud of hot ash and dust came billowing down the shaft.

The air was getting thick with smoke. Hannah's mind was racing, scrambling for a way to get the children back, but for all hers and the witch's combined knowledge, there was nothing she could think of. She was sure the floor above them was about to collapse.

Jake's body ached and he wanted nothing more than to lie down. At least he'd got to see Hannah again before his time was up. All he wanted to do now was cuddle her until the inevitable end. But Hannah was preoccupied. 'What's with the mirror?' he asked and lowered himself to sit on the dusty floor with his back propped against the rough cave wall. 'Is it the *gateway* everybody keeps talking about?'

She didn't answer. 'I have to get them back,' she muttered to herself. 'Please help me.'

She wasn't talking to Jake, but he answered anyway. 'Get who back?'

She gave him a look. 'I can get us out of this,' she said.

'Can you?' Jake sat straighter.

'I think so.' Unless her new memories were misleading her, but she didn't believe they were. 'But we can't leave the kids.'

'What fucking kids?' But he already knew.

'It's a long story.'

'Try me.'

'There's no time!' she said.

'Then get us out of here,' he looked around. 'If you say you can?'

Hannah relented a little. 'They're trapped.'

'In there?' Jake tilted his head towards the mirror.

'On the other side,' she said. 'There's got to be a way.' Hannah could feel certainty in the pit of her stomach that she was supposed to save them. She couldn't bring herself to admit failure.

'But we need to hurry.'

'I know we do.'

'Who are they?' he asked.

'Victims.'

'What the fuck has been going on?' he asked.

She said, 'I'll explain later.'

'Do we have to go through and get them?' Jake pointed limply to the mirror

'We can't,' she said. 'Not unless we're dead.'

'Are these children dead then?' he asked.

'I don't think so.'

'Because if they're dead I don't know why we're wasting time.' He didn't mean for the words to come out so harshly.

She glared at him. 'Don't you see?' she said. 'They're lost. We need to save their souls.'

Jake shut up. The cogs of his mind were whirring, trying to form an idea, but not quite catching, until something dawned on him. 'Or asleep?' he said.

'What?'

'I've been there, I think. In my sleep,' there was tinge of

excitement in his voice. 'The priest told me.'

'Father Hamilton?'

'Yes, that's the one,' he continued. 'But I don't know how that would help us now.'

'Did the priest help you, when you were there?'

'Yes.'

'The crafty beggar,' she mused. It could have been the witch talking. 'So, you can travel there in your sleep?' she asked. 'Is that why I thought I saw you, at the cottage?'

'You were all tangled up in thorns. It was a terrible nightmare.'

'It certainly was,' she said. 'What can you do when you're there?'

'Absolutely nothing,' he said. 'It was a dream. I was floating in the dark, you were trapped, I smashed the window and then I woke up.'

'So, you can do something then?'

'I'm not sure.'

She was formulating a plan, working with her newfound wisdom of spells and necromancy. 'It's worth a shot,' she said.

'What is?'

'You're going to have a nap.'

Tired as he was, sleep was something he wouldn't be able to manage, or so he thought. 'Am I?'

'Lie down,' she instructed. 'It's a simple trick, putting someone to sleep.'

'What if I can't get back?'

'I'll wake you up.' She uttered a few unintelligible words and with a small wave of her hand across his face, Jake began to quietly snore.

38

He was back in the void, which felt so empty, yet filled with voices so numerous they dissolved into cosmic babble. 'Back again?' asked a voice at his shoulder. 'I may be able to help.' Jake felt someone near him in the dark. 'Here, take my hand.'

Jake did.

Gradually the background noise died away and the monochrome dream-light started to filter through, as a scene floated into view. It was the cottage, as it always appeared in his dreams but this time it was burning. The thatch was gone, exposing charred beams and gaping holes where the roof had collapsed inwards.

Many shadowy figures crowded the cottage. Although all vaguely human in form, they were not of the material world. Their shapes were constantly shifting, and so Jake struggled to get a grasp on what he was seeing; a tentacle here, antlers there, were all but glimpsed.

'We have to go down there,' said the priest. His eyes were sad and honest. Soft creases went up towards his receding hairline.

Jake knew. 'And then what?'

'You need to run into a burning building.'

'Really?' he groaned.

'Afraid so.'

'Sounds legit.'

The priest chuckled without mirth. 'Yeah, it's a bit shitty, I know.'

'What about them?' he asked, pointing to the throng of demons and spirits.

Geoffrey Hamilton sighed. 'I think I found my calling in life,' he said.

'Aren't you dead?'

'A figure of speech.'

'Oh.'

'Are you ready?'

Jake nodded and they were at the front door of the cottage. Jake could smell the wool of his jumper starting to singe.

At their arrival, the shadows which were congregating around the cottage turned their attention towards Jake and the priest, flames flickering at their backs. They came as one to rush across the ground between them. 'Go. Now,' shouted Father Hamilton.

'I'll be incinerated,' Jake shouted over his shoulder.

The priest had his back to Jake, both arms thrust out in front of him, palms facing forward and the demons were a few feet away, held back by some invisible force, but they wouldn't be held back forever, judging by the strain etched into his face and the sinews of his neck. 'It's not as bad as what will happen if you don't. I'm sacrificing myself for you here Goddammit, the least you could do is have a little faith,' he shouted. 'Now go.' With that, the inkblot shadows surged over Father Hamilton and he was overcome.

In the same moment, Jake took a deep breath and dived into the fire. For a fraction of a second he burned all over and his ears were full of crackling and hissing, but then he was in the hallway, unharmed.

The cottage appeared the same as when Hannah had been caught up in the thorns, although now the brambles were dying, their drooping leaves slimy and black. He chanced a glance backwards. A shaft of moonlight shone in at the end of the hallway, tinged orange by fire. Dust floated up with every hollow footfall and the house creaked as if it had remained undisturbed for centuries. Smoke was beginning to hang lazily under the ceiling.

Jake went to the bottom of the stairs and listened. Upon hearing nothing he started up. The bottom step cracked when he put his weight on it, the stair sagged but didn't break and nervously he continued, hoping the aging planks would hold his weight.

The banister pulled away from the wall and he almost fell. The wood was full of rot. The wall was deteriorating before his eyes. It was as if the house was dying around him. More than that, he was sure the cottage was already dead and rotting. Each time he moved up another step he was terrified of crashing through to the floor below.

The upstairs of the cottage had fared no better than the ground floor. The door to the old nursery was hanging askew by its bottom hinge. Beetles scurried across the floorboards. Long deserted webs billowed across the partially collapsed ceiling, which was disgorging boxes from the attic to spill onto the rotten carpet. He listened and the house was silent apart from the floorboards, which groaned and splintered beneath his weight. Jake trod carefully, feeling along the walls to their bedroom.

Hannah had been right all along, they were sharing the

same nightmares. There were seven children, huddled around the walls, little more than indistinct shapes amongst thick shadows. The kids were confused and afraid. In the middle of the floor lay the dog, in a pool of its own congealed blood which had dried black. Jake went cold. Rooks were picking at its leathery hide, discarding scraps of dirty fur and tearing strips off the tough meat beneath.

They all took to the wing at the same time, flinging their feathery bodies at Jake's head and face, pecking and clawing, going for his eyes, so Jake's first instinct was to cover his face with his hands. If he didn't fight back he'd be eaten alive; he could feel the intent behind their pointed beaks. His timing needed to be perfect, and so he waited until one of the corvid's feet brushed against his hand. Striking fast, he got lucky and grabbed a leg and was swinging the screeching rook before the others had chance to realise what was happening. The bird shrieked as it slammed into the plump, feathery bodies of its cohorts. There was a ruckus of cawing and in the commotion, Jake gained his feet and threw the broken rook into the room, where it landed with a thump and didn't move. He'd managed to regain the advantage and was able to swipe the birds with his hands as they flew at him. He caught one with full on punch to the beak and it fell to the floor, broken and twitching while glaring up at him through one shiny eye. Within moments the rest of the birds had returned to their various perches around the room, eyeing Jake warily but keeping a respectful distance.

With a close eye on the birds, Jake hobbled towards the children. 'Come on,' he said. 'We've got to go.'

The children cowered against the back wall. They were grimy and dressed in rags. Jake realised he had no plan, nor even any half-formed ideas. *The priest thought I could do it?* he thought. *But the priest's dead, and most likely a construct of my own crazy mind. I don't even know what this is. A dream?*

Have faith. What else have you got? The answer was *nothing*, and if he was only dreaming then there was nothing to lose.

'Please?' he begged. Desperation made his voice tremble.

Smoke was billowing into the room and Jake heard the crackle of fire. The kids were becoming agitated.

'Quickly, we've got to go, *now*!' Jake tried to put as much urgency in his voice as he could muster, but in the end it was the fire that made the decision for them. There came a clatter from downstairs as part of the building collapsed. Jake ran to the window, but it was painted fast shut and he knew it wouldn't do any good to try and smash the glass. The crash had sounded like it had come from the kitchen and Jake thought they might be able to make the front door if they hurried. 'Go,' he urged, frantic.

'Where?' asked another of the kids.

Exasperated he said fiercely; 'Just. Go. Now,' and via numerous shoves in the right direction, Jake propelled each of the children out of the door and followed. 'You've got to trust me,' he pleaded as he bustled them across the landing.

Once they were moving, the troupe, having little choice, seemed to accept him as their rescuer and clattered downstairs at full pelt. With each footfall, Jake expected the staircase to collapse beneath them. When the first of the children reached the foot of the stairs and spilled into the hallway, they pulled up short and Jake crashed into the back of them. Flames were licking the inside of the front door and the kitchen was an inferno. Along the walls, brambles and splinters of wood were igniting.

'Run,' he screamed, shoving them in the direction of the cellar door. They flew down the steps in a tight pack with fire roaring at their backs and burning their lungs.

'The trapdoor!' yelled Jake. He and the older children scooped up the smallest without missing a beat. They dropped through the trapdoor into the grotto below. Jake landed hard, knocking the wind out of himself, but at least he cushioned the fall for the baby. The others, whether through youth or pure chance, all landed comfortably.

The mirror was swirling light out into the room. Through it they could see a mirror image of the temple under Picker's Bleed. Hannah was there, kneeling on the floor and cradling Jake's sleeping head.

The children shied away, terrified.

'It's okay. She's not going to hurt you.'

'But...,' said the girl again.

'She's not the one who hurt you,' said Jake. 'She's gone away.'

'It's a trick,' said another of the raggedy kids.

'No, it's not,' said Jake. 'Now I need you to come with me.'

'No.'

Jake guessed the boy who'd spoken to be about twelve or thirteen and like the others, he was emaciated to the point his face was skeletal and his belly distended and round. His hair looked like it had once been a bowl-cut, but it had grown long. 'Who are you?' he asked with a faltering voice.

'My name's Jake, and I'm trying to save you?'

There was a murmur amongst the children, a mere ripple. 'You're tricking us,' the older child said. The glint in his eye said he wanted to believe.

'No,' he answered. 'I'm not.' He begged them. 'We're out of time; please we have to go now.' The crackle of fire from above was getting louder. The children milled about, agitated. 'Trust me,' he said, trying to project a touch of Father Hamilton into his voice. *Trust me?* He thought. *That's a good one. I have no clue what I'm doing or what happens next!* Jake faltered. 'The mirror!' he yelled.

When he tentatively touched two fingers to the glass he

could feel the pull, elongating his molecules, stretching him out like crossing the event horizon of a black hole. The sensation was warm and although he didn't want to, he pulled back his hand. 'Through the glass,' he said.

At first the children looked confused but soon, one by one they placed a hand on the mirror and disappeared into the reflection. Jake took a deep breath and followed.

39

Jake opened his eyes, lying on compacted earth in the grotto under Picker's Bleed. After a glance about he was as sure as he could be that he was back in the real world. The first thing he noticed was that the children were nowhere to be seen. 'Where are they?' he said. The disappointment was crushing. The smoke was a lot thicker now and the air was hot.

Hannah was perplexed, she guessed he must be talking about the kids. 'I don't know,' she said. 'But we're out of time, the cellar's burning.'

Jake couldn't help thinking they must have achieved something. What, he didn't know but deep down in his gut he knew it was all over. Now all they had to do was make it out alive.

'We need to shut this, pronto,' Hannah said, before beginning to chant. It was the same primal language Vincent had used. Jake was too exhausted to register surprise, or even wonder what she was doing. Instead, he gave her elbow a reassuring squeeze, just as the sickly light dimmed and the mirror's strange surface went black. With a gust of rotten air they were plunged into complete darkness. The temperature rose drastically. Jake could smell his own hair burning. The heat got into his lungs, making him choke. It was getting harder to breath.

'Over here.' Hannah took Jake's arm and guided him past the empty mirror before fumbling along the back wall. 'Yes!' she exclaimed. There came a click from out of the dark and the squeal of a door opening.

'Light,' she said and a glowing, white orb formed, floating just above the upturned palm of her left hand. The cold light revealed a narrow tunnel, carved, like the grotto, out of the bedrock. It wasn't wide or tall, but was large enough for them to comfortably walk upright without fear of banging their heads. Here and there, cave spiders fled from the light into little nooks and crannies in the rough stone.

After only a few feet the passageway widened into an oblong chamber. Both of them pulled up short. About a dozen alcoves were chiselled into the wall, and in seven of them lay seven children. Although their clothes were old, rotten and crumbling, the children appeared as if they only slept.

Jake recognised them immediately. 'It's them! These are the ones from my dreams!' he said. 'What happened?' He looked down on the bodies, dressed in the rags of different eras.

'Their souls were stolen,' said Hannah.

'What can we do?' he said.

'I think we've already done all we can. What happened when I put you to sleep?' she asked.

'They vanished into the mirror. I followed and woke up back there.' He pointed back the way they'd come with a manic look about him. 'Is it all real?' he said, fighting back tears. He shoved his face into his hands.

'I'm so sorry,' Hannah said to the lifeless bodies. Now the witch was part of her she couldn't help but feel in some way responsible, as if the crimes were hers. 'I don't know what I can do.' She could feel the witch burning bright behind her eyes, curious and spiteful. She fought back the sensation. 'You should be better now, perhaps it's been too long?'

'We ought to go,' said Jake. Smoke was beginning to drift down the tunnel, bumping along the ceiling.

'We can't.'

'We have to. There's nothing we can do for them.'

'We can't just leave them here,' she snapped. Desperate for answers, knowing he was right, and they might soon run out of air made her all the more angry. 'They had names, you know! See, this one here,' – she strode to the biggest of the boys. 'His name's Tim. He had dreams of travelling to art school in London or Bath, but the land 'round here was cursed and so he worked sixteen hours a day to scratch enough food to keep the rest of his family going. They all did. When he disappeared, his mother and two of his siblings starved.

'This baby here is called Joshua,' she wiped her mouth with the back of her hand, 'He lived in the cottage before us. He was too young to experience any kind of life. Her there, that's Katie...'

'Stop it,' said Jake as he bundled her into his arms. 'Stop it, you're torturing yourself,' he said through tears of his own, caused by two parts smoke and one part emotion. 'And how do you know all this stuff?'

'Believe me, I do,' was the only answer she was capable of. The new thoughts, knowledge and emotions which were surging through her were overwhelming.

'Come on,' he tried to lead her away with an arm around her shoulders. 'We'd best be getting out of here.'

She sighed a heavy sigh. 'You're right,' she said and allowed herself, begrudgingly, to be led away.

There came another sigh from behind them, the sleepy kind. Hannah spun around, breaking free of Jake's grip. 'Isabelle!' she cried. Jake turned to see a young blonde girl waking up and yawning. She was wearing a yellowed, cotton nightie. Woodlice tumbled to the floor when she moved. Her face was a picture of confusion.

'Tim. Agatha!' Hannah cried again as the rest of the children started to wake with pathetic groans and whimpers. She was crying herself and ran to the children, gathering them in her arms. They looked around meekly, too exhausted to resist.

'Quick,' said Jake. 'We need to get out of here, now!' Between them they bustled frightened children out of the chamber and along the passageway, which ran pretty much straight. Tim tried to voice a protest, but Hannah gave him a shove in the right direction and told him to get a move on. The smoke and heat penetrating the tunnel convinced them to comply and there were no further protests.

Here and there tunnels branched off, but Hannah kept to the main passage, confident of where she was heading, until eventually the tunnel came to an end at a set of rough, stone steps, which rose to a square hatch in the tunnel roof. They emerged into the temple beneath Marsham Hall, in the middle of the inlaid pentagram, by means of a loose floor tile which lifted to expose the tunnel's egress. Jake breathed a sigh of relief at knowing they were safe from the fire, marvelling at how far they'd travelled and thinking he must have lost track of time underground.

Their footsteps echoed on the tiles, as if the building itself was telling them it was empty, and a safe place to spend the night. They went up into the old mansion-house and found a room with a dusty old sofa, armchairs and a huge fireplace. A threadbare rug covered the slate floor in front of the fireplace and to one side of the chimney was a decent pile of chopped logs and to the other, a basket of kindling. The front door was still blocked open by snow and wind whistled through the empty hall, but once the fire they'd built was fully alight their dilapidated room felt almost cosy.

Despite their extended stasis, over four hundred years in the case of Tim, the children dozed on the sofa, chairs and at the edges of the rug where the fire warmed through to their souls. 'Shock, I imagine,' Hannah said.

'So, what happens now?'

'Well, we always said we wanted a big family.'

'This isn't quite what I meant,' he said, but there was no argument in him. 'I'm sure we'll figure it out.'

'I'm sure we will,' she said, her tone much more optimistic than his. 'She's still in here you know?'

'Who is?' said Jake with fresh alarm.

'Ella Jameson. The witch.'

'Shit,' said Jake.

'I think it's okay,' she said, twiddling her fingers. 'It's a bit strange and I'll need some time to figure it out, but I think I've got her under control. It's sort of like my dark side has been given a personality all of its own, but it's okay, because I'm still at the helm, so to speak. I can still tell what's right from wrong.' She took his hands in hers and looked him in the eyes. 'But it's very early days, so if that changes you need to tell me, okay?'

He nodded.

'I need you,' she said.

'And I need you too.' He shuffled on his bottom a bit, trying to get comfortable. He ached all over, but the tips of his fingers and nose hurt more than the rest of him. Once again, Jake found himself wondering if he'd lose any body parts, but then figured a missing finger or two was the least of his worries. Although it would mean he'd have to find a new career, but all that was a long way distant. 'So, practically speaking, what are we going to do?'

'What do you mean?'

'We need somewhere to live. Did we sort out the insurance?'

'I'm not sure they'd pay up for this?' She almost laughed.

'Seriously,' he said. 'It's all stuff we need to think about.'

She ruffled his hair 'You're such a stress-head. Being a witch has its perks.'

'What do you mean?' Jake asked.

Hannah reached around and pulled a twenty-pound note from thin-air behind Jake's left ear. 'I think everything's going to work out just fine.'

They could hear sirens drifting from the direction of Marsham. 'Will it?'

She gulped, a sombre moment while they paused for thought. 'Yes,' she said. 'I think this village is due a little prosperity all round.'

Acknowledgements

I feel I should write something clever or witty here, but it's late and I want to go to bed. It's a fact of life that writing a novel takes more than the grit and determination of the author alone, but like many independent authors, the kindness and generosity of others is what makes a book.

Extra special thanks goes to my fantastic partner, Fay, without whom this wouldn't be possible and my stories would make even less sense than they do now. I'm eternally grateful, my books would be crap without you.

I'd also like to thank Kath Middleton, who came in and cleaned up at the end, helping with my dodgy grasp of the English language and mopping up the last few typos. Check out her books.

At the time of writing, there are no reviews for Picker's Bleed, but I would like to thank any potential reviewers, bloggers, and those who just like to talk books, in advance. Those are the people who enable a book to find readers, and readers to find books. Without them I could write the best book in the world, but I'm pretty sure no-one would ever hear about it. At this point, I'd like to apologise to the handful of reviewers who received advance copies that contained errors. I wonder how the reviews will be?

The internet can be a fantastic space, full of people who happily impart their wisdom and experience, and they've been crucial, especially when it comes to formatting and publishing. So thanks to all of those. You know who you are.

Anyway, that's all from me for one night. Tomorrow I'll upload the final files and send Picker's Bleed out into the world. Let's see where the journey takes us.

Also by the Author

FLUX

THE DARK STONE

INFESTED

CPSIA information can be obtained
at www.ICGtesting.com
Printed in the USA
BVHW052134141222
654304BV00006B/48